Blizzard

Also by Ron Schwab

The Lockes
Last Will
Medicine Wheel
Hell's Fire

The Law Wranglers
Deal with the Devil
Mouth of Hell
The Last Hunt
Summer's Child
Adam's First Wife
Escape from El Gato
Peyote Spirits

The Coyote Saga
Night of the Coyote
Return of the Coyote
Twilight of the Coyote

The Blood Hounds
The Blood Hounds
No Man's Land
Looking for Trouble
Snapp vs. Snapp

Lucky Five
Old Dogs
Day of the Dog

Lockwood

The Accidental Sheriff
Beware a Pale Horse
Trouble

Sioux Sunrise
Paint the Hills Red
Grit
Cut Nose
The Long Walk
Coldsmith
Ghost of the Guadalupe
Bushwa

Blizzard

Ron Schwab

Uplands Press
OMAHA, NEBRASKA

Copyright © 2024 by Ron Schwab

All rights reserved. No part of this publication may be reproduced, distributed or transmitted in any form or by any means, including photocopying, recording, or other electronic or mechanical methods, without the prior written permission of the publisher, except in the case of brief quotations embodied in critical reviews and certain other noncommercial uses permitted by copyright law. For permission requests, write to the publisher, addressed "Attention: Permissions Coordinator," at the address below.

Uplands Press
1401 S 64th Avenue
Omaha, NE 68106
www.uplandspress.com

Publisher's Note: This is a work of fiction. Names, characters, places, and incidents are a product of the author's imagination. Locales and public names are sometimes used for atmospheric purposes. Any resemblance to actual people, living or dead, or to businesses, companies, events, institutions, or locales is completely coincidental.

Ordering Information:
Quantity sales. Special discounts are available on quantity purchases by corporations, associations, and others. For details, contact the "Special Sales Department" at the address above.

Uplands Press / Ron Schwab -- 1st ed.
ISBN 978-1-943421-72-5

Chapter 1

November 1887

"FIFTEEN BUZZARDS BY my count," Chloe Downs said. "They're making a perfect circle. That means there's going to be a lot of dying in these parts next year."

Gage Kraft sat silently with Chloe on a weathered, sturdy bench in front of her dugout in the heart of the Nebraska Sandhills. She was a wiry woman of seventy years. She might still reach five feet, and he doubted she would weigh a hundred pounds. The formerly golden hair tied back in a ponytail had turned snow white now, and the flawless, tanned skin of her face was webbed with creases, but he still found her as beautiful and alluring as ever.

He watched as Chloe, her fingers steady, dumped tobacco from a leather pouch held in one hand upon a paper resting in the other. She set the pouch beside her and deftly rolled the cigarette, then pressed it to her lips, struck a match on her belt buckle, and lit it. He allowed her a few puffs before he spoke.

"The buzzards circle because they've got their sights on something dead, not because they're making predictions," he said.

"I won't argue with you. A Sioux medicine man told me that once. I'm just saying 1888 is going to be a bad year for folks dying."

"I ride over here on a perfect Indian-summer day to chat a spell, and you've got to talk about bad things ahead. The buzzards are here because they've got their eyes on something behind the barn." He started to get up. "I think I'll just mosey over there and see what kind of supper they've got in mind."

"Sit down, Gage. No hurry about it. He's dead. He ain't going anywhere."

"Who's dead?"

"How the hell would I know? He showed up here the night before last and was trying to break through the door long after I'd gone to bed. If Inky hadn't woken me up and told me somebody was out there, those buzzards might be feeding on me."

Inky was a black tomcat with half of his left front leg missing and shared her bed most nights. "So, how did he end up dead?"

"I got up and grabbed the loaded double-barreled I keep next to the bed, went out and released the bolt lock—didn't want him to break it loose from the door. I just stepped back, and he almost fell on his face when he put his shoulder to the door and it flew open. Instead, he stumbled backwards and fell just outside the door when the shotgun blast tore into his guts. That was handy, so I closed and locked the door and went back to bed."

"And you just hauled his body out behind the barn?"

"Charlie and me. Yesterday morning I took a rope and hitched him to Charlie, and that old mule drug the corpse back there for me easy as you please. I got me a new unbranded, sorrel gelding, a nice saddle and tack, a Winchester, and a Colt revolver in the bargain. Feller had two double eagles and over fifty dollars in paper money stuffed in his pockets, so yesterday was a good day."

"You don't have any idea who it was?"

"Nope, but I suppose he's the feller that's been nosing around the place a spell."

"What do you mean?"

"I've seen him slinking around for three or four days. Caught sight of him at least a half dozen times. Figured he was up to no good. With the money he was carrying, I don't think he was fixing to rob me. I might flatter myself and say he was wanting to plant his pizzle in my nest, but it doesn't seem likely. I'm thinking he was looking to leave me dead."

"But why?"

"That's the question I've been trying to answer."

"I want to take a look at this guy."

"It won't be pretty. I suspect scavengers have already been feeding on him. The buzzards are just getting started. They like the meat to ripen a bit."

They walked together to the barn and went to the rear of the barn's north side, which was hidden from the dugout's view. A fenced horse corral took up much of the west, which gave Chloe a view of the horses she loved so dearly. More often, however, the critters grazed in an expansive fenced-in pasture off the east side that was sometimes shared with ailing or injured cows or calves. The barn was probably the largest and best built in the Nebraska Sandhills, yet the owner still insisted upon residing in her dugout.

Gage was surprised to find the naked body not ten feet from the barn wall. Coyotes and a few hungry buzzards had already been at work and made off with the man's nose and male parts and peeled much of the flesh from his face. "You stripped his clothes off."

"Less nuisance for the buzzards."

"Digging is soft enough. I'll get a shovel from the barn and bury him."

"Seems like a waste of time, and I'd rather feed buzzards than worms."

"It's hard to tell, but from the gray streaks in his hair, this wasn't a kid."

"No, he'd been around a spell. Not old like you and me, but seasoned, it appears. You're hellbent on burying him, aren't you?"

"Yes, I don't feel right just leaving him here for the scavengers."

"They're nature's friends. It doesn't hurt to help them out now and then."

"We've got to talk about this."

"Are you staying the night?"

"If I'm invited."

"If you don't mind sharing my bed."

"Now, I've shared that same bed well over a thousand times for close to thirty years now. Why would you think I'd have a problem sharing it tonight?"

"Well, you ain't been around so much lately. It's been a month since I last saw you. I thought maybe you'd gone and died on me."

"Don't give me that bushwa. Sam drops by at least every other day to help where he can. Do you think my grandson would not have told you? We've got a lot to talk about. I already told Monique not to look for me home tonight. Now, you go on back to the house, and I'll tend to the burying after I put my tired old horse up."

Chapter 2

CHLOE RETURNED TO the dugout, sat back down on the bench and rolled another cigarette. Inky meandered up from the barn, jumped up on the bench, and nestled on her lap. As was her habit, she had a conversation with him. "Well, Inky, I suppose Gage interrupted your nap in the hayloft. He didn't bring Rip with him today. I didn't think to ask why not." Rip was Gage Kraft's old shepherd-mix dog, and the cat and dog were good friends, often napping side by side in the sun after they had played a spell.

The cat shifted positions and started kneading on Chloe's belly with his single paw. She scratched the back of his neck and behind the ears, and he purred appreciation. "Gage is a dang good man, Inky. None better. Maybe I should have married the ornery cuss, but I just wasn't sure I wanted a man underfoot all the time. They're good to have around for bed warmers now and then but a nuisance when it comes to doing things a woman's expected to do—meal fixing, laundry and the like. I had all that I wanted when I was married to Hank and raising those kids. I'd just as soon be working cattle."

Inky meowed and rubbed his head against her chest.

"Yeah, Inky, I ain't trading you in for no man, but you ain't sharing the bed tonight. You know that by now." The cat curled up and fell asleep on her lap. She brushed her fingers back and forth over his soft coat. Chloe had always liked cats, taken by their independent ways—just like herself. She had a passel of barn cats, too, but Inky had somehow wangled his way into sleeping nights in the dugout as a kitten almost five years earlier. When the weather was not unpleasant, he still roamed some and spent time in the barn, especially during mating season when he might also disappear for several days at a time. The cat owned her, and she did not deny it.

When Chloe finished the cigarette, she dropped the butt on the ground and crunched it into the dirt with her bootheel. She figured the smoke would be her last till Gage left. He never complained, but she knew he was not fond of her habit, and she didn't need the tobacco so much when Gage was around. She moved a complaining

Inky off her lap and got up and went into the dugout to see what she might round up for supper.

After completing his chores, Gage opened the thick oak door to the dugout and walked in. "This is better," Gage said. "Sundown's not more than an hour off, and the usual chill is moving in from the west."

He walked over to the fireplace where part of the wood had already burned down to cooking coals. Chloe did not have a steel or iron cookstove like most ranchers and other settlers did these days. She saw such contraptions as a waste of good money.

The fireplace heated the entire dugout, which consisted of a single front room containing what might be called a kitchen-parlor and two rooms deeper into the cave-like structure, both of which had once been bedrooms. Since she was now the only occupant, one had been drafted for storage. The dugout had been the result of hollowing out part of a limestone bluff that erupted like a giant tooth from among the seemingly endless waves of grass-covered sand dunes and canyons. Early explorer Major Stephen F. Long had dubbed the area, which included much of central and western Nebraska north of the Platte River, the "Great American Desert" and had written that it should remain "the unmolested haunt of the native hunter and the bison." The vast water resources of this misnamed desert had not yet been discovered.

The first front wall of the dugout had been fashioned from large blocks of sod but had been subsequently replaced by limestone slabs. Packed clay, dirt, and sand formed the dugout's floor, firm and smooth after years of wear. Scattered buffalo and deer hides carpeted much of the surface to add a bit of warmth. Two narrow windows in the stone front furnished the only natural light, so the two rooms at the rear were virtual caves. And Chloe loved her domicile that would seem primitive to many.

"I've got biscuits in the Dutch oven and beef stew in the pot," Chloe said. "No dessert. You'll have to settle for an extra biscuit or two and lots of blueberry jam. You can see I've got coffee brewing, too."

"That'll do me fine, Chloe. You've never disappointed me with stew and biscuits."

It occurred to her that she rarely prepared anything else for him. She liked simple fare. Besides, she didn't like cooking all that much. "Why don't you get the bowls and cups out while I get the jam from the storeroom? You know where everything's at." She lit a small lamp with a handle extending from the stem and base and disappeared into the storeroom. The room was packed with canned goods and tins of staples on shelves that spanned every wall. She figured that maybe she was oversupplying. She nearly had enough food to open her own store. She recalled vividly the days as a child when she went without a bite to eat three and four days at a stretch before a woman took her from the St. Louis streets and delivered her to an orphanage. She would have been seven years old then.

She had hated the place and did not get along well with the other children, but they did see that she got schooled through eighth grade before she ventured off on her own, vowing she would never go hungry again. And she had not. She supposed she ate like a dang horse, but she never gained a pound except when carrying babies.

Gage had the table lamp lit when she returned. He had set the table and removed the Dutch oven from the coals. He was kneeling at the fireplace stirring the stew now. They had always worked together like a matched team of horses, each instinctively knowing what had to be done and doing it.

She stopped and watched him. Damn, he was a handsome devil, still had his wiry hair, a distinguished salt and pepper, not white like hers. Trim and muscled. Clean shaven. He might have shrunk a bit with his seventy-two years, but he would still be an inch or two over six feet, although dwarfed by his grandson Sam, who would reach six feet five inches in stockinged feet.

"I found a can of peaches, too," she said.

Gage looked up and smiled. "That doesn't surprise me. God knows what you've got hid out in there." He grabbed the handle of the stew pot and got to his feet, towering over her.

She watched him as they ate, noting for the first time the lines etched in his face, especially the webs extending from the flesh about his indigo blue eyes. She guessed he was not entirely resisting the passing years either. "You're quiet," she said.

"Chloe, how many times have we eaten a meal without speaking a word?"

She rolled her eyes and surrendered a small smile. "More than I can count. I guess we get lost in our thoughts."

"I like it that we can be quiet together, Chloe. But I've been thinking about that guy I just buried. I'm worried about why he was here. You really don't have any notion of why he might have been gunning for you?"

"None."

"I don't think you should be staying here alone at night, and maybe you should find a fulltime hand or two to help here. You haven't had anybody except temporary hands staying in the bunkhouse for over five years now."

"During spring roundup, I generally have a few."

"That doesn't count. Does Mort Boone ever stay over?"

"He comes every other day and takes the wagon for supplies into Broken Bow once a month. He doesn't stay over. His wife wants him home at night. She's a jealous sort. She thinks I might take advantage of poor Mort. She's safe."

"Hire Mort to take care of daily chores here and come stay at the K Bar K. You're tight as bark on a tree, but I know you can afford it. You don't spend your money on much but food and tobacco, and we've had some good years in the cow business lately."

"You've got plenty of folks there already."

"I've got three fulltime hands in the bunkhouse. Monique and Bruce Potter live in one end of the house. Sam insists on living in that fancied-up line shack between our two places, so I have two spare bedrooms. Of course, I figured you would share mine. Nobody would think anything about it. We haven't been fooling anybody these past thirty years, but if you are worried about respectability, you can marry me."

"That's a piss poor proposal."

"Do you want something better? Alright." He got up from his chair and stepped over to her side of the small table, took her hand and got down on one knee. He looked up at her with those seductive eyes of his. "I love you, Chloe Downs. Will you marry me?"

She was sorely tempted this time. Age had not subdued her feelings for this good man. "You have been asking me a half dozen times a year for most of the last thirty years, Gage. I can't imagine why you'd want this broken-down old hag in your bed anymore."

Gage's eyes turned sad, and she thought they glistened with a few tears. He sighed and got to his feet. "You're a beautiful woman, Chloe, and you are my dearest friend. I love you, and I'm selfish. I want more time with you for whatever time I've got left."

He was making this very difficult. "Gage, you know I love you. But the answer is the same. I've got to think about it. Let's just enjoy the now, the time we've got tonight. And I don't want to talk about the no-good you buried out there. Maybe in the morning before you leave."

Gage nodded, sat down, and returned to his meal, eating silently again. But she knew his brain was working and that they would have another talk in the morning. She shrugged off the thought. She was not about to let that prospect spoil her night with this special man.

They headed for the bedroom immediately after supper clean-up, as was their usual routine. They were both early risers and enjoyed sharing their time in the intimacy of the bedroom, sometimes talking for hours after they had properly tended to business, which tended to take more time and perseverance than in their younger days. But they would both be sated and satisfied before their lovemaking was finished. Of course, the repeat performances had faded away somewhere along their journey together.

Just as she reached the bedroom, she heard Inky scratching and yowling at the front door. "Go on to bed," she said, "I've got some meat scraps to feed Inky. I'll be right along."

"He's not sleeping in here tonight, is he?"

"I've got his blankets folded on the couch for him. He'll go there, I think. We'll freeze our butts if I shut the bedroom door."

Gage went on into the bedroom and lit the lamp, and by the time she joined him, he had removed everything but his undershorts, and as he pulled those off, her heart started to race, and urgency struck her. He watched as she undressed, and she wondered why he did not gag, but she saw as he stood near the bed that there was life in that old pizzle.

They wasted no time crawling beneath the blankets and soon she was wrapped in his arms, and she could tell that tonight he would be ready. Suddenly, a thump on the mattress signaled a guest had arrived, and Inky appeared on her pillow, his yellow eyes fixed on Gage, obviously viewing him as an intruder. She could feel Gage's passion dying.

"I can't do this with that dang cat watching, Chloe. Things just won't work. Maybe he's already killed it for the night. I don't know, but I'm done if the cat stays."

"I'll put him out and shut the door. We can open it after we've had our time." She swung her legs out of bed, grabbed the black cat and placed him back on the couch. Then she raced for the bedroom and got the door closed just before Inky beat her to the room. The cat started scratching on the door and yowling again, but she would be damned if he would take away her time with Gage.

Gage was laughing as she climbed back under the blankets. "Now that was a sight, a naked lady running into the room with a cat chasing her."

"I ain't going to miss special time with my man. Can you ignore the racket he's making? He'll give up soon."

"With your help, and as long as he's not watching, I'll be okay."

And Chloe Downs went to heaven not just once that night, but twice.

Chapter 3

WHEN GAGE AWAKENED, he heard the clanging of metal against stone from the front room, obviously Chloe stoking coals in the fireplace to get a breakfast fire going. He rolled to the side of the bed, tossed off the covers and then pulled them back on. Dang, it was cold in here, and his back was so stiff and sore, he wasn't sure he could stand. He remembered that he had dropped his clothes on the buffalo hide rug next to the bed. He reached over the bedside and raked his fingers over the rug till he located his undershorts and shirt and pulled them under the blankets to warm a bit.

The stone-walled room was pitch-black except for a sliver of light that made its way through the half-closed door. He pulled on his undershorts before tossing the blankets back again and dropped his legs over the bed, sat up, and slipped on the shirt. His eyes, adjusting to the darkness now, helped him retrieve socks, boots, and britches, and he got up and made his way out of the bedroom, noticing the heat instantly when he stepped into the front room.

Chloe, who was looking at him from the fireplace where flames were starting to dance, said, "Good Lord, Gage, you're all hunched over like an old man."

"I am an old man, woman, if you haven't noticed."

"Sure wouldn't have guessed it last night. I thought I was bedding a young stallion."

Her praise was welcome this morning, but he knew she was exaggerating his lovemaking prowess. "I had the help of a frisky young filly. Anyhow, I guarantee I'll loosen up in a half hour or so and maybe won't look so beat-up. What's for breakfast?"

"You know I ain't much for cooking, but I got leftover biscuits I'm warming up some and plenty of bacon—and coffee, of course. I've got plenty of eggs if you want to fry or scramble some."

"I just might do that." He looked around the room. "Where's Inky?"

"He headed for the barn early. He slept out here even after I opened the bedroom door last night. I think he's pissed that he got booted. He'll claim his spot tonight—unless you're staying another night."

"No, I've got to get back home. Work to do. But it appears the sun is coming up, and we've got another good day ahead. I thought we might take a ride before I leave this morning."

"I already got my riding britches and boots on."

"You've always got your riding britches and boots on. You know, all these years have gone by, and I've never seen you wearing a dress."

"They're a damn nuisance. I owned a dress once, but I eventually cut it up for rags. I think dresses were dreamed up by men who wanted to keep women from looking after themselves. Do you know a better horse wrangler than me?"

"Nope."

"And can you imagine me doing that work in a dress?"

"Nope."

"There you are."

After breakfast, they went to the barn to saddle their horses. Gage saddled his gelding, Keeper, a grayish-yellow dun with a black dorsal stripe and dark ears and legs below the knees. The mount had been born at the ranch over fifteen years earlier, the same year a nearly starved Rip, just recently weaned, had shown up on the ranch house veranda.

Chloe thought it was silly to name a horse, although she loved them all like an indulgent mother. Today, she claimed a sleek, sorrel mare that she rode more often than most. He did not offer to help saddle the gentle critter. Chloe would have rebuffed any attempt, and she slung the saddle on the mare's back with ease. She was fitter than most seasoned hands, Gage thought.

As they mounted their horses, Gage said, "Slow and easy today. I want to talk. You take the lead."

"No race?"

"That sorrel of yours would whip Keeper. It might embarrass him. He's sensitive about his age."

"Keeper or you?"

"Me? You just said I was a young stallion."

"I said I thought I was bedding one. That doesn't make it so, and I ain't no filly either."

As they rode away from the barn, Chloe said, "We're going up to Eagle's Nest Bluff. It'll take us above the fork of the Dismal and Middle Loup Rivers. A perfect day for that visit. It might be the last till spring with winter coming on. It's going to be a bad winter."

"They're all bad as far as I'm concerned, but what makes you say that?"

"You ain't seen the birds heading south?"

"Yeah, birds are always heading south."

"Not this many. Winter birds are going, too. They might stop in Kansas, but they don't want any part of what's coming our way."

He did not possess knowledge to contradict her, so he was not about to argue. If he won, it would be the first time. "You could be right," he said.

They followed a trail that snaked between the wide dunes and led to sloping terrain that took them higher until the riders approached the face of a stone-covered bluff and moved onto a narrow trail that forced riding single file, Chloe, of course, in the lead. The bluff was not comparable to the cliffs in the Rocky Mountains in Wyoming to the west, but a 150-foot climb along the ledge was plenty high for Gage. Chloe had always been more daredevil than he.

When they reached the top, they dismounted and staked their horses. There was a fair stand of grass on a table-like top that was well over one hundred feet wide at this place, and scattered cottonwoods offered a bit of shade. Gage guessed that the temperature was over seventy degrees today, but in this country it could be well below freezing tomorrow.

The bluff ran for several miles above the Middle Loup River before it tapered off and merged into the grasslands below. The slopes were gentler further northwest with trails that eased into the lowlands. Chloe would willingly take one of those when they left, but he would be forced to suggest it. He would. He was far past the days of bravado.

Chloe took his hand and led him to a cluster of rocks near the edge of the bluff overlooking the Middle Loup that flowed past the bluff's base below. In spring or summer, they might watch bald eagles or their fledglings in nests along the sheer wall below. They had been here many times, and he knew they would share the flat surface of a large stone that nature had deposited for a lovers' bench.

When the pair reached the stone, Chloe pulled Gage to her and planted a lingering kiss on his lips. He held her in his arms for a bit before releasing her. They sat down on the bench-rock and gazed silently at the panorama below. The view extended for miles over the seemingly endless Sandhills, split only by tree-lined streams and rivers and occasional ponds where water had broken to the surface. A half mile upriver on the presently slow-flowing Middle Loup, they could see where the rushing waters confined by the narrow Dismal River's banks poured into the Loup.

"Remember when we built a raft and took it down the Dismal?" Chloe said.

"How could I forget? We both about drowned that day when the rapids tossed us off the raft, and it went on without us. Then there was a long walk upstream to the horses. I'd figured on a slower ride and a place where we could pull over."

"Oh, but the thrill. We've had a lot of good times, Gage." She wrapped her arm around his waist and squeezed.

"We have, Chloe, and we're not done yet. But it's probably best we pass on the rapids."

"I hope there is more time ahead."

She seemed doubtful, and it worried him. She had always been given to premonitions, good and bad, and the number of times she had been correct was plain unnerving. "Chloe, we really need to be together all the time. It bothers me to have you living at your place alone. Marry me. Come live at the K Bar K. We've got a cook there. No house chores. We're not more than five miles from your place. You can check on things there every day if it suits you, but my hands could look after the stock."

"You could come live with me."

He thought for a moment. "I would do it if that's what it takes to be together. Just marry me."

"I wouldn't let you move to my place. You would hate it soon enough. But I will marry you."

Gage could not believe what he was hearing. He looked at her and saw that her eyes were already fixed on his face. She was serious. He kissed her gently. "When? Next week? Sooner the better."

"Not till April."

"Why April? Will you come live with me now?"

"I want to spend another winter here. I've got things to settle in my head first about my property and such. And the cats."

"Bring the cats with you. We can always use mousers in the stables and other outbuildings. Inky can live in the house. He and Rip are pals."

"You are making it too easy."

"I want you to be my wife, and I don't like you staying at the Circle D alone, especially after the stranger tried to kill you. I worry that it's related to something else going on in this part of the hills."

"And what's that?"

"Sam says we've got a rustling problem. We're missing cattle, and he's sure you are, too. Probably other ranchers have the problem and don't know it yet. Sam and the hands are going to start taking the best cattle count they can. We should have about 750 cows plus their calves from last spring. Then we've got nearly twenty-five herd bulls. We'll get a count on yours, too, if you like."

She sighed. "I guess you'd better. I'll cover the cost of your hands doing this."

"I don't want your money. Unlike some folks I know, I keep some year-round help just for unexpected things that come up. You might put pencil to paper and figure out how many we would be looking for."

"Twelve herd bulls, 297 cows and 282 spring calves. I don't think anybody's made off with horses. They're fenced off separately, and the ones not in the lot here get checked every other day by either Mort or me. All told, I should have fifty-eight. I'm hoping to sell anything I don't hold back for breeding next spring after breaking the young ones."

"You don't break any yourself anymore, do you?"

She smiled impishly, "What do you think?"

"I was afraid so. It's been a long time since I broke a horse, and I have no longing for those days. I still get aches and pains from the broken bones."

"I'd have never guessed it last night. Anyhow, I thought I would write to Fort Niobrara and Fort Robinson and see if the Army's got any interest. They could come and get them, and I wouldn't need to hire wranglers to drive the critters someplace."

"Local ranchers are always looking for good horseflesh, too."

"And most don't want to pay a fair price. They treat me like I'm a dang fool. I don't have time for that nonsense. Now, you thought that would-be killer might be connected to the rustlers?"

"Well, I just thought it was a possibility to consider."

"And how many cattle do I keep in the house?"

"Maybe he figured if they killed you, they could run off the whole herd and that it would be days before anybody noticed. You said he had been watching the place. He would've known you didn't keep any fulltime hands around."

"You always get back to that, don't you?"

"Well, I guess I've moved you a bit this trip. We're still going to get hitched in April?"

"I said so, didn't I?"

"Yeah, so I'm counting on it."

"That's providing I'm still alive, of course."

"Now, don't talk like that. That could work two ways, you know."

"I ain't got plans to die. You know how I feel about 1888 coming up, though."

"I don't want to hear any more about 1888 or buzzards circling or anything like that. I've got to head back to the K Bar K. One more thing, Chloe. We need to report what happened here to the law. My ranch is in Custer County and so is your house, even though all but a sliver of your land lies north in Blaine County, so I thought I would ride into Broken Bow and talk to the county sheriff there. Any objection?"

"I don't give a dang. Wally Barnes ain't going to get off his fat ass and ride clear out here anyhow, especially since as a female I can't vote. I'm just a fart in a whirlwind to him. But I know it will make you feel better to make your report. You always want things done right."

Custer County, the second largest county in Nebraska area-wise, consisted of over 2500 square miles, twice the size of the state of Rhode Island and second largest Nebraska county next to Cherry, also located in the Sandhills. Vast lands with few people and many cattle. A trip by the sheriff from Broken Bow would likely require an overnight stay, and Gage shared Chloe's expectations so far as an investigation was concerned.

"Well, it's best we make a record of this with the authorities. You really don't have any idea why a man might try to kill you?"

"Nope."

Somehow, Gage did not quite believe her.

Chapter 4

GAGE ARRIVED AT the K Bar K headquarters just before noon. He dismounted and led Keeper to the stable. He was pleased to find his grandson, Sam Kraft, putting up his own mount in the stall next to Keeper's. It never failed to strike him that Sam was the spitting image of Dalton, the young man's father, at the same age albeit a half foot taller.

Sam had just turned twenty-five a month back. Dalt was twenty-three years old the last time Gage saw him, the day Dalt and his best friend, Robert Downs, went off to enlist in the Union Army. Both died at Gettysburg and were buried there among the unknowns with over 3500 Union soldiers. It always perturbed Gage that the Army knew that their sons were dead but could not identify them for burial, but maybe it was better that he did not know the reason.

Dalton Kraft had departed unaware that his wife Jenny was carrying a child. Gage did not know if Dalt had ever received the letter informing him of the birth of his son and the death of Jenny following childbirth. Gage had received no confirmation, but mail to and from the battlefronts was a roll of the dice. Regardless, Dalton, not yet grown, had been the second "K" on the K Bar K's ranch brand for nearly a decade before the war.

"Hi, Gramps, you look like you're lost in deep thought. Monique said I should be here for noon dinner and that you would be back from the Circle D for dinner. How's Grams?"

"She was fine when I left her, but we need to talk about her. We'll sit down in my office after dinner."

Gage and Chloe had been maintaining their unconventional relationship since before Sam's birth, and there had been an extended stretch of years when Chloe would join them for a meal now and then. That had stopped abruptly several years earlier when she started declining invitations and became more reclusive.

She had once been a cheerful, easy-going sort. Now that side of her erupted only occasionally from the cloak of sadness and black moods she had taken on. Still, he savored the moments he shared with her. His deepest regret was that they had not spent more of their days and nights together.

Meals for family and all the hands were served at the expansive headquarters house. During roundups, when extra hands were taken on, meals were often served in shifts. Monique Potter was not more than a few years past forty-five, but she had been chief cook for the outfit for nearly thirty years, having joined Gage less than three years following his wife's death from what the doctor called consumption. That diagnosis usually meant that he did not know. In any case, she had wasted away and suffered great pain during her final weeks, and Gage would not have wished her another day.

At the table today was Monique's husband and ranch foreman, Bruce Potter, who had been with Gage when he claimed a parcel of Sandhills land almost thirty-five years earlier after pulling up stakes in Missouri. Bruce had been no more than seventeen-years-old then, but he had been a hard-working, smart kid and proved loyal, even working for room and board for months at a time during tough years till Gage could raise the money for back pay.

White-haired and bearded Smoky Fletcher, a crusty character in his late sixties now, had hired on during the Missouri years. He had no ambition beyond herding cattle and wrangling horses, but there was none better at what he did. The other hand who showed up for dinner was a relative newcomer with only ten years' service. Ricky Meeks, stocky and thickly muscled in his mid-thirties, was a quiet dark-haired man with a brushy mustache who never talked about his past like most did.

So far, Gage had found nothing that Ricky could not do. He did a lot of blacksmithing and repair work for the ranch, but when called upon, he could handle livestock or any other task that needed attention. The other fulltime hand, Alex Paul, had taken a week off to visit family in Broken Bow, and rumor was that the young man also had a lady there he was courting.

The men were in good humor today, partly because of the unseasonably warm weather, Gage suspected, but it did not hurt that tomorrow was Saturday and a day off except for a few stable chores. They had a Saturday off once a month and every Sunday during slack times, but with a hard day's ride to the nearest town with more than one saloon, a visit to the trading post a bit over five miles southwest was the closest to sporting adventure a man might find in these parts. Smoky and Ricky would likely make that trip Saturday afternoon or evening.

There was a small tavern connected to one end of "Orville's Oasis" that included three or four card tables, as well as an upstairs room hosted by Kitty Kat, a young lady who provided a half hour's company for a dollar. The only other prerequisite was a bath, available in the rear of the Oasis for another dollar. Kitty Kat had been hosting the room for fifteen years now, but Gage was told that a half dozen women had played the role over that time.

As usual, Smoky did most of the talking at the dinner table. In his boots, he might crowd five and a half feet tall, but he stood above them all when it came to tall tales, some of which might carry a grain of truth but no more than that, Gage thought. Monique and her fifteen-year-old daughter, Vega, emerged from the kitchen carrying trays packed with bowls and serving plates, which they placed on a counter that separated the spacious kitchen from the dining area. A huge platter of roasted beef caught all eyes, and the large baked potatoes and other canned vegetables from Monique's huge garden assured the usual feast. Cobbler or pie would top off the meal later.

Monique was a treasure. A dark, slim woman of mixed French and Sioux heritage, she always seemed to have a reservoir of energy to call upon, and she made the household function. She had also been a surrogate mother for Sam through the years, starting with wet-nursing the orphaned baby with her own newborn at the time of his mother's death. The two had been like twins until Everett Potter died an agonizing death from diphtheria at age eleven. Everett had been the Potters' eldest, and they had raised four others without serious incident, Vega being the youngest.

The men were already eating when Monique and Vega took places at the table, Monique traditionally sitting next to Gage and Vega claiming a chair on the opposite side of the table by her father. Monique and Gage did a lot of their business during meals while others ate and talked. Gage finished a few bites of the succulent roast beef before he spoke. "Delicious as usual, Monique. I don't know how you do it day after day. I think my hands hang around more for your cooking than the money."

She smiled. "I think it's the way the boss treats them. Those of us who can work for the K Bar K are very fortunate. You treat us more like family than hired help."

"You are family. Now, I am going to be taking the wagon to Broken Bow on Monday. My guess is you are needing some food supplies."

"I will make a list. I have a favor to ask."

"Granted."

"I didn't tell you what yet. I would like you to take Vega and me with you. I want to see if I can arrange for her to enroll at the high school in Broken Bow next term. It starts in February. Her teacher says she cannot teach her any further and believes she would qualify to enter as at least a junior. She is helping the teacher now, and she thinks that is what she wants to do. As you know there is a boarding house for students in Broken Bow. The other kids had to board in North Platte two years to finish schooling. They didn't like it then, but they're glad now."

"I would enjoy your company. I have other errands there, too, and I would be glad to have you help deal with the general store folks. We will stay at the hotel, and I will get another room for you and Vega. We may need to stay two nights. It will be a long day with the buckboard both ways, and that will give us a full day in between to take care of business."

"There will only be four eating here. I will prepare food ahead as much as possible, and Bruce claims he can handle the kitchen. I know Sam will help. He is handier there than my dear husband, but I would never tell Bruce."

"You spoil all of us. They'll be fine." Monique and Vega would lighten the journey, and he welcomed any opportunity to keep Monique happy at the K Bar K. Vega was an exceptionally bright and hardworking young woman, as well as the recipient of her mother's exotic beauty. It was time for her to move on.

The diners were rewarded with apple cobbler and, of course, an extra round of coffee. Before they began marching their plates and dinnerware to the kitchen, where any uneaten food would be scraped into a twenty gallon can before placing the plates and utensils in the big sink, Gage called for their attention. "Starting next week, fellas, we are going to make a livestock headcount as best we can. Tally the horses, cows, calves, and bulls by location on the range. I will be in Broken Bow for a few days. Work on K Bar K land till I get back. Then I may split off a few of you to help me with the Circle D."

Smoky never hesitated to question. "Rustling, boss?"

"Could be. We need to see if anything is disappearing for reasons we can't account for."

Chapter 5

LATER IN THE ranch office, Gage sat in his swivel chair, and Sam was perched in a leather-cushioned chair on the opposite side. Gage said, "I just wanted to bring you up to date on a few things, Sam."

"About Grams?"

"Yep. I'm worried sick about her. Somebody tried to break into her place the other night, and it appears he intended to kill her. Why else would a man break into a dugout like that? Fortunately, she killed him with a shotgun blast."

"How is she doing after that?"

"I'm more shaken than she was.".

"Somehow, I'm not surprised. Maybe he was trying to rob her, heard that she doesn't trust banks much. She said she keeps an account in North Platte to deposit drafts from cattle or horse sales, but she doesn't leave the money there long—tries to convert as much as possible to silver and gold. She doesn't like paper money much, either. Of course, you know all that."

"Yeah, she's got some strange ways, but she's smarter than the devil. I can't keep up with her thinking. Most folks hereabouts think she's on the edge of destitute. Well, we may have a bigger spread, but she's better at handling her money than I've ever been. Some years, we're land and cattle poor. No cash money. God knows how much she's got stashed away someplace."

"And you love that woman," Sam said.

"Yep, for nearly thirty years now. Can't help myself. I've asked her to marry me I don't know how many times over those years. She never said 'no,' only that she had to think about it. This is just between you and me. This morning she said 'yes.'"

Sam grinned, "You're serious. When's the date? Before Christmas would be nice."

"April, she told me. No sooner."

"Why wait?"

"I've been thinking about that. She thinks 1888 is going to be a terrible year, that lots of people are going to die. I'm wondering if she plans to die before April and trying to make me feel good because she agreed to marry me."

"That could give a man the shivers."

"She's a strange woman, but I guess that has always been a part of my attraction to her. I am going in to Broken Bow with Monique and Vega next week. I would appreciate it if you would keep an eye on Chloe's place. Check in once a day, maybe circle the area around the farmstead to see if anybody's there that shouldn't be."

"Of course, I will."

"Maybe you could stop over tomorrow and tell her I'll be headed to Broken Bow with the wagon and see if there is anything she wants me to pick up. She knows I was going to report the shooting to the county sheriff. I didn't ask her to go, because I knew she wouldn't. Just as well, I guess. Monique wanted to see about enrolling Vega in high school next term."

"I'm glad to hear it. The girl is smart as a whip. Maybe even quicker than John. Monique told me he loves school at the Omaha Medical College. He still wants to return to the Sandhills when he finishes and gets licensed."

"Yeah, and Marie is teaching school in Lincoln. Good kids."

"I still think about Everett every day. Never had a close friend after he died. Too much of a loner, I guess. I wonder about Ben sometimes, too. After schooling here, he just up and left, and nobody's heard a word since. At least six years, I'd guess. That's got to be a load for Bruce and Monique to carry."

Sam just shrugged. "He was a different one. I don't think there was a falling out with his folks. He just took his horse and tack and pulled out early one morning. Maybe we should hire a detective and see what can be turned up. When we get through this, I'll see what Monique thinks."

"Yeah, I like that idea. I worry for Monique's sake. She's been like a ma to me, but she carries her wounds so privately."

Like Sam, Gage thought. He wished his grandson would socialize more. He rarely left the ranch, not even on Saturdays when the others went to the Oasis. Not many miles to the east there were a good number of homesteaders settled on quarter-section claims, most with large families. He had kept company with several young women, been serious about one, but social life in this country was at best a barn dance once a month during summer months, perhaps a wedding now and then, but more often funerals. He was married to his work, Gage feared, but he guessed he hadn't been much of an example to guide the young man differently.

"Well," Gage said, "I mostly wanted to talk about my concern for Chloe. I know you keep an eye on her and think of her as grandma. I felt you should be aware of what took place."

"You can count on my keeping a watch out. It's sad that her daughter never comes out this way. I gather she doesn't write, either."

"No, she hasn't heard from Darla in twenty some years. Darla was five years older than your dad and Robert. I guess she would be in her early fifties now. She hated it here and tried to run away twice as a girl, saying she would rather die than live in the Sandhills. That's when Chloe and Hank, shortly before he was killed in that Sioux raid, agreed to send her away to boarding school back east. She married some Harvard-educated lawyer by the name of Churchill—Richard Churchill. Prominent Boston family. Chloe always figured her daughter would have been mortified to bring her husband back to the dugout."

"But she doesn't even write?"

"Chloe writes every three months, but her letters have gone unanswered since a few years after the end of the war. Of course, it's possible Darla never receives them. Chloe doesn't know for certain that Darla is alive. She has likely moved during that time, but the letters never come back. That doesn't mean much, though. There are a lot of complaints that the Post Office doesn't return undelivered mail."

"So she's just disappeared?"

"Darla wrote after she got married—Chloe, of course, was not invited to a wedding, but she supposed Darla would have been embarrassed by her mother's appearance among the elite guests. She just shrugged it off. We didn't have train connections anywhere near in those days."

"Grandchildren?"

"There was a granddaughter born a year or two before you were born. Colette was the girl's name. If she survived childhood—and that's uncertain—she could have children of her own by now. For that matter, Darla could have had more children."

Sam said, "I wonder if that's what Chloe meant when she asked me to ride along with her to North Platte last month. I know she told you she was going to visit that lady lawyer there, Audra Scott Adams. The lawyer clerked in her husband's law firm for three or four years before she passed the bar examination. She worked for a private detective firm in Kansas before that. Chloe said she had legal business, but she intended to investigate some family things while she was there, too. Maybe she is trying to find out something about her daughter. I didn't ask, of course. She never talked family things with me."

"I've always just got bits and pieces. Chloe's very guarded about her history. She will say something when it suits her, but I never pry."

"Well, Grams has been more than good to me over the years, and that's all I will judge her by."

"That's how I look at it. Be slow to judge anybody harshly. We never know what ghosts they carry on their shoulders."

Chapter 6

MADDIE SANFORD STEPPED off the Burlington and Missouri River Railroad Company's passenger car onto the platform in front of the small, clapboard depot. She was followed by a huge dog bearing over 160 pounds on a tall, long frame.

The two were incapable of disappearing into the melee of passengers and greeters flooding the platform, and they were given ample room by the others. Maddie stood a strong six feet tall with her regal bearing, a rare height for women of her time. She was a striking young woman with long, reddish-brown hair tied back with a green ribbon and flowing almost to mid back.

Sharp features and high cheekbones came together to give Maddie an exotic look, but some might find the dusting of freckles on her nose out of place. Regardless, she was aware of men turning heads her way as she made her way to the station and noted a few frowns from the wives of the married lookers.

She wore a long beige skirt and matching jacket over a white blouse, although her preferred attire was denim britches over cowboy boots. She had learned to dress for occasions, however, and she knew that she would procure more assistance in town dressed like a lady of social significance. Safety was not a concern. Her dog, Pirate, on command would dispense with anyone who made a threatening move toward her. He had killed more than once.

Pirate was a mixed blood creature, likely sired by a wolf that mated with a domestic female, a large shorthair of some kind, since his own hair was short. Erect ears seemed constantly alert to foreign sounds and his coloring was an unusual calico of blue-black, orange and white splotches. Eerie yellow eyes tended to make strangers wary, and coal black fur surrounding one eye like a one-eyed pirate's patch had earned his name.

Maddie hoisted her large carpet bag and made her way through the crowd toward the ticket window. She had seen the white-haired balding man inside watching her with curiosity, and he was either not busy or folks were keeping their distance from her and Pirate. She knew they sometimes affected people that way, and she rather enjoyed it.

She walked up to the window, and the man opened it and peered at her over spectacles that were pushed down to the end of a prominent nose. "Yes, ma'am?"

"I require lodging for a night or two. Can you recommend a decent place?"

"No shortage of hotels here, ma'am, and several more in the works. Since the B and M showed up with rails a bit more than two years back, this town is booming. But I think you might like the Grand Central just a block north. They got dining for those that want it, and if you give the clerk fifty cents or a dollar, he'll likely let your friend share the room."

"Thank you, sir. I'll look at the Grand Central."

"There are buggies lining the street off the platform if you need transportation."

"Thanks again, but I can handle a block or two with what I've got."

"Figured as much."

She headed toward the dirt street off the west side of the station, and turned onto the walkway that was boardwalk here but appeared to be brick farther north. She was just glad for the chance to stretch her legs after embarking from Kearney several hours earlier. Her long legs were not made for cramped passenger cars, and, of course, poor Pirate was not structured for confinement. That was one reason they had taken a day off the rails in Grand Island to the southeast after their journey from Manhattan, Kansas. They had walked for some hours along the banks of the Platte River there.

As they walked along the street, she was surprised at the new construction recently completed or in progress in the town. She assumed this had been triggered mostly by the railroad, but the area must have a significant population to serve. She counted at least four law offices, two on second floors of main street buildings, a newspaper office for the *Broken Bow Republican*, several restaurants, a brick building for the First National Bank, a butcher shop, clothing stores, and she could only guess at the commercial activity on the streets stretching out in all directions beyond.

When she reached the two-story hotel, she opened one of the double-doors and stepped inside, pleased to find a lobby that was clean and carpeted. A thin man of average height wearing a white shirt and a string bow tie stood at a counter off to one side, and he was eyeing Pirate uneasily.

She walked over to the counter. "My name is Maddie Sanford," she said, "and I would like a main floor room for one night. I won't know till tomorrow whether I will require a second night."

"My name is Morris Withers, at your service. Main floor, they're more expensive ma'am. Two dollars a night. Now about the dog . . ."

"Another dollar for the dog." She reached in her shoulder bag and plucked out three silver dollars and laid them on the counter.

He pointed to the hallway that led off to her right past the stairway to the second floor. "I think this can be arranged. I have Room 110 at the far end of the hallway near the rear door. That might be convenient for the dog."

"It would be. You are very considerate. Thank you, Mister Withers."

He handed her a pencil and nodded to a register for her to sign. "It is almost noon. I will need to know before noon tomorrow if you wish to keep the room for another night."

"I should know by then. Tell me, I am traveling to the Circle D Ranch. I am told it is in the northwest part of the county. Do you know where that is?"

Withers turned and went to the desk behind him and pulled a folded parchment sheet from the drawer and spread the sheet out on the countertop. "This is a county map. Nebraska's got ninety-three counties. Custer is the second largest area-wise. This map marks the location of the headquarters of the major ranches."

Maddie said, "The eastern part of the county doesn't show so many."

"You don't find so many in the eastern part because that is homesteaded by would-be farmers. Most are 160-acre tracts—quarter sections—the amount allowed by the Homestead Act. The land is granted by the government, and if a man proves he has worked it for five years, he owns it. Even many of those who last the time, sell out and leave. Not an easy life out there. There has been a glut of folks swarming in the past few years—a lot of Germans. They seem to be prospering more than most."

Maddie said, "I see the Circle D on your map. It's almost on the county's north border."

"The B & M has a track that will take you to Anselmo, which I guess would get you within about ten miles of the place. That town was just platted not more than a few years ago, and they don't have the homesteader population nearby to support a boom like Broken Bow has had. There is a house there that takes lodgers but not much of anything else just yet beyond a little general store, maybe a tavern. The rail spur to the north will likely be for cattle shipments back this way and on to the Union Pacific south of here for transporting east."

"Does that train go out daily?"

"No. Once a week right now. I think. I'm not sure how regular the schedule is. You would need to get back to the station agent about that." Withers looked toward the front door that was opening. "Wait, here is someone who may be able to help. Gage, could you spare a moment?"

An older man wearing faded blue jeans, boots, and a Stetson walked toward them. Obviously a cattleman, she decided. He was about her height, maybe an inch or so taller, a slender man who had not gone to fat with the years—distinguished looking, clean shaven, wearing a buckskin jacket, and string tie. He tipped his hat to her and nodded a greeting when he reached the counter. She liked him.

"What is it, Morris?"

"Gage, this is Miss Maddie Sanford. Miss Sanford, meet Gage Kraft of the K Bar K Ranch. He neighbors with the Circle D."

Gage said, "My pleasure, ma'am."

She extended her hand, catching him momentarily by surprise. "Pleased to meet you, Mister Kraft." He accepted her hand, and she gave him a firm handshake.

Withers said, "Miss Sanford is wanting to get to the Circle D. I was thinking you might be able to help."

"Certainly. Would I be too forward if I asked you to join me in the dining room for lunch, Miss Sanford? I'm hungry, and I gather you just got off the train. They would not have fed you on the B & M. We can talk over lunch."

"Well, I would love to, Mister Kraft, but I must take my bag to my room and freshen up a bit, and I must find something for my dog, Pirate, to eat. He is well behaved, but I don't know how dining room guests would take his presence."

"Will he remain in your room willingly?"

"That's not a problem."

"Would he come with me?"

"If I tell him to. I have a leash and collar in my bag. He is not fond of leashing but accepts it."

"Where is your room?"

"Room 110 at the end of the hall."

"Just across from yours, Gage," Withers said.

"Very well. Let me take your bag and escort you to your room. I have a few items to pick up in my own, and if you will collar and leash Pirate, I will take him across the street to Schwartz's Butcher Shop for lunch. By the time we return, perhaps you will be ready to dine."

"Uh, well, yes, I guess that will be fine." This elderly rancher had her head spinning. He was decisive and did not waste time, but certainly a gentleman and very kind.

Blizzard

After Gage Kraft left her room with Pirate, Maddie had a chance to catch her breath. She was accustomed to setting the pace for those around her and was quick to grab command at first opportunity. Ordinarily, she would have declined an offer by a man to carry her bag, but this gentleman just made things happen. Pirate liked him, so she had no qualms about the rancher's intentions, but she welcomed some time to regroup.

She looked about the room, which was simply decorated with a double bed, clean and welcoming but not luxurious. There was a bedside table with a kerosene lamp and a small dresser for clothing with a washbowl and water pitcher on top. She peered under the bed and found a chamber pot. She had been pleased, however, to see in the hallway separate men's and women's water closets for common usage by guests of the wing. Maddie was accustomed to outdoor privies but welcomed the luxury of more convenient facilities. She would take advantage of the accommodation shortly.

She was much refreshed when Gage Kraft returned with Pirate. After rapping lightly on the door and being admitted, Kraft stepped aside while Maddie unbuckled the dog's collar and placed it and the leash on the room's only chair. "Did you find something for Pirate to eat?"

"Oh, yes. Hans Schwartz always has meat scraps to sell. His butcher shop feeds a lot of dogs and cats in this town. Hans suggested three pounds of beef scraps for Pirate. Your friend made short work of it but seemed satisfied. Hans is open till eight o'clock evenings and said you will probably want to bring him by again before closing. Scraps are a dime a pound, so they're cheap enough."

"Thanks so much for doing this."

"On the way back, we stepped into an alley, and he relieved both bowels and bladder. I thought you would want to know."

She had wanted to ask about that and had been seeking words to do so without the crudity she might more commonly spit out. "Then, I think Pirate will be ready to nap a spell. I filled my wash basin with water and placed it on the floor in case he gets thirsty."

Chapter 7

THE WORST OF the lunch crowd had started to clear out by the time Gage and Maddie entered the hotel dining room, and they found a table for two in a corner near the front window. They both ordered the day's special of steak, fried potatoes, and beans with apple pie for dessert, and now they sipped on black coffee while waiting to be served.

Gage noticed that the young woman seemed entranced by the pedestrians and horses passing by on the street and brick walk outside. "Busy town," he said.

She turned her head toward him. "I'm sorry. I'm not being very businesslike, Mister Kraft. I just can't quite believe all the activity in this town. New buildings going up all over, more people than I ever dreamt I would find here."

"Please, call me 'Gage.' I won't feel so old."

"If you will call me 'Maddie.'"

"Fair enough. The hustle and bustle out there can be easily explained. Broken Bow was just laid out and platted as a town six years ago with no more than a shack for a post office. I'm told the town has now reached over fifteen hundred people. That is in large part because of winning a fight to be county seat for Custer County and then the B & M arriving with its rails a mite over two years back. And then there are ranchers and homesteaders over a large territory who have been desperate for the goods and services of a full-fledged town. The demand has been there for a spell but not the supply. It may take some time to balance out with some homesteaders pulling up stakes and too many of some businesses setting up. I'm guessing there will be an oversupply of hotels soon enough, for instance. But this is a boon to those of us who live out in this country."

"I've seen cattle covering some of the hills, but they seem to be small ranching operations."

"If you are headed out to Circle D, you will see more cattle and a lot fewer people along the way. You're not quite to the Sandhills here. The whole county is best fit for cattle operations in my view, but much of the south and east are homesteaded by farmers. Cattle reign in the north and west, and most of what was homesteaded there has been surrendered to ranching operations. At least a third of my ranch on the east end was once homesteaded."

The waitress appeared with their heaping dinner plates, and as they turned to their meals, Gage decided it was time to get to the purpose of their little talk. "So you are trying to figure out how to get to the Circle D, and Morris thought I might be able to help you?"

"He saw you coming through the door and seemed to be inspired. That's why he called you over, I guess."

"And I assume you are wanting to speak with Chloe Downs there."

"Yes, that's my mission."

She obviously was not going to tell him more than that, and it was none of his concern. Not now, anyhow. "Morris told you about train connections at Anselmo."

"Yes, and they did not appear too promising. I would have to find the right day, and there was the question of transportation after I got there."

"My headquarters place is about five miles from Chloe's. She and I have been friends for over thirty years. I am going to have a buckboard loaded with supplies. I am also transporting the lady who runs the house and her fifteen-year-old daughter. They are looking into high school arrangements for the girl in Broken Bow. I've got a team of mules pulling the wagon, but we've got more load than I like. I brought my horse with me in case I needed him for getting about town, but I haven't so far. Can you drive a team or ride for a long day?"

"Either, but I like mounted better."

Gage was silent for a time, watching the young woman tear into her food like a starving cowhand.

"You don't need a sidesaddle?"

Maddie about choked on her food and started laughing.

"What's so funny?"

"Mister . . . Gage, I was born on a horse, raised on a ranch in Colorado till I was fifteen. I've never been on a sidesaddle. And I wear a dress as seldom as possible. If you take me along, I'll be wearing boots and britches. I can't wait to get rid of this clown outfit I'm wearing."

"You will get off to a better start with Chloe if you stick with the britches."

"I hope you will tell me more about her along the way—that is, if I am invited."

"Yeah, you're invited. We will pull out after breakfast in the morning, so if you have business here in town, you will want to tend to it this afternoon. You can stay at our ranch house while you're visiting. We've got plenty of room. You'll find that Chloe is a bit cramped for space."

Blizzard

"I appreciate that, but let's just see how this plays out. Right now, an enormous slice of apple pie is calling me."

Chapter 8

A WARM DAY LIKE this was a bonus in late November even farther south, Maddie thought. It energized her to be astride a horse again with sunrays warming her neck and shoulders. Pirate bounded along beside her, disappearing now and then to chase a rabbit or explore the wooded areas along the creeks.

She loved Gage's horse, Keeper, a seasoned, gentle critter that responded to neck-reining and no doubt would remain near the buckboard if she dropped off to sleep. She was too enthralled, of course, for that to happen. The gelding was a strange-colored animal with his yellowish coat and the dark dorsal stripe. On her father's ranch in Colorado, the gelding probably would have been called a coyote dun.

She had loved getting acquainted with Monique and Vega Porter, who might have passed for sisters with their dark beauty. She hoped she would have the opportunity to get to know them better. Her stay in the area was to be for an indefinite time. She was on assignment from the Crockett Detective Agency headquartered in Manhattan, Kansas.

She had been attending college there and was not a fulltime employee of the agency but took assignments occasionally when they were shorthanded. Having resided with the owners, Trace and Darby Crockett, for over four years now, she figured she owed them that much, and the pay was good.

Maddie had attended Kansas State Agricultural College in the town for two years but had taken the fall term off to experience other things and to decide the next road to take in her life. She was tired of school and did not seek a career as a detective. Audra Scott Adams, a former Crockett agent and now a newly admitted member of the Nebraska Bar, was a dear friend and had been trying for the past year to lure her to North Platte for an extended visit.

Audra had employed the detective agency on behalf of her client, Chloe Downs, and asked the firm to send Maddie if she was available. Audra had joined her husband, Ari Adams, in the North Platte law firm where she had clerked, and Maddie knew her friend had visions of convincing her to try clerking in her firm.

She had already done a stint as a bank clerk before taking on the Crockett assignment and knew that working within the confines of a law office was not for her, but she wanted to visit Audra. First, however, was her interview with Chloe Downs. She had no clue what the client expected of her beyond reporting on the results of the investigation the agency had completed to date.

"We will be moving into the Sandhills from here on," Gage hollered at her from the wagon. "You've probably noticed some changes as we moved along, fewer farmsteads and such, the rolling prairie starting to get hillier. We won't be on public roads anymore, such as they are."

She reined her mount nearer the wagon. "Yes, I've noticed the change, but the endless hills ahead are breathtaking—like a vast desert, but with grass-covered hills and dunes and haystacks rising above the flats. Cattle country, obviously. I like the Kansas Flint Hills, but this is more like home than anything I've seen since leaving Colorado five or six years ago. Yet, these hills are different. I have never seen anything like this country. How far are we from your ranch?"

"Probably three hours taking the wagon trail with our load. A rider, of course, taking a route more as the crow flies would cut that in half, or by pushing the horse a little could do it in an hour."

"I can't wait." She slowed Keeper's pace to allow the wagon to move ahead and then rode alongside the rear of the wagon where Vega was perched on several bags of flour. "Where is your school, Vega? I could see schoolhouses dotting the prairie, especially to the east when we started. I haven't seen one for a few hours now."

Vega, brushing wind-blown strands of raven hair away from her face, said, "I have always attended Cedar Creek School about three miles east of the K Bar K ranch house. We have one of the larger schools, almost twenty students most years. Most are from homesteads east and south of the school. Ranch kids come in from the north and west, maybe five or six of us. Some of the schools that are further north and west might not have more than a half dozen kids some years, and some kids far away from homestead areas in the Sandhills go unschooled except for what mom or dad can do."

"You said you will be going to Broken Bow to high school. When does that start?"

"I won't transfer in till early February. Miss Galbraith is the only teacher at Cedar Creek right now. There are usually two, but the other—Miss Lowe—disappeared a few weeks back. I think she up and married a cow puncher who'd been courting her, and they just pulled up stakes and left. She was the head teacher. Miss Galbraith just turned seventeen and is overwhelmed by the notion of teaching that many kids on her own, so I agreed to stay and help her for a few months while the school board looks for a replacement. I was offered the job for the rest of the school year, but I don't want to delay my education."

"You are very wise."

Pirate's frantic barking from the west interrupted their conversation. Maddie's eyes, partially blinded by the sun's glare, searched the horizon before she saw the dog no more than fifty yards distant digging at the base of a low bluff on the near side of one of the larger sand dunes. She reined Keeper away from the wagon and nudged the horse toward her wolfdog.

When she reached Pirate, Maddie dismounted, and the dog stopped his work and turned to her, his expectant look summoning her to his side. The footing was soft here, the earth a mix of dirt and sand. Part of the bluff's bank had been caved off above where Pirate stood.

"What is it, boy?" she said, when she stepped over beside him. The dog looked down, and then she saw the shredded clothing covering torn, rotting flesh on the bones of a skeleton with the jawbone of a skull displaying grinning teeth. The size and clothing indicated male, and patches of short brown hair remaining atop the head pretty much confirmed it. Of course, her own height and attire might cause some to wonder under such circumstances.

Maddie had seen enough death that the scene did not stun her. She was mostly curious and knelt on the ground to study the remains more closely. Other creatures had obviously been digging in the soft soil before Pirate's discovery. Most of one arm and a foot had apparently been dragged away. She could not be certain how the person died, but what seemed to be an unnatural hole in the middle of the forehead suggested a bullet might have entered there. She figured that someone, presumably the killer, had rendered token burial by caving off a portion of the bluff overhang to cover the body.

She saw something of dull, tarnished silver on the leather belt draped over the man's hip bone, almost hidden by the remains of what her railroad executive father called a "lawyer's coat." She unbuckled the belt and pulled it free, dislodging the metal object from the leather and examining it. A badge in the shape of a shield. She rubbed the surface clean and read the imprint: Pinkerton National Detective Agency.

"Good Lord, what have you and that hound of yours come across, young lady?"

She started at hearing Gage Kraft's voice behind her and got to her feet. "It appears that Pirate found a dead Pinkerton agent." She handed Gage the badge.

He nodded, returned the badge and walked over to the makeshift grave that Pirate had uncovered and looked down at the remains. "Took a slug between the eyes, probably up close. Do you agree?"

"Yes, that's what I figured." It occurred to her that he was testing her, already guessing that she was not a virgin when it came to dealing with things gruesome.

Gage sighed, "We've got to get the law involved. We can't get the remains in the wagon. I will send a few hands over here first thing in the morning. They can roll everything into a blanket and put the remains in an empty supply chest. One man can take the buckboard back to Broken Bow and turn everything over to the sheriff. He won't come out to investigate. I've already tried that. We don't have enough votes this far out in the county. He would likely contact Pinkertons, though, and see who they might be missing. They might even send an agent."

"If they can find a paying client."

Gage's eyes narrowed, and he cocked his head to one side as he looked at her. "Yeah, I suppose. I wouldn't know about that. Let's get back to the wagon so we can get home before dark."

Chapter 9

BRUCE POTTER WAS at the ranch house to greet his wife and daughter, and after quick embraces and kisses and a brief introduction to Maddie, hurried to the bunkhouse to fetch Smoky Fletcher and Alex Paul to help unload the buckboard. When he returned with Smoky, he told Gage, "Smoky and Alex and me finished up inventory of the K Bar K herd this afternoon, Boss. Alex got back a day early."

"I'm anxious to hear what you turned up. What about the Circle D?"

"Sam and Ricky split off at noon to start the Circle D. Supper will be late, so they ought to make it in time to eat. If not, Monique will hold something back for them. Thank the Lord, I've been booted out of the kitchen. She'd have me washing pots and pans that I didn't get cleaned up while she was gone."

Gage said, "I'll put up the mules and Keeper and let you deal with Monique on where to put things. If it's not foodstuffs, you know where things go. I've got a nastier job for tomorrow. We'll need the buckboard, so you can just leave it out tonight."

Gage was mildly surprised when he saw that Maddie was already unhitching the team when he turned to the task. The lady was certainly no novice at the ranching business. After they led the critters to the stable, she unsaddled Keeper and rubbed him down, put him in a stall, forked him some hay and watered and grained him while Gage tended to the mules. They worked silently, Maddie asking only a few times where she might find something.

On the stroll to the ranch house, Gage said, "Thanks for the help. You mentioned you were raised on a ranch?"

"Till I was fifteen and my folks got divorced. Dad had to sell the ranch then—he was a vice-president of the Atchison, Topeka and Santa Fe Railroad then and tried to trade some of his stock for Mother's interest in the ranch. She hated the ranch, but insisted on cash, so the ranch got sold. Then she loaded me up on a train and shipped me off to Dad, who had settled in Kansas City by then."

"So you became a city girl?"

"Nope. I hated it there, so Pirate and I ran off to Manhattan, Kansas to my friends, Trace and Darby Crockett.

They took me in at their Flint Hills ranch after getting Dad's approval. That's the short story."

She obviously did not want to pursue the story, but Gage suspected the long version would be quite interesting. He tossed a look to the north, hoping he might see Sam and Ricky riding in. He worried that Sam would head to his own place and not check in at headquarters. He really wanted to fill Sam in on everything that was happening. He gave a sigh of relief when he saw two riders on the horizon.

Maddie said, "Two riders coming this way."

He could not stay a jump ahead of this mysterious, young woman. "That would be my grandson Sam and one of the hands, Ricky Meeks. Appears somebody took your carpetbag inside. We'll go on in and see if Vega can put you up in one of the spare rooms and help you get settled in before suppertime. You'll meet Sam and Ricky at supper."

"Pirate. I'm not sure what to do about him."

Gage nodded toward the big dog that sat side by side with Rip on the veranda that stretched the entire front of the house. "Looks like he and Rip have made friends. He can come on in and share scraps with Rip."

"He generally shares my room."

"Rip shares mine. I don't see how we can treat our guests any different."

Later, Sam and Ricky appeared just as the diners were lining up to be served chuckwagon-style at the counter that separated the kitchen from the dining room. She had met Smoky and the foreman, Bruce Potter, Monique's husband, upon arrival.

Gage introduced Maddie to the new arrivals and Alex, a fair-haired young man perhaps a few years over twenty who looked like he had not yet escaped the teens. He was a wiry cowhand with a slight build, and the six-foot Maddie towered over him. Alex was on the shy side and blushed when she offered her hand.

In contrast, Sam stood significantly above the visitor, and his face was impassive when he met Maddie, however his coffee-brown eyes betrayed him. Gage saw that his grandson studied Maddie as if putting every feature to memory. But all he said was, "Pleased to meet you, ma'am." He was obviously mystified by her presence, but no more so than Gage.

Conversation was initially awkward at the supper table. Maddie sat next to Vega directly across the table from Sam who mostly focused on his plate of ham and beans but cast furtive glances at the supper guest from time to time. Maddie, Vega and Monique, who sat on Maddie's other side, carried on their own soft dialogue about life in the Sandhills while the men talked mostly about news from Broken Bow.

When they were nearly finished with seconds, Monique announced she would break out the cherry pies she had hidden before leaving for Broken Bow. "Limit of two pieces tonight," she said, as she got up to put the pies on the serving counter.

Smoky was in line before the sliced pies were laid out. "Ain't taking no chances. I'll claim my two now."

Gage said, "Go ahead and grab dessert. We've got business to talk tonight, and I'll get started now. I've already introduced Miss Sanford. She is staying here for a spell, I hope. She is going to be visiting Chloe tomorrow. You can speak freely in front of Miss Sanford. First off, I've got an unpleasant chore for two of you first thing in the morning." He told the men about the body Pirate and Maddie had discovered and explained what needed to be done.

Alex said, "I'll help with the body, Boss, and take the wagon in to Broken Bow if you like."

Gage knew that the young man's lady friend lived only a few miles off the trail to Broken Bow and that the journey would give him a chance for another visit. He would not begrudge him that in exchange for an unpleasant chore.

Ricky said, "I can go with Alex for load up, Boss."

Gage nodded approval. "You are both elected, then. Use the back-up mule team."

Smoky said, "What in blazes is going on, Gage? What would a dang Pinkerton be doing out here in the middle of nowhere?"

"Good question, Smoky. I don't have an answer—yet. Now, where do we stand on the cattle count?"

Bruce Potter said, "Finished the K Bar K today. Of course, with the canyons and creek bottoms and such, some will be too hid-out to find. Short three herd bulls, but they wouldn't likely have been rustled. We run about 750 cows and our count was 642. I'm thinking we could have missed forty or fifty but not more than that. Last spring's calves are pretty fair-sized now, of course. Near impossible to get a heifer-steer count of them critters, but total was 626. Seem to be more of them missing, but again there would be some we didn't find."

Somebody was making off with cattle, Gage thought, enough to wipe out a year's profits so far. He looked at Sam. "What about the Circle D?"

Sam said, "I guess there will be three of us to count tomorrow, but . . ."

"Make that four. I'll ride with you."

"Well, with four of us, we should finish up in a short day, but right now I'm guessing Grams is losing at a greater rate than we are, and she doesn't have more than half the herd size to start with."

Gage sighed. "Well, it appears we've got our work cut out for us tomorrow. When you're stuffed with pie, call it a day."

After the hands left, the dogs were fed all the scraps Monique could collect, and Maddie joined her and Chloe in the kitchen to help with cleanup. Only Sam remained at the table, and he looked at Gage expectantly.

"Yeah," Gage said, "we should talk a bit before you go. Let's take our coffee mugs and go in the office."

"What is this Maddie Sanford here for?" Sam asked after they were both seated at their respective sides of the office desk.

Gage sensed suspicion in his tone. "To visit Chloe. That's all I know."

"But why? She's just a kid. She wouldn't show up out here in the Sandhills for just a social call."

"I'd guess she's a strong twenty years old, maybe a year or two more, and I'm thinking she's done a lot more living than most that age. Hell, you're just twenty-five and have been doing a man's work for over ten years now."

"But she's a woman."

"Well, at least you noticed that much. A very attractive young woman unless you're blind. Most women I've known out in this country work harder than men and are tougher, too. Look at Chloe."

"Grams is different than most."

"Yeah, she's different alright. Anyway, we'll know when or if Chloe or Maddie decides to tell us. In the meantime, it wouldn't hurt if you got to know Maddie, make her feel at home here. I've got a feeling she won't be leaving anytime soon."

"Right now, I've got cattle to count. I try to make a few rounds a day in the hills about Grams's home place to see if unwelcome strangers are snooping around, but I haven't seen any sign yet. Of course, with the intruder just recently killed, I wouldn't expect anybody else just yet. Who would know about that fella? There might not even be anybody else."

Gage said, "I wouldn't have thought all that much about it if Chloe had not seen signs of the guy for several days before he tried to break in. I would have passed him off as a passing saddle tramp looking to take advantage of a woman alone and steal whatever was handy. And he could have been. We may never know."

"But this Pinkerton agent is a new twist. I'm wondering if this all ties in somehow."

"And you can add the rustling to that. Is it all related? Or none of it? Anyway, as to the rustling, we're going to need a few men to make daily rides over the ranchlands to keep a better eye on what's going on out there. I'd like to hire that Sioux tracker friend of yours—Coyote Hunter, I think is his name—to see if he can find where somebody's been driving cattle off our ranges. What would you think about taking him on as a fulltime hand?"

"He goes by 'Jim Hunter' these days. He's Santee Sioux and living in a sod house about two hours' ride east of here. It was abandoned by a homesteader who didn't stay long enough to prove up on his quarter section. The man disappeared, and the place is sort of 'no man's land' till the government office works out legalities. He does handyman work for neighbors who are just starting to trust him. He's not going back to the reservation, and nobody cares so long as he doesn't cause trouble. He's close to my age and got a decent education at a Quaker school near the Santee Reservation while he was growing up. He might like a steady job. They're tough to come by for someone with his coloring."

"Talk to him."

"I'll work on the cattle count tomorrow and head over to Jim's place the next."

Chapter 10

MADDIE RODE AWAY from the K Bar K astride a spirited sorrel gelding shortly after breakfast. It was interesting, she thought, how the ranch hands all gathered at the main house for meals, and she liked how they were all treated as family. She had already judged Gage Kraft to be a good and kind man, and it bothered her some that she had to be so secretive about her visit to Chloe Downs. Kraft was obviously fond of the woman, maybe more than fond. There was a history there that was no doubt interesting.

Pirate raced along beside horse and rider, deviating now and then to scare up a rabbit or prairie chicken. He had eaten well enough this morning that he was not scaring up food. Darn dog hadn't even slept with her last night, and when she came out of the bedroom this morning, he and Rip were sleeping side by side on the bearskin rug in front of the fireplace. Pirate and Rip even went outside together to enjoy a morning piss, and Rip had watched with sad eyes as Pirate departed with Maddie.

With Vega's help she had made up a bedroll in case she needed it for an overnight stay at Chloe Downs's house. She brought some extra undergarments, and Vega had persuaded her to leave her laundry at the K Bar K and that she and her mother would include it with the household wash. A homestead wife came every other week to tend to the cowhands' laundry, something that Maddie never gave thought to before. She knew most hands she had been around started smelling gamey after too many days in the saddle, but at her father's ranch laundry had been the wearer's responsibility. Most might take care of it in a nearby creek where they did their bathing. On her, she preferred clean undergarments but did not worry much about anything else.

Ahead on the faint trail, she caught sight of the old line shack that Gage said she should pass on the way to Chloe's dugout. Sam had not joined them for breakfast, and Gage had explained that Sam lived here and generally took care of his own morning meal, supper, too, depending upon where he concluded his workday. She was surprised to see that the so-called "shack" had an extra room attached to the rear and had been recently whitewashed. The residence appeared cozy and inviting.

She wondered why Sam did not reside in the headquarters house. It was a big sprawling residence with a second story in the wing where the Potter family resided. Gage had only mentioned that Sam was a "private sort." Well, he was a handsome devil even if he was a bit standoffish. She was going to ride on past what she thought of as a cabin when Sam Kraft came around the corner of the building leading a big stallion with scattered white splotches on its face and hip. She thought the horse might be an Appaloosa or descendant of one. He was a large, muscled critter, but of course, a man Sam's size would not be riding a small mare.

She could not very well pass by without speaking, so she reined in her sorrel and gave him a small wave. "Good morning. I didn't see you at first, and then you came around the corner of your cabin."

He doffed his hat and brushed a few strands of his unruly black hair off his forehead. "Morning, ma'am. I was fetching King here from my little three-horse stable out back. Sun's out. Going to be a good day to be in the saddle."

"Perfect for the last day of November."

He offered a small smile. "You could have told me it was October, and I wouldn't have known the difference. Some men lose track of the days out in this country. Gramps doesn't. I suppose you're headed to Circle D?"

"Yes, I'm going to meet Chloe Downs for the first time. Your grandfather told me that she's a different sort, but he seems to think quite highly of her."

He chuckled and reacted with a big smile now that she liked. "Gramps and Grams have been . . . uh . . . good friends for thirty years or so. Yeah, she's a different sort, for sure, but I'm betting you'll like her when you get to know her. I'm working on the cattle inventory at her place today, and I'm starting from the east end. If you don't mind my company, I'll ride with you as far as the house and introduce you."

"That would be nice."

He mounted the stallion, and they rode at a slow trot toward Chloe's ranch, riding side by side so they were near enough to talk along the way. Maddie said, "You called Missus Downs 'Grams.' Is she your grandmother?"

"I think of her that way, but there are no blood ties. My mother died when I was born, and I never knew my father. I was born shortly after he went off to war, and he and Chloe's son were both killed at Gettysburg. Gramps and Monique mostly raised me, but I spent a lot of time with Grams. She spoiled me some, I fear." He pointed to the northeast, obviously looking to change the subject. "See that big bluff sticking up above the hills. A person goes up there, and you can see the juncture of the Dismal River and Middle Loup. It's a sight to behold."

"I'd love to see it." She thought he might offer to take her there sometime, but he said nothing. For the next fifteen minutes, she asked questions about the Sandhills, and he answered them with enthusiasm. This was a different Sam Kraft than she had met last night, or, for that matter, the one Gage had spoken of. As they neared the ranch buildings, she had learned something about this man. He was born in the Sandhills, loved this country and would spend his life here. This is where he would be buried.

"There's Grams," Sam said, nodding toward a tiny figure, who had just emerged from the big barn, wearing a slouch hat, faded denims, well-worn boots and a tattered sheepskin jacket. At first glance, Maddie would have guessed her for a small man, but as she walked up to them, she saw a still-pretty face and stunning sky-blue eyes offsetting snow-white hair.

The woman looked first at Maddie and then at Sam. "You brought a fiancé here to meet your grams?"

Sam's face flushed a bit. "No, Grams. This is Maddie Sanford. She stayed at Gramps's house last night, but she came all the way out here to see you. Business, I take it."

Chloe turned back to Maddie. "Business, huh? Hope you're looking for horses. I could use some cash now."

Maddie said, "Not that kind of business, Missus Downs, but I do want to speak with you. After that, you decide if I can be of further help."

"Now you've got me curious, young lady. Sam, you've got work to do. Get the hell on your way. Maddie, get down off your horse and follow me to the barn. We'll unsaddle the critter, put him in a stall with eats and water, and then we'll go up to the house and grab some coffee, treat it with something stronger if you like."

Before they led the horse into the barn, Chloe nodded at the dog, "What about that big animal that tags along with you? I've got a passel of cats in the barn. Does he eat cats?"

"Only cougars and the like. I've taught him to ignore house and barn cats. He's been known to make friends with a few."

"We'll get along then. Inky—that's my black cat—shares the dugout with me most of the time. Your dog can join us in the house then."

"I appreciate that. He's happier if we're not separated."

Leading her horse, Maddie followed Chloe into the barn, Pirate following. Four or five cats disappeared but several stayed put and watched the dog curiously. As she unsaddled the sorrel, Chloe forked some hay into one of the stalls, fetched a pail of water from the pump just inside the door and retrieved a tin can of grain from the barrel.

"I ain't ever seen a hound that big," Chloe said. "Looks like he's got some wolf in him."

"Half wolf, I think, but I don't know his history for sure. He found me and saved my life out in No Man's Land. Do you know where that's at?"

"Yep. Read a book about it a few years back. Strip of land on the end of the Indian Territory panhandle. Touches Texas, Kansas, and Colorado. The government messed things up as usual and didn't give the land a home."

"Yes. It's a long story. Pirate took me up on a plateau atop a wide ridge and led me to his former home. I found his dead owner there and tended to the body. Pirate adopted me and has stuck by me ever since."

"Most ranchers don't want wolves around, but I'm fond of wolves. Did you know they never eat corpses? They won't touch dead animals or people, unlike their coyote cousins. They spend their entire lives with one partner and stay alone if the partner dies. A male wolf won't mate its mother or sister."

"Well, I can't say that Pirate has been that loyal about the mating business. I think the fancy word is 'promiscuous.' He's not too choosy when it comes to mating."

Chloe laughed. "You could probably say that about most men and maybe more than a few women. Anyway, a wolf always remembers its pups when they meet up someplace, and they're the only wild creature that helps its parents in old age and brings them food. They're smarter than dogs, but they don't train worth a darn. The dog side must be showing up in old Pirate here in that regard."

"He wasn't more than a year or so old when he came to me. Maybe that helped with the training."

"If a man kills a wolf, it will look him in the eye till its soul gives out."

"How do you know such things?"

"Living out here and reading now and then. Hell, for all I know some writer made up all that, but it sounds good anyhow."

Chapter 11

WHEN CHLOE AND Maddie entered the dugout, they were greeted by Inky, who was not pleased with the wolfdog guest at first. He hissed at Pirate and backed away. When Pirate ignored him, he sat down and watched the dog's every movement warily but did not back off again.

Maddie dropped her bedroll and saddlebags on the dirt floor that was so packed and shiny it might have been tile. Perhaps it was clay of some kind. Chloe told her to sit down at the little table while coffee was brewing in a pot set on coals near the edge of the fireplace bed. Pirate lay down on a buffalo hide rug while the cat continued to glare at him.

Maddie noticed that the cat was missing a front left leg just below the elbow, but it didn't appear to affect the feline's movement that much. Maddie said, "What happened to your cat's leg?"

"Can't say for sure. He showed up here about five years ago and moved in. Lots of trappers along the creeks and rivers out here. I think he likely got his leg caught in a steel trap and then chewed it off to break free like wild animals do sometimes. It's a rough-ended stump, but he doesn't let it bother him. He doesn't seem much interested in taking up roaming ways again, though."

Chloe set two mugs on the table and poured steaming coffee in them. Then she retrieved a bottle of whiskey from a cabinet and brought it to the table, pouring a generous jigger of the contents in her cup. "How about you, Maddie? Would you like a bit of seasoning?"

"Sure, why not?"

Chloe obliged, and they sat there silently stirring their coffees with a spoon. Maddie thought Chloe seemed a bit fidgety. Perhaps it was time to discuss the reason she was here.

Chloe said, "I need a smoke, sweetheart. Then we will talk." She plucked rolling paper and a little tobacco pouch from her shirt pocket. "I don't suppose you smoke?"

"Not much, but I might enjoy a cigarette today."

In truth, she had not smoked since she was fifteen and spending every minute she could with Wally, a young ranch hand, who had led her into smoking and drinking, and, of course, taught her how to spread her legs and please a man. Luckily, she thought, Wally had pleased her also, in ways that the several other men she later slept with had not. She had planned to run off with Wally but then he suddenly disappeared from the ranch. She was never certain whether her mother, Alexandra, had paid him to leave or whether she had him killed. She realized now that from her own standpoint Wally's disappearance was best, but she hoped he was alive and happy someplace and not feeding the worms.

The two women smoked and sipped at their coffees for a spell, and when they snuffed out their cigarette butts in a charred dish, Maddie thought Chloe was noticeably more relaxed. She figured it had not hurt that Maddie shared a bit of wickedness with her, and Maddie thought it had been rather fun, not that she intended to take up smoking regularly again.

Chloe said, "You're from the Crockett Detective Agency, aren't you?"

"Yes, I am. I guess I didn't cover my identity very well."

"Wasn't hard for me to figure out. Who in the hell else would come all the way out here to visit a crazy old lady? When I asked my North Platte lawyer about hiring an investigator, she suggested the Crocket outfit."

"The Crockets are good people."

"She said she would ask for a young woman she'd worked with to be sent out to talk with me after they found out what they could. That suited me fine. With a few exceptions, I ain't real trusting of men. Of course, I don't trust a female right off, either, but I'd sooner take my chances with one of my own kind. That's why I went to Audra Scott for my law wrangling. She's the only woman lawyer in the west two-thirds of the state. Only two or three in the whole danged state that I've heard of."

"I'm glad I got the chance to make the trip. I love what I've seen of the Sandhills country."

"Might change your mind if you don't get out before winter sets in."

Maddie bent over and reached into her saddlebags next to the chair, plucked out a binder of papers and laid it on the table in front of Chloe. "The official report."

"You got a dang book there. Hope you folks don't charge by the pound."

"You will find several sheets showing an accounting of time and costs to the day I took the train out of Manhattan. Your retainer hasn't been used up yet. I'm costing you ten dollars daily including travel time, which you will only pay to here. I plan a personal visit to Audra in North Platte, and you will not be charged for the return trip."

"I guess that's fair enough. That's pretty much what my lawyer told me. I hope you get most of that."

It wasn't any of Chloe's business, but Maddie told her, "I get half."

"Better than a cowhand's wages, I guess. I'll read this later. Give me a short version of what's in this report."

"Certainly. First, I'm very sorry to inform you that your daughter, Darla Churchill, is deceased. She died almost six years ago of complications from pneumonia. Her husband, Richard, died almost five years earlier. Dates are in the report."

Tears glazed Chloe's eyes, but otherwise she was silent for several minutes before she spoke. "I guess I shouldn't be surprised, but still, I didn't hear from her for nearly fifteen years before she died. I wrote and tried to contact her, but it was like she just disappeared. It's a wonder she didn't come to me for money after her husband died."

"She wouldn't have needed it. He was very wealthy."

"I always had a notion he came from money."

"Enough that he could pay the fee to have another man take his place during the war."

"And her brother died beside Gage's son at Gettysburg. I wonder if she ever knew that. The last I heard from her she had a child—a girl. 'Colette' was her name."

"The daughter still lives in Omaha, where Darla and her husband spent most of their years following the war—where they both passed on."

"My Lord, just down the railroad tracks a ways. Less than a day's travel time now. Of course, not more than a few years back, it would have taken two or three times that long just to get from here to a mainline depot."

"You will find in the report that Darla also had two sons, both born in the late 1860s. George died from diphtheria before his second birthday. Grover only three years ago at age sixteen. He was the younger of the two boys. An apparent murder, but the killer was never apprehended."

"No. That's terrible. How?"

"Gunshot. His body was found in a downtown alley, a good mile from where he lived with Colette and her husband. She had become his guardian after the mother's death."

"I need to think about these things and read the report. One question, though. Who is Colette's husband?"

"Her name is now Colette Walton. No children. She is married to a man approaching fifty, a little less than twice her age, which isn't unusual. But I think you should read about him before we talk any more about the situation."

"I am not optimistic about what I am going to learn, but, yes, I need some time. I want you to stay for a bite to eat. I harvested eggs from my layers this morning, and I'll fry some up with bacon, and I do have biscuits left over from breakfast. I hope you will stay on at the K Bar K. I know Gage would be more than glad to have you there."

"He said I was welcome." She obviously was not welcome for an overnight stay, and the K Bar K appeared better suited for unexpected guests. Maddie was not disappointed. She would have stayed overnight if asked, rolled her blankets out on the floor, but she thought Chloe should read the full report alone, digest all the sad news a bit before they spoke further. She hoped to learn soon if her mission was concluded or just beginning.

While they ate, Chloe said, "I want you to come back day after tomorrow, and we will talk more. Tell Gage I want to see him tomorrow. I assume he knows nothing about this report?"

"I haven't given him a clue about why I came to see you. He is obviously curious, but I cannot imagine him asking."

"I would rather you not say anything to him tonight. I will tell him everything I have learned tomorrow. After that, you can feel free to discuss this matter with him, and Sam, too, for that matter. I'll explain why you didn't say anything. I don't suppose Gage has told you about me and him."

"That you have been good friends and neighbors for many years."

"Well, you should know, I think, that Gage and I are betrothed."

"Betrothed? You're planning to marry?"

"Yep. Sometime in April if we both last that long."

"Well, uh, congratulations. I'm very happy for you both."

"Thought it was about time maybe. I'll have to go and live over at the K Bar K most of the time, but I'll keep this place to get away to when I feel the need, and I'll still have chores over here. I suppose I'll have to get a fulltime hand or two to stay in the bunkhouse and look after things. Sometimes, especially in winter, it would be near impossible for me to get here. Anyhow, I thought you should be getting the lay of things in the neighborhood."

Maddie was a long way from figuring this woman out. She had waited thirty years to marry Gage Kraft. She would bet Chloe had slept with Gage in those early years, but she supposed that was long past. At least she did not want to think about it. She got up from the table and picked up her saddlebags and bedroll and moved to the door. "Well, I had better be on my way. I'll be back day after tomorrow."

"Sometimes Gage will stay over a day or two. If he doesn't show up the night before, put your visit off a day."

"Yes, certainly. I can do that. I can see you might have a lot to talk about."

Chloe winked. "We don't spend all our time talking."

Chapter 12

GAGE WAS RELIEVED when he peered out the window and saw Maddie ride into the ranch yard with Pirate bounding along beside her. His first instinct was to head out of the house and go out to the stable and help her put her horse up, but his second thought was that she might be offended.

She obviously knew horses and was perfectly able to see to the mount herself. In some ways Maddie Sanford reminded him of a young Chloe. Tough, independent, almost fearless. The young woman had obviously not lived a sheltered life.

"Maddie's back," Gage said, when Sam walked into the parlor.

"Just in time for supper. I wondered if she would be staying over at Chloe's."

"Yeah, with all that's been going on around here, I was uneasy about not knowing."

Ricky Meeks had rejoined the crew after helping Alex Paul load the presumed Pinkerton agent's remains on the buckboard for Alex to deliver to the Custer County sheriff in Broken Bow, and they finished the Circle D cattle count by midafternoon. They gathered at the headquarters house to tally numbers and then the foreman assigned chores for completion before supper. Sam was staying for supper before heading back to his place.

Supper turned out to be a relatively quiet affair with conversation limited to the foreman's plans for the next day's work. Today, Gage had told the men about the shooting at Chloe's place nearly a week earlier and his worry about the Pinkerton agent's killing so near in time.

The cattle count at the Circle D was worse than the K Bar K's totals in proportion to herd size. The situation was sobering, and nothing made sense. He did not see how the rustling and killings could be related, but the events were making everyone uneasy. He could not see any help coming from the law and figured the remoteness of their location would handicap the best of lawmen.

After supper, Maddie insisted upon helping the other women with cleanup again and then joined Gage in his office for a private conversation. He had invited Sam to stay, but his grandson had demurred, saying that he thought it best that the conversation with Maddie be one on one and that he had chores to tend to at his own place. Something was eating on Sam, too, but he knew that Sam only spoke when he was ready.

Gage and Maddie sat in two cushioned side chairs next to the desk in front of a wall of books. Maddie was looking over her shoulder at the filled bookshelves. "You have an impressive library, Gage."

"If you see something that interests you, help yourself."

"I've never read Henry James's book, *The Portrait of a Lady*. I might take you up on that."

"I think you would enjoy it. I liked it well enough, and I think Chloe did, but she tends to be stingy with her praise. Vega absolutely loved it. The library is available to everyone on the ranch. A few avoid books like they are coiled rattlers ready to strike, but you often get surprised at who the readers are. Smoky, for instance, has probably read every novel in this room two or three times. Not interested in non-fiction, though."

"No, I would not have guessed that."

"Now, how did the visit with Chloe go?"

"I loved her. She is an interesting and fun lady. Congratulations, incidentally."

"Uh, I'm not sure what for."

"She told me that you are betrothed."

Gage's face flushed. "Yeah. I haven't told anybody but Sam here. I wasn't sure how she felt about making the news public—and she tends to be an unpredictable sort. I guess I can tell folks now. It's not like I was sworn to secrecy."

"She wants you to go over to her place tomorrow. I think she expects you to stay overnight."

He did not want to talk about his visits with Chloe and changed the subject. "Did she say what she wants to talk about?"

"She has a lot of information that she considers important to share with you personally. I'm not free to talk about it now, but I will be when you return. You should know that she could be in some emotional turmoil when you arrive, but she wasn't showing it when I left her place."

"I've got to say, you have set up an intriguing mystery here."

"I'm sorry, but it truly is best that you hear the story from Chloe. I gave her some important information. That's all I can say."

Gage shrugged. "Just know that you and Pirate are welcome to stay here for as long as you wish, Maddie."

Chapter 13

December 1887

CHLOE WAS GLAD this was a Mort Boone workday. She felt a change of weather in the air, and she had endured a restless night's sleep after receiving Maddie's news and studying the Crockett Detective Agency report. She rarely cried, figured the last time was when she learned of her son Rob's death the same day Gage got word of Dalt's. But yesterday afternoon, after the young detective's departure, she had spent several hours racked with sobs before the tears dried.

Mortimer Boone rode in a half hour after sunrise, dismounting in front of the dugout and hitching his horse to the two-horse rail there before leading his mount to the barn, never knowing whether the horse would be needed or not on a given day. She opened the door and motioned him in, and he took a seat at the table while he waited for the ritual cup of coffee to start his workday.

Mort was a sixtyish, small-boned man who might reach five and half feet tall in his boots. His long black hair streaked with white dropped to just above his shoulders, and a matching beard fell onto his upper chest.

When she placed the steaming mug on the table, Mort said, "What you got in mind for today, Chloe?"

"I'd like you to do my morning chores at the barn and lots, maybe take down the fencing around the haystack in the barn pasture, I think our first real winter storm may be blowing in, and I'd rather not be opening a fresh stack in the midst of wind and snow. I'll tend to the chickens and egg gathering. I'll be frying up a chicken and taters for noon and heat up some canned beans. Fixing up a cherry cobbler in the Dutch oven."

"Sounds mighty good, Chloe."

"We may be crowded at the table. Gage might join us for dinner, too."

"Me and Gage get along good. Don't worry none about that."

"If you got time, see what you can do with the south barn door. It won't open all the way. It feels like something's jamming it, or maybe it just needs a little grease someplace. Anyhow, I think you got plenty to tend to this morning. I'll let you know at noon what else is on my list. We'll keep an eye on the northwest in case you need to head home early."

As she was finishing dinner preparations, she peered out the window and saw Gage leading Keeper to the barn. As anticipated, he had arrived just in time to eat. Gage was almost totally predictable in his habits, unlike herself, she admitted, who was anything but. Maybe they were each attracted to an opposite.

Gage and Mort walked up from the barn together, and when they came in Mort was still talking about some youthful hijinks of his. Mort was a storyteller, and he would enjoy having a bigger audience this noon, which was fine since she and Gage would have little to say in Mort's presence.

They ate while Mort told his stories, and she wondered how the man ate so much between words. The spindly little man ate twice as much as she and Gage combined. Chloe waited for Mort to finish and then got up to remove the cobbler pan from the Dutch oven. She placed the pan with a big serving spoon on the table. "Eat all you can handle, gentlemen. I don't need a lot of leftovers. Cats won't eat the stuff."

"Mighty good, Chloe," Mort said. "I wouldn't tell my missus, but you do the best fried chicken in Custer County. And your cobbler ain't never left me without wanting more."

"Thank you, Mort. I know you love your chicken, so I fried this up just for you. And I know cherry is your favorite cobbler."

"You got me figured out good, Chloe."

"What's it looking like to the northwest, boys?"

"Snow coming," Gage said. "Temperature's dropping outside, below freezing by now, I'd guess."

"I figured as much. Mort, you had better head home. Hilda will be worrying about you. I'd hire you for an extra day after the storm's run its course, if you like. I've got things I'd like done before winter really sets in after the first of the year."

"You got my extra day. Hilda complains I ain't working enough, but I got work farming my quarter section, too. Of course, this time of year that ain't so much, but I do have my few cows and five brood sows that keep me running when they're farrowing the piglets. Gotta save them pigs. They're my mortgage lifters, only thing on the place that turns a decent profit."

"Wait a minute, I'll get your pay." She left and went to her storage room, returning with coins in her hand. She gave Mort two silver dollars.

"But that's a full day's wages, Chloe."

"Storm ain't your fault. Now skedaddle out of here."

"Yes, ma'am, and thank you, Chloe. Hilda won't find out about one of these dollars."

As soon as Mort disappeared out the door, Gage stepped over to Chloe and took her into his arms. She clutched him tightly as his lips met hers with a lingering kiss. This felt good. And so right. She could have had so much more of this over the years, but you could not get passed time back. This much she had learned.

"Thanks for coming over," she said.

"You doubted that I would?"

"Not for a minute. But we should talk now. Let's sit down and finish the coffee."

"We've got the rest of the day, as well as the night, if I'm invited to stay."

"You're invited. I can't have you out in that storm that's coming anyway, but I don't intend to spend the whole night talking."

"I was hoping not."

They sat back down at the table with the coffee pot between them.

Gage said, "For starters, why don't you tell me who this Maddie Sanford is?"

"No secrets after today. I told Maddie that, too. All the cards will be on the table, and she's been told she can talk freely with you. She's been in an awkward position from the beginning. But to answer your question, Maddie is a private detective."

"Somehow, I am not surprised. She notices things that most don't. Of course, that dang wolfdog clues her in on a lot. The reason I'm scratching my head is that I can't figure out why she's here."

"I hired her agency. Remember Sam riding with me to North Platte last summer?"

"Yeah, because you didn't want to take the quickest way and catch the new train connection at Broken Bow."

"I wanted to see the country from horseback while I can still sit in the saddle for a few days. Folks are getting soft, grabbing trains every chance they get. Someday, nobody will know how to mount a horse. Anyhow, I went to see a lawyer there I'd heard about—a young lady. Name's Audra Scott Adams. Partners with her husband, Ari, and another young feller there."

"We've done business with the firm. I'm acquainted with Ari."

"Anyhow, I had some law work I needed done. I wanted to deal with a woman, and there ain't but one law wrangling female this far west. So while we were talking about my business, I learned Audra used to be a detective with an agency out of Manhattan, Kansas."

Gage said, "Which happens to be where Maddie Sanford is from."

"Yep. The Crockett Detective Agency. Audra thought it was important that I find out what became of Darla and what she had in the way of heirs who might make a claim on my estate someday. It made sense, so I went ahead with making my will and then asked Audra to contact the Crockett people. I don't like banks, but I've got to do some business through them, so I left a draft for what Audra thought the Crockett people might require—too dang much. But I've got to say they dug up more information than I think I wanted." She got up, walked away from the kitchen area and went into her bedroom. She returned with the Crockett report and placed in front of Gage.

"What's this?" Gage asked.

"The Crockett outfit's report"

"You've got a dang book."

"Yeah, and it reads like a novel, only sadly, it ain't. You can thumb through it, but I'll give you the guts of it."

"I'm listening."

"Well, Maddie gave me the gist before she left yesterday. That's one reason I didn't want her staying over. I needed to be alone a spell." She continued, telling Gage about Darla's death and the fates of her daughter's two boys.

Gage reached across the table and took her hand. "I'm sorry."

"I know. I've done the worst of my grieving, but it never ends, of course. We both know that with our boys and the war after all these years. I wanted to know what became of Darla, but maybe I would have been better off not knowing. And, you know, they were living right here in Nebraska for many years—Omaha. Not that far distant since the railroad came across the state all those years back."

Gage shook his head in disbelief. "It's hard to figure."

"I wanted you here, Gage, to help sort this out, and, well, I needed you with me tonight."

"I'm glad I can be here, Chloe, you know that."

"That ain't the worst of it. The Crockett report says that young Grover was murdered at age sixteen not long after Darla died."

"Murdered? How? Who killed him?"

"I can't answer the last question. The killer was never found, but he took a lead slug in the back of his head. An up-close shot in a downtown alley."

"His mother was gone. Who was he living with at that time?"

"His sister, Colette. She was his guardian, and, of course, inherited his share of Darla's estate, since he had no other kin."

"You aren't suggesting Colette had him killed?"

"Ain't saying she did or didn't. She's married to a man that would rank high on the list of the state's no-goods. He doesn't rob banks, but he's got a history of skullduggery, mostly using crooked government agents to feed his money appetite. Roscoe Walton is more than twenty years older than Colette, which would make him near fifty. He's outlived two wives—always married money."

"Are you thinking that he might have killed Grover or hired someone to do it?"

"Farfetched, I suppose, but this man seems plenty short of scruples. He's never been jailed or arrested, but his name has come up plenty during government scandals, mostly with Army and Indian reservation purchases of horses and cattle, sometimes other supplies. He's been connected to a half dozen companies with Indian agency contracts and supplying frontier fort needs. Turns out, these companies all have the same owners. Roscoe Walton is the president of all the outfits."

Gage said, "I suppose they make their money by bribes to the government purchasing agents. I've heard of these things. Sometimes, especially with the Bureau of Indian Affairs, the cattle delivered by the seller are short of the number contracted for, and the agent doesn't notice for a percent of the contract. Or he might pay above market price and take his commission from the difference. I suppose it works the same way with the Army, although I'm guessing that's starting to dry up with fort closings and troop reductions in the west."

"Yep. The report says that Roscoe Walton is hurting because of that, and he spends a lot of money on failing ventures besides him and Colette living in an Omaha mansion and moving in high society up there. He's got two different bank lawsuits going against him right now for unpaid loans, one for a bit over fifteen thousand dollars and the other near thirty. That's a hell of a lot of money. The fifteen involves foreclosure on their mansion. I'm thinking I might meet my granddaughter any day now, maybe on a scouting visit to see if I got money."

"I wonder if Roscoe is in the rustling business?"

"What do you mean?"

Blizzard

"We've finished the cattle tallies. Allowing for some we didn't pick up, Sam and I think you're down close to a hundred head, a mix of cows and spring calves. We're somewhat more but not a lot. Our herd loss percentage would be less, of course."

A rage swept through her. "Those sons-of-bitches. Who? We ain't had serious rustling problems for half dozen years now. Oh, maybe somebody makes off with a head or two now and then. Some of those are to feed a hungry family, and I don't begrudge them, but this could put me out of business."

Gage said, "This would put both of us out of business if it keeps up. I'm thinking most of this has taken place since September. We need to check the stockyards at North Platte and Broken Bow to see if any of our brands have shown up there. I'm thinking they more likely went to one of the reservations north of here or to Fort Robinson to the northwest."

"You wondered if Roscoe Walton is in the rustling business. It could be he does some killing on the side."

"I thought about that, especially if he thought your granddaughter as next of kin would end up with your ranch and everything else you've got."

"We've got to think about this." She nodded toward the window. "The snow's starting to fall. Looks to be heavy.

We're going to have plenty of thinking and talking time, but I think we'd better tend to barn chores early today."

Chapter 14

COYOTE HUNTER, NOW known as Jim Hunter, was a lean, sinewy man, who stood a few inches short of six feet. His clothes were those of a western cowhand including faded denims, scuffed boots, and a battered, low-crowned hat. His black hair fell just below his ears, and only his bronze skin suggested his Sioux ancestry. Sam thought that most young ladies who saw beyond a man's coloring would find Hunter rather handsome.

"Are you serious? You're offering me a fulltime job at the K Bar K?"

"Darn right I'm serious. Sixty dollars a month, bed and board. Includes feed for two horses. After you've worked a few months, the ranch will up your pay if you and Gramps are both satisfied."

"When do I start?"

"That's your call."

"How about today?"

"Well, yeah, I guess so. I figured you would need a few days to get ready."

"There's a snowstorm coming. If you can give me a hand, I'll have everything I own on my packhorse and ready to move in an hour. Your bunkhouse can't be any colder than this place."

"We've got a good woodstove, and the cracks in the walls are all sealed tight. The hands have never complained."

"Let's get my two critters out of that lean-to that's about to fall over. I've been in your stable over there. They'll think they're lodging in a first-class hotel."

As Hunter had promised, the Sioux's black gelding was saddled, and his sorrel mare packed in less than an hour's time. Sam said, "A pair of fine-looking animals you've got there, Jim."

"The mare's insulted by pack duty, but I use her as a cow horse, too. I got her bred to a good stud in exchange for some work I did. She'll foal come May. Someday, maybe years from now, I hope to have my own small horse ranch. If you've got horse work over at the K Bar K, I'm glad to do it—breaking, training, whatever you need. I like vet work, too. Cattle or horses."

Blizzard

"We'll find a place for you, but your first job will be some tracking. We'll talk about that later. It's starting to spit snow, and the wind's coming up. We'd better hightail it out of here."

When they arrived at the K Bar K, it was well past noon, but Monique warmed up roast beef and fried potatoes for the two riders. "We're eating in shifts today anyhow," she said. "The boys are out taking down fence around some of the fenced haystacks, and dropping by when they can. I got some cakes when you're ready for sweets."

When they were filling their plates at the counter, Sam said, "Monique, I apologize. I didn't introduce Jim Hunter. He's a new fulltime hand."

She smiled. "I know Jim. We've talked a few times when he was here doing some repair work on the house. We're relatives of sorts, aren't we, Jim?"

"Yes, ma'am."

"Some might call it shirttail. We figured out that Jim's a third or fourth cousin on my mother's side. Mama was half-blood Santee Sioux."

Sam said, "Well, Jim, I guess you're having a family reunion here. Monique, I know Vega's at school today, and Gramps is over at Grams' place, but where is Maddie Sanford?"

"Oh, she went to school with Vega. She wanted to see what the school was like. She's an educated woman, you know."

"What do you mean?"

"She's had two years of college. Went to Kansas State Agricultural College at Manhattan, Kansas, where she's been living the past four or five years. That young lady has led an interesting life, let me tell you. And how she came to be with Pirate is quite a story. It would make a good dime novel like those Gage keeps stacked in his office for folks to read. I've sneaked more than a few, and I know you have, too."

Sam was an insatiable reader and had read most of the classics, but he admitted only to himself his addiction to dime novels that could be read in an evening—and rarely told the story of the real west. "Yeah, you got me on that. How do you pump all this information out of her? It's like pulling teeth for me to learn anything about that woman."

"Be patient and be nice to her. She'll come around. She's been fun. I forget what it is like to have another woman to talk to. And Vega adores her."

Sam shrugged. "Let's eat, Jim. We'll talk about the first job Gage has got in mind for you. I doubt if Gramps will make it home tonight." Lord knew how long his grandfather would use the storm as an excuse to stay at Grams's dugout. With the luxuries the headquarters house offered, he could not imagine what that near-cave offered to lure him there—not that Sam did not love Grams dearly.

As Hunter and Sam ate, Sam told the new hand about rustling problems at the K Bar K and the Circle D and the murder of the man who was apparently a Pinkerton agent. "Gramps wants you to try to track cattle that have been moved from the ranches the past few months. Rustlers wouldn't be taking one at a time. I would think they would be driving off at least twenty-five, maybe twice that."

"If we get much snow, it might be spring before I can pick up much to follow. Let's think about where the market is."

"I don't think they would be driven someplace for rail shipment. Too dang risky, especially nearby."

Hunter said, "Two Nebraska Army posts within reasonable distance without many people in between here and there. Fort Robinson in the northwest corner of the state and Fort Niobrara more directly north. They're both just across the line from Dakota Territory where the Great Sioux Reservation runs and drops down in Nebraska places. Niobrara is within walking distance of the reservation, and there is an agency headquarters not far from the fort."

"Of course, if the cattle have already been slaughtered, you wouldn't turn up much."

"But I can ask questions, and I have several friends near the reservation agency. They would not be disappointed to see the agent in trouble for buying stolen cattle. A white man would not learn much, but sometimes my skin color can be useful."

"You are making sense. I think you should do this. If you can leave before Gramps returns, I will furnish money to cover expenses." Sam and his grandfather were well beyond the days when he needed to wait for Gage's decision on such matters.

Chapter 15

THE TEACHER DISMISSED school at two o'clock after Vega's urging. Harriet Galbraith had been the junior teacher at Cedar Creek school when the twenty-year-old head teacher abandoned the school a few weeks earlier. Maddie judged her a competent teacher, but she was obviously overwhelmed by the responsibility for twenty pupils spread over first through eighth grades.

A petite, blondish young woman, Harriet resided with one of the homesteader families during the school term as was the custom in rural communities. Two of the younger pupils lived in the same house, and she agreed to accompany them home, which was less than a mile north of the school. Eleven other homesteaders' children were from three families, all residing within two miles east and south, the nearest with four children only a half mile from school. These all included a sibling old enough to assume responsibility for escorting them home. The storm was not near its worst yet, Maddie figured.

Maddie and Vega would see that the five ranch children who lived to the north and west got home. They were the children of ranchers or their ranch hands and came from two different ranch neighbors, three children residing three miles distant and two with a five-mile trek. The two with the longest journey shared a horse, but the others were afoot, so Vega settled Ben, a ten-year-old boy, behind her on the bay mare she had ridden. Maddie pulled Ruthie, a six-year-old, up in front of her on the big sorrel gelding she had chosen before helping the girl's eight-year-old sister Mary mount behind her.

"Somebody tell us how to get to where we are going," Maddie hollered as the wind whipped around her face and lifted her hair, burning her cheeks and ears.

Vega yelled back, her voice muffled by whistling of the wind. "Just follow me. I know the way to the Walking Five, where the Gable bunch live. Ben can tell me if I go astray." She turned her head toward twins Mason and Martin Timmons mounted on the chestnut gelding off to her left. "Mace and Marty, you stay with us. We'll ride with you on to the Box T unless the storm lets up."

Blizzard

Maddie could not tell the difference between the two boys, but Vega demonstrated in the classroom that she could unfailingly tell them apart. She did not know which one sat in the saddle now, but Maddie had told her the twins alternated. One got the saddle coming to school, and a switch was made for the journey home after school.

As they headed out, Maddie noticed that Pirate was loving the adventure, bounding about in the snow, racing away to chase some creature, real or imagined, then returning to the riders. She could feel Mary pressing against her back and squeezing her arms tighter about her waist as they advanced, probably seeking warmth. Little Ruthie had worked her way mostly onto Maddie's lap now, searching for the same thing. Not that much time had passed, she supposed, but it seemed like they had been in the saddle for hours.

Houses had suddenly disappeared, it seemed, like there was a twisting invisible line that separated farm and ranch country. The homesteaded farmlands had homes on almost every quarter section, and section-line wagon roads in many instances, but the trails in ranch country were few and widely separated. A rider could get easily lost in weather like this. Three miles was not so far to home in decent weather, but in a storm like this, it was a treacherous passage. How did parents cope with these changes?

Her question was answered when Pirate stopped and started barking, and a ghostlike rider emerged from the white curtain of snow on the road in front of them. He was leading an extra mount. The party reined in.

"It's their father," Vega yelled. She waved, "Mister Gable, the kids are with us."

The snow-caked horses and rider reined up beside them. George Gable was featureless so far as Maddie was concerned. His upper body was wrapped in a bulky sheepskin coat that reached over a chin already covered by a wool scarf hiding the lower part of his face, and a coonskin cap with earflaps was pulled down to just above his eyes.

Gable tugged his scarf down to expose his mouth. "Vega, thank God. Susie and me was worried sick. Ain't seen nothing like this in a few years—especially this early. I can't thank you enough for bringing the kids. I was headed for the school."

Vega said, "We wouldn't have let them leave afoot. We would have waited out the storm if you hadn't got there."

"Well, I'll take over from here. You can't see the home place, but we're less than a mile from the house. You can all come and stay there, if you like, or you can head home, and I'll ride on with Mace and Marty once I leave the kids with Susie."

"No need. We'll be fine. I've got my friend, Maddie Sanford, and her wolfdog with me, and the boys know their way. We'll ride with them till we know they're safe. Then we've got pretty much a straight shot to the K Bar K."

With the Gable children turned over to their father, they continued with the Timmons twins. Maddie was starting to worry now. Every snow-covered dune and hillock looked the same to her, and they were forced to move the horses at a slow pace because of the uncertainty of the footing underneath the white blanket. She did see drifting along fence lines that told her they were on a trail that led to someplace.

The twins seemed unperturbed, and they were better dressed for a snowstorm than the Gable children had been. Of course, they had a farther distance to travel to their home from school and were even more detached from the better-marked characteristics of the homesteader land than the Gable Walking Five homeplace.

She could tell that the boys were probably astride a horse before they walked and between them likely doing a man's work at home. She suspected the mother was insisting on the schooling as so many did. The father likely would just as soon have the boys home working. She chided herself for pre-judging a man she had never met, but she knew from experience that mothers seemed to be the driving force for education where farm and ranch kids were concerned.

Finally, she thought she saw a stream of sideways smoke coming their way through the snow's haze. Soon, she smelled it, and shortly they trudged into the ranch yard. A bundled-up woman stood on the porch of the two-story, box-shaped, frame house, obviously searching the near-blinding storm for some sign of her sons. When she saw the riders, she hurried down the steps and tried to run out to meet them before she bogged down in the drifts in front of the house. As they rode up, Maddie could see the woman was choked up with sobs.

"Boys," she said, "get your horse to the stable. Your pa's down there getting ready to ride out and look for you. I feared I was going to lose the lot of you."

She turned to Vega. "I can never thank you enough for getting the twins home. You and . . ."

"Meet Maddie Sanford, May. She's a guest at K Bar K and went with me to the school today."

Maddie just raised her hand and offered a little wave.

"You girls can stay here if you like, or at least come in and warm up with coffee."

Vega said, "I think we had best keep moving. I don't want folks back at the ranch to start a search for us. If it gives you any comfort, I think Mace and Marty would have made it home just fine without us."

Maddie said, "You've got a pair of top wranglers there, Missus Timmons."

"But they are still just boys, although sometimes their father won't admit it."

A few minutes later, Vega and Maddie headed south. Now the wind was at their backs, and Maddie found that an improvement. "I take it you have some idea of where we're at," she said. "I don't. I'm lost. With the blowing snow, I can't see that far, and everything I can make out looks alike."

"Off to the right is Cougar Creek. It runs through the Slash T and winds southerly till it cuts through the east end of the K Bar K not more than a hundred feet from the stable. You've seen it from there."

"Yes, I guess I just never heard it called by name. So, we just keep the creek in sight, and it leads us home?"

"Yeah, we need to edge over that way. There is an old trail above the creek bank that follows the creek flow between the hills. We will have some tree cover, too, that should help break the wind and snow."

Maddie looked down at Pirate. The dog had ceased straying so much now but otherwise seemed unfazed. He would likely welcome a spot in front of a fireplace now, though. She knew she would. "You just lead the way, Vega. We'll be right behind you."

In less than an hour, they arrived at the K Bar K stable. After they put up the horses, they raced to the house with Pirate taking the lead.

Chapter 16

THE MORNING FOLLOWING the snowstorm, a bright sun appeared, and calm settled on the white-blanketed land. At breakfast, Smoky reported the temperature at fifteen degrees on the Fahrenheit thermometer tacked to the wall just outside the stable door. "Going to freeze our asses off checking on the herd today—pardon me ladies," he said. "So cold out there, the two milk cows in the barn are going to be giving icicles, speaking of which, are you milking this morning, Vega?"

Vega said, "Of course I am, Smoky. If I'm here, I never miss. I heard you got stuck with it last night because I was late getting home. Sorry, I know you don't like milking."

"Beats riding out there in a storm, I guess. Just be glad today we ain't got a wind making the chill worse. Days like this make me wonder why I ever left south Texas."

"I should have done the milking before breakfast like usual, but I didn't get around so early this morning."

"I'll help with milking," Maddie said. "That'll cut your time in half."

Vega's brow furrowed, and she looked at Maddie. "You've milked?"

"Of course I have. Thousands of times. I need to make myself useful while I'm here. I won't know if I'm staying longer till Gage gets back. In the meantime, I'd like to do my part."

"Okay, we'll milk and feed the horses and barn stock."

"What about chickens?"

"We get all our eggs and poultry from Grams Chloe. She's got lots of laying hens. Gramps will be bringing eggs back when he comes, but I'm betting we don't see him till tomorrow, if then."

Monique interrupted. "Vega . . ."

Maddie thought mother was warning daughter to tighten her loose tongue some. "Well, that's fine. I don't mind an extra day or two here. It's hardly fit for travel back to Broken Bow just now anyway."

Bruce Potter spoke to Jim Hunter. "What about you, Jim? Sam said you might be pulling out for a spell to look into the rustling problem. I don't think you will find any tracks out there today."

"No. That'd be a waste of time. I'm heading north to the Sioux reservation and to see who has been selling cattle up there and if anybody noticed the brands."

The foreman said, "Now that makes sense. Good hunting, Mister Hunter, and watch your back."

After breakfast and helping Monique with clean up, Vega, carrying clean rags and a small bucket of warm water, and Maddie went to the barn and retrieved the two haltered milk cows from a shared pen at one end. Vega put grain and hay in a bunker in front of two side by side stanchions.

Vega said, "You can take off the halter ropes. They'll stick their heads through to eat."

Maddie released the lead ropes, and the cows stuck their heads between the wooden bars to eat. Vega closed the movable stanchion bar just enough to keep a cow from backing out and shoved a huge bolt through a hole to anchor it. Barn cats were gathering now, and Vega spread some bowls out ten feet or so from the cows.

Vega said, "They'll be up here pestering us if they don't get milk as soon as you squeeze the first tit. I'll take Polly. She's the big Holstein. She'll kick if she doesn't like your touch. Smoky hates her. The Guernsey is Margaret. She's a sweetheart. She won't kick. You can milk her. I'll be right back."

Vega disappeared through a door to what appeared to be a storage room and returned shortly with two one-legged wooden stools and three buckets as well as two large tin pans. She handed Maddie one of the stools and a bucket, dropping the pan on the packed dirt floor. "Does Pirate like milk?"

"He does, but I don't let him drink much. He's had a big breakfast, and he tends to puke up his food if he drinks too much milk."

"You can decide what he gets. I'll milk enough for the cats to start and take care of them."

They each took one of the rags, dipped it in warm water, and washed off the teats and udder of their respective cows. After the dog and cats had been given their portions, Vega commenced to chat. "You are the strangest woman I've ever encountered, Maddie. Don't be offended. I'm like a curious cat where you're concerned. When I first saw you in Broken Bow, I thought you looked like some highfalutin type. But that dang wolfdog had me puzzled. Pirate didn't appear like the kind of dog a society lady would have. You speak like a woman of education, for sure, but you can match any of our hands when it comes to riding a horse, and the woman I first saw for darn certain would not be saddling her own horse. She would likely be riding sidesaddle."

"I've lived in many different worlds, Vega, and learned something from all of them, but I like the ranching world best of all. Someday, that's where I'll end up. I wouldn't mind going back to Colorado if my mother weren't there, but that's another story."

"You just keep feeding me enough to make me curiouser and curiouser."

"I want to know you better, Vega, and I would like for you to learn about me. Maybe we can each teach the other a few things. I'm hoping that when Gage returns, I will be freer to talk and satisfy some of that curiosity."

"Then he had better get his butt back home soon."

Chapter 17

ROSCOE WALTON PACED the creaky wood floor of the second-story offices which served as headquarters for nearly a dozen companies, including Colorado Beef, Wind River Farms, Sandhills Cattle Company, and Nebraska Bargain Ag Products. The company offices consisted of a front room with an old desk, several straight-back chairs, and a file cabinet, where Lulu Perry worked. His private office had nearly identical furnishings with the addition of a cot with a soft feather mattress where he might nap on occasion or couple with Lulu when the mood struck.

Walton was the president and sole owner of all the businesses, although he could not instantly recall every name. Lulu had served as secretary for the pseudo-firms for over five years now, and he paid her well above what she had made whoring. Well, he *had* anyway. She was getting restless because he was three months behind on her pay, and he was damned tired of her bitching about it. She handled the books and knew he couldn't scrape up the funds to pay her.

Gar Ford was waiting for word from him in Broken Bow right now. Gar had deposited funds from the Sioux agency sale with a bank there under the name of Sandhills Cattle Company, but Walton had decided not to transfer the money to the Omaha account just yet, because Lulu would learn about it and demand her pay. He sighed. Lulu was a problem. She knew too much, and she was too smart for her own good. She had information that could likely send him to prison if not the gallows. Would she risk implicating herself? She might, especially if she could make a deal with a prosecutor. Her own involvement was secondary, and she could claim ignorance until a recent discovery.

Lulu, blonde and buxom, was in her early forties but could still pass for ten years younger. She had learned her first trade well and pleased him in ways that his pretty, young wife did not. The flaxen-haired Colette was a willowy beauty that many would call stunning, but she showed little enthusiasm for him in the marital bed. Of course, with Lulu available, his demands were not that frequent, and he supposed that Colette suspected his infidelity.

He had been pacing around his private office, exiting from time to time and circling Lulu's domain, then returning to his own. This time, when he walked out, Lulu lifted her head from the papers spread out on her desk and glared at him.

"You know, you're starting to get on my nerves with this walking back and forth," she said.

Lulu never could resist speaking her mind. At one time, he loved that tendency. Lately, he had found himself getting tired of it. "I pay for this space. I'll walk it where and when I please."

"You haven't paid for it for three months. Did you remember the eviction notice? In three days the sheriff's deputies will be here to kick us out on our asses. I ain't going to be here that day, and I want my pay tomorrow."

"You do the books. You know I don't have any cash money. Let me have a poke, and we can talk about it afterward."

"You can go poke yourself. How dumb do you think I am? I know about the Sioux agency job. I never saw money come through here. It should be in the Sandhills Cattle account. The bank says there's not a nickel in that account. Gar Ford's holding it for you someplace."

"I'll go to the telegraph office right now and stop at the bank first and let them know to expect contact from another bank. It's not yet noon, so there should be time to get this done. Then I will send a wire to Gar before I head on home. I need to talk to Colette."

"Are we closing down shop when the sheriff's people come?"

"No. Maybe I'll set up an office at home."

"Then I'm done?"

"You can come there and work."

"I'll just bet Colette would love that arrangement."

"Why would she care? It's business."

"She likely already knows that we don't always tend to business. She's been by here when she's downtown. She's made clear enough her dislike for me."

"I'll talk to her about it tonight. Anyway, we can discuss this tomorrow. I'll have your pay and a bonus by noon." He went back into his office, grabbed his top hat and frock coat and walked out.

Chapter 18

ROSCOE WALTON, OF course, did not go to the bank. He did wire Gar Ford to let him know that he would be joining him in Broken Bow within a week. Gar had wired him that he needed to bring Walton up to date on important matters. That was a signal that they should meet up someplace. Gar could catch a train back to Omaha, but that seemed a waste given that it was nearing Christmas season and a good time for Colette to meet her grandmother.

He enjoyed a hot dog, something new out of St. Louis, at Percy's Pub and indulged himself with a slice of cherry pie. He asked for a cup of coffee and nursed it for a half hour before he decided that one whiskey might shore him up for facing Colette. And then another, and another.

It was nearly five o'clock when Walton arrived at the mansion atop the hill overlooking the Missouri River. He led his bay gelding to the stable, where it was now the lone resident. He still had a three days' supply of grain in the feed barrel, and a like amount of hay in a small stack near the bay's stall. A month earlier, the twelve-stall stable had been full, but he had been forced to sell the animals, first because he needed the money and then because the stableman had quit, taking one of the horses with him for back pay. The bay was a fine animal, and a purchaser was ready to buy when Walton needed the cash in a day or two.

After taking care of the horse, he went to the house, grateful that Omaha had missed the snowstorm that struck the western part of the state. There were no more than a few scattered patches of snow on the ground in the city, and those were quickly disappearing with temperatures well above freezing the past week. This would not be an unpleasant night to go out again and complete his mission.

Colette was waiting at the door, her eyes red and swollen, her full lips set in a pout. Now what?

"Hulda's son picked her up in a buggy a few hours ago," Colette said. "She's packed her things and left. She's finished here. Hulda said you haven't paid her in weeks."

Hulda Schrum had been the family cook for some years before Colette's mother died. When Walton dismissed the housekeeper a few months back, the German woman had been assigned the housekeeping duties as well for an additional twenty dollars monthly. Of course, he had not come up with the money to pay her. "You are the cook and housekeeper now," he said.

"What do you mean? I can use a broom, and I can mop, I guess, but I know nothing about cooking."

"Then learn, damn it. That's what most women do. They cook and clean and do the laundry and spread their legs for husbands at night. It's time for you to become a real wife."

Her eyes narrowed, and the set of her chin said she was angry. She stepped up to him. "I am not going to be your slave. I am going to leave you."

His arm flew out and the back of his hand slammed into her cheek. She stumbled back a few steps, and he expected her to race to their bedroom as usual. But this time she did not. She charged him, yelling expletives he did not know she even knew, her fists swinging and landing a stinging blow to his chin. She continued to pommel him, and he was unsteady on his feet from his drinking and was forced to regroup, shielding his face with his arms until he finally cleared his head. He slammed his fist into the side of her nose and targeted another blow above her right eye before she went to her knees and then collapsed on the floor.

She lay there whimpering while he drove his shoe into her ribs and triggered a mournful scream. "Now listen to me, you worthless bitch. You are not leaving me. Where would you go? You have no family here besides me. You have no way to make a living unless you take up whoring. This house will be sold at foreclosure sale in a few weeks, and we will be escorted out of here. Like it or not, you're stuck with me. I own you, and you will do what I say. Understand?"

She was consumed by sobbing but nodded her head.

Walton said, "Now, I am going to change clothes. You find something in the icebox for me to eat. A sandwich will do. I'm betting Hulda left some bread behind, maybe something else if you look. Can you brew coffee on the coal stove?"

"I think so, but Hulda said we have less than a week's coal left."

"That's plenty long. We will be leaving very soon to visit your grandmother. I will be back downstairs after I change and then I will expect something to eat. I will be going out to meet a potential customer and will be gone an hour or two. When I return, you will be prepared to join me in bed and behave like a good wife. Do you understand?"

She was slowly lifting herself off the floor now. She stood stiffly, clutching her ribs where she had been kicked.

"You didn't answer me, woman. Do you understand?"

She nodded, "I understand."

Later, mounted on the bay again, he reined his horse toward Lulu Perry's house not more than a mile distant. The house was set off by itself not more than a hundred yards from the Missouri River's edge. It was a small frame structure with a kitchen, parlor, and single bedroom. The residence was at the end of a dirt road surrounded by woods, assuring privacy for her and her guests. This would change soon when she agreed upon a sale price with the firm that owned the remaining land and intended to convert the property to business and residential uses. Omaha investors were gobbling up land like hungry bears with real estate demand far exceeding availability. She would have received a good price had she lived long enough.

When he arrived at the house, he was distressed to see a horse tied to the rail out front. It was not Lulu's black mare. She would be settled in the three-stall stable in back.

He dismounted and led his gelding into the woods off to the east side of the house. With the cover of both darkness and trees, he did not think he risked being seen, and he had a decent view of the house front from here. He had not been totally surprised to find Lulu with a visitor. She made no secret that she had retained a half dozen or so of her wealthier patrons when she went to work for Walton. These were prominent men who did not wish to be seen in the usual bawdy houses and had become increasingly uneasy by being caught up in police raids generated by new municipal ordinances restricting prostitution.

Lulu was a sole proprietress of her enterprise with a reputation for discretion. She could probably live comfortably enough without Walton's job, he figured. He suspected she had a fair amount of money stashed away and wondered how much of it she kept at home. He would make a search.

He heard the visitor's horse nicker, and he hoped his bay did not respond. Thankfully, the gelding remained quiet, seemingly bored by the wait. A man emerged from the house, unhitched the horse and mounted, then wheeled his mount and headed the animal down the road at a gallop. Walton gave a sigh of relief. He had not wished to use his Smith & Wesson. The likely prominence of the customer would not have gone unnoticed by authorities and would have created complications.

Walton hitched his horse to a tree branch. He walked toward the house and, reaching under his coat, he caressed the bone hilt of the dagger sheathed on his belt and slipped it out. He rapped on the door and heard footsteps moving toward the doorway.

"Who is it?" Lulu said.

"Roscoe. I've brought your pay and next month's, too, if you will stay on."

She opened the door a crack and peered out, "Let me see the money."

He slammed his shoulder into the door, knocking her backwards, and the dagger entered her belly before she could regain balance. Her eyes widened in disbelief, and she opened her mouth to scream but no sound came out as Walton ripped the knife upward nearly gutting her like a caught fish as her entrails slipped through the severed flesh. In seconds she was flattened on the floor, blood saturating the silk robe she wore. Walton looked down and saw that the front of his shirt, coat, and trousers were blood-soaked, too. He would deal with that later.

He rushed through the house searching for any money Lulu might have squirreled away. He immediately discovered the ten-dollar gold eagle on the bedroom chest of drawers, presumably payment for her services to the visitor. He stuffed the coin in his pocket and rummaged through the drawers, uncovering a tin box packed with gold eagles, maybe two hundred dollars and certainly enough to get him out of Omaha with Colette. A bonanza. Lulu had an even higher class of patrons than he would have expected. She held information that might have been valuable, but it was too late for him to mine that possibility now.

He froze when he heard a rapping on the door. No. Another customer? Surely she did not entertain more than one in an evening these days. Greedy bitch. He pulled his Smith & Wesson from his coat pocket, readied it to fire. He went to the door and opened it slowly. The grinning face was that of his lawyer, Calvin Lockhart.

"Roscoe, what in blazes are you doing here?" Lockhart said.

Walton raised the revolver and squeezed the trigger and sent a lead slug into the man's forehead. Walton's ears rang and stung from the blast, but he was pleased to see that his ex-lawyer had fallen forward and was halfway into the house. He put his weapon away, dragged the dead man into the house and shut the door. He doubted Lulu would have yet another customer coming, but he dared not chance it and take time to haul two bodies to the river. Besides, Lockhart was a big man, so he doubted he could manage anyway.

He dropped his pistol on the floor next to Lulu and pushed his dagger blade through the pool of blood on the floor before working the dead lawyer's fingers around the hilt. He did not delude himself that the law would buy the notion that the two had killed each other, but there was always a chance that a moron would be investigating. He figured that the scene would at least confuse the issue for a time.

He took the derringer and ammunition he had seen in the dresser drawer. Better that she did not have a second gun in the house, and he could use the weapon. He would dispose of all the ammunition for his Smith & Wesson as soon as possible, although he could think of nothing to conclusively tie him to the incident.

When he departed the house, he unhitched the lawyer's horse, gave it a slap on the rump and hollered, sending it back down the road. Perhaps it would wander home, or if picked up as a stray, at worst it would be matched to the lawyer who would become a missing person. It should be at least a day, or maybe two or three, before Lockhart was found in the house with his whore. He decided he should not take Lulu's horse as he had previously considered. It should last some days till the bodies were discovered. If not, too bad.

Chapter 19

COLETTE STOOD IN front of the mirror above the sink in the water closet and studied her swollen nose and eye. She was ugly now and would be uglier tomorrow when the flesh turned blue and purple. She hoped the nose was not broken and would not turn into a twisted turnip. The damage appeared to be mostly to the base of the nose nearest her right eye which had absorbed most of the other blow. She knew it would not open in the morning. All of this was nothing compared to the unrelenting pain that stabbed at her ribs.

Roscoe had not resorted to more than a slap now and then when angry at her about something in the past. Of course, his tongue lashings were constant. She was such an incompetent fool. All her education at elite private schools had been for naught. Her husband was right, she had no idea how she could support herself without the family money, which appeared to be quickly disappearing.

She had taken normal training in high school with the thought of teaching primary students in a private school, but her mother had forbidden her from taking a position in a public school after she finished high school. Her strong-willed mother insisted she stay at home and focus upon finding a suitable husband, which meant one with lots of money.

As usual, she had obeyed, and eventually Roscoe Walton appeared to meet her mother's requirements. Colette barely knew the man when she married him, but he had seemed nice enough and was quite prominent in their social circle. It had seemed a little strange marrying a man old enough to be her father, but such pairings were not unusual given the premature deaths of women from childbirth and other hazards peculiar to the gender. A man taking his third or fourth wife was likely to marry a much younger woman.

While Darla Churchill lived, Roscoe had treated Colette well enough, although they had little companionship outside the bedroom and on those occasions he chose to join her and her mother for evening dinner. He had been especially attentive to Darla and spoke more often with her. Of course, only a few years younger than

Roscoe, she had been nearer his age, and she supposed they had more in common.

One night, she had awakened with an urgent need to relieve her bladder. Roscoe was not in bed, and she thought he might already be occupying the water closet. He was not there, however, and after she had completed her business was heading down the hallway to the bedroom when she heard a door open at the far end of the six-bedroom second floor and saw Roscoe exiting her mother's bedroom wearing only his undershorts. She slipped back into the bedroom, pushed the door shut softly and rushed to the bed, feigning sleep by the time her husband joined her again.

Thinking back, she realized that this was not the first time he had disappeared for significant times during the night. Surely there was an explanation for what it seemed was taking place. She had refused to think about it further, and most of the time did not.

When Darla died, it had been no surprise that Roscoe was named executor and trustee of her sizable estate. Colette freely admitted that she was ignorant of business and property matters. Roscoe had been granted total control for ten years at which time the estate was to be distributed to Colette and her brother equally. When Grover was murdered, Colette became the sole beneficiary. Of course, she realized now that she was likely beneficiary of nothing.

Roscoe had procured total power over the remaining Churchill money when Darla died and commenced ruling with an iron hand. Immediately, the old charm dissolved, and his requests turned to edicts, and she and Grover would be punished like small children if they did not obey. They still made social appearances among the monied class, but otherwise Colette became a virtual prisoner in her home. Grover ran away after razor strap beatings on several occasions, but Roscoe always dispatched one of his lackeys to find the boy and bring him back. At least Grover rebelled at his treatment. She just obeyed. The battered face she gazed at in the mirror was that of a coward.

She started when she heard the door slam downstairs. She hoped that Roscoe had been with another woman who had left him sated. Perhaps there was a chance she would be spared tonight.

Colette descended the open stairway to the expansive parlor. She had fed wood into the fireplace flames only minutes earlier so that the room would be warm when he returned. She found Roscoe on the thick rug in front of the fireplace stripping his clothes off down to nakedness.

She froze when she entered the room and realized that the garments were blood-drenched.

Roscoe turned to her and fastened a glare at her face that made her shiver. "Boil water for the tub. Add enough cold to make it more hot than medium. I'm chilled, and I need a bath. You can boil water, can't you?"

She did not bother to answer.

"When you're done with that, get your butt down here, and burn these clothes in the fireplace, one piece at a time. I want ashes. Understand?"

She nodded.

"Now get moving."

She boiled water in a huge steel kettle that Hulda used for pan and dish washing, dipped the hot water into buckets, and carried them upstairs to the tub, thinking she had never worked so hard in her life. On her third trip upstairs, she noticed that the study off the parlor was lighted and paused a moment. Roscoe was at his desk with a blanket wrapped about his shoulders seemingly absorbed with a task there.

When the bathwater was ready, she went to the study and told him, "The tub is filled. I hope it's warm enough."

"Damned well better be." He got up, brushed past her, and headed up the stairs, then stopped and hollered back,

"Turn the oil lamp off in the study. Then get upstairs and get yourself ready for company in the bed."

She sighed. Well, knowing Roscoe, he would not take long. She went into the study to kill the lamp flame. The unfamiliar tin on the desktop tempted her, however, and she risked another beating and opened it. It nearly took her breath away. A small roll of paper bills, but the remaining contents were gold coins, mostly ten-dollar pieces, it appeared. She closed the lid, turned off the lamp and went upstairs wondering who her husband had robbed and murdered. He had bragged of killing men over their years together, thieves and outlaws and those who deserved it, he always assured her. Not for the first time, she wondered if Grover might have been one of those who deserved it.

In bed, she moaned as Roscoe claimed his spousal privilege, but it was not from ecstasy as he might have deluded himself. Her injured ribs were protesting, and the pain was excruciating. Fortunately, it was over in five minutes. As he pulled the blankets over his body and lay back, she got up and slipped into a high-necked flannel nightgown, not wanting to do anything to ignite his interest again.

When she climbed back in bed, he spoke from the darkness. "Tomorrow, we get prepared to leave. We will catch a train the next morning. I will get the furniture man out here tomorrow to make a deal on the contents. I also need to sell the horse."

"This is happening too quickly. There are so many things to do."

"Get done what you can. This can't wait. Anyhow, take only what you can carry in a few bags. I have some papers and things. If we don't have enough to wear, we can restock in Broken Bow. I have some money in a bank there."

"You said something about my grandmother. I have never met her. I doubt if she knows I exist."

"She will soon. We will talk about the family reunion on the way."

Soon he drifted off to sleep, and she was grateful when she heard his snoring. She wondered if she could kill someone. Not tonight, she decided. She did not want to face the gallows, although she was on the edge of not caring.

Chapter 20

GAGE STAYED WITH Chloe two nights because of the storm, even though the worst of it had ended after the first night. He estimated nearly a foot of the white stuff cloaked most of the countryside, which would not have been so difficult if not for the drifting. He stayed on to help Chloe clear the drifts and make paths to the privy and the woodpile, and then they dug out the snow that nearly covered the barn entrances.

He even milked the single milk cow that morning, the first time he had done that chore in some years. Thankfully, Mort Boone showed up shortly after noon to help with some of the chores, and by the time Mort departed with dusk coming on, a semblance of order had been returned to the Circle D.

That evening, they shared a stuffed, cowhide couch in front of the fireplace while nursing cups of coffee. Gage noticed that the sheep's wool stuffing was starting to leak out of the ancient furniture piece that had been in the room the thirty-some years he had been visiting the place. It was warm enough here; downright cozy, he admitted, but the thought of Chloe alone in the place most of the time, with chores to do in the middle of storms and possibly someone trying to kill her, downright frightened him.

It was time to have the talk he had been thinking about for several years. He reached over and took her free hand in his. "Chloe, are you still going to marry me?"

"I said I would, didn't I?"

"But not before April?"

"Nope."

"You're a stubborn woman, Chloe."

"So you've told me at least a thousand times."

"How about coming over to live at the K Bar K till then? I'd feel a whole lot better about that. I don't like you being here alone."

"You know you're welcome anytime. Move in if you want."

"I've got responsibilities at ranch headquarters to tend to."

"You're a stubborn man, Gage."

Blizzard

Now, how in blazes had she maneuvered him into that corner? It reminded him of when they used to play chess, and she would checkmate him three-fourths of the time. "I've been thinking for a long time, Chloe, that the K Bar K and the Circle D ought to partner up."

"Whoa, mister, you ain't taking my ranch with the bride."

"You know me better than that. This would be sheer business. You would keep ownership of your ranch and livestock, but the day-to-day operation would be combined. I'm going to take on a few extra hands. You've got a decent bunkhouse. I thought I would lodge two of them over here. They'd take care of daily chores. Your milk cow and the chickens would move over to the K Bar K when we marry, but there will always be horses and cattle needing special care over here. You've got the biggest, best barn in the hills, and we could use some of that space."

"So your outfit would take over the homeplace?"

"No. But you won't be here to look after things daily once you move in with me. You can come over here to check on things whenever you want, but there should be several hands here all the time, and you know that, dang it. We've lost a lot of cattle, because we haven't had enough men checking the herds. We can't keep our fences repaired because there's too much else to get done."

"I know I ain't done my share on the fencing between us. I've offered to pay, and Sam's been like a free hand for me, looking after my place as best as he can when he can find time."

"We wouldn't need a fence between us if we run the herds together. Your calves would still carry the Circle D brand, but the K Bar K would pay all expenses and take a one-third share when calves and cull cows are marketed. We would be living together, so we would be able to consult about things anytime. I also thought I would put Sam in charge of coordinating operations between the two places."

Her eyes finally showed interest at the mention of Sam's name. He wasn't playing fair. He knew that Chloe worshipped Sam, and he hoped his grandson's involvement would open her mind a bit.

"Well, I guess it's something to think about."

"I'd like to see us start the first of the year. And I think we ought to get married New Year's Day."

"That's only a month or so off. You're pushing things, Gage. You know I don't take to crowding."

"Unless you're doing the crowding."

She looked at him and squinted her eyes. He just grinned mischievously.

Blizzard

"Let's go to bed, and I'll show you some crowding, you old rooster."

Chapter 21

SAM AND MADDIE were seated in Gage's office waiting for his grandfather to join them. His curiosity had certainly been piqued when Gramps asked him and the mystery woman to meet in the office after supper. He liked Maddie well enough, and she was more than pleasant to look at, but it was difficult to carry a conversation with someone who shared so little of her background.

Maddie broke the silence. "This Jim Hunter you hired on . . . he's Indian, isn't he?"

"Uh, yeah. Santee Sioux."

"I spoke with him briefly. He seemed very nice. He's obviously had some education."

"He attended a Quaker school on the reservation before he left."

"He escaped the reservation?"

"Not exactly. If you don't cause trouble, nobody is going to arrest you and take you back. He has decided to make his way outside the reservation world. Times are changing. Some will stay, and others will go elsewhere. There are already a lot of mixed bloods in the west. Gramps says that someday so-called white folks will be bragging about the Indian blood in their veins."

"He rode off just before the snowstorm struck. I hope he is alright."

"He'll be fine. He knows this country. I sent him on a job up north." He thought there would be no harm telling her about Hunter's mission, but he wanted to know where she fit in the puzzle before he said much. He was rescued from the awkward conversation when Gage entered the room and sat down at his desk.

Gage said, "I haven't had a chance to speak with either of you since I got back from Chloe's, and I thought it was time to clear up some things, maybe make it a little easier getting to know each other." He looked at Maddie. "Chloe explained to me about your job here, Maddie, and she shared all the information in the report you gave her, let me read it as a matter of fact."

Gramps was not making any sense to Sam, but he was reluctant to say anything.

Gage quickly answered his questions. "Sam, Maddie is a private detective for the Crockett Detective Agency out of Manhattan, Kansas. Remember when you took Chloe to North Platte to visit a lawyer there?"

"Sure. That was several months back."

"Well, Chloe's lawyer, a young woman by the name of Audra Scott Adams, used to work for the agency and arranged for an investigation into the whereabouts of her daughter Darla. The agency learned of Darla's death, and Maddie was sent here to deliver a written report. No more secrets. We can all talk freely now, Chloe says. Darla lived in Omaha for many years, and she left behind a daughter who appears to be married to a no-good. Maddie and I will fill you in as we get opportunities, and you can ask any questions you want of either of us. Is that okay with you, Maddie?"

"Of course. This is a great relief. Will you inform Monique and the hands of my purpose here?"

"If you don't object. I think it will make it more comfortable for everybody."

"Of course not, but I would prefer word was passed from you. I think the details of my report should remain among the three of us and Chloe, though."

"I agree. No reason to share that beyond, perhaps, making Monique and her family aware of Darla's death and the existence of Chloe's granddaughter. I don't think anybody else knows much about Chloe."

Sam knew of Darla, Chloe's long, lost daughter but had never met her, so news of her death struck him only slightly harder than a stranger's passing. The sadness he felt for Chloe, however, brought tears to his eyes.

Maddie said, "So did Chloe say what she expects me to do? Am I to leave now?"

"She wants you to stay on till the end of the year at least. She will pay the Crockett firm for your services till then. She will decide at that time if she requires your help beyond that time."

"But there is nothing for me to do. I won't feel right if I am not earning my salary."

"You have probably heard us talking about this. We have a rustling problem at our two ranches. You are Chloe's contribution to getting this resolved. Your part in this isn't clear right now, but I have a feeling you will be able to help us over the next several weeks."

Sam said, "Gramps, there is something else I'd like to discuss. I've been thinking about the dead Pinkerton agent. Do you think the cattlemen's association could have hired him? Smoky heard a rumor from some hands to the south that they've been having rustling problems, too. I don't think the losses are as heavy as ours, though, but sometimes the association steps in when there are problems like this."

"That's a good thought. I pay dues to the outfit, but they include eight counties and headquarter at North Platte in Lincoln County. Sometimes, there's a meeting in Broken Bow, but I have not gone to one the last five years. I don't even know who's heading up the organization these days."

"Rance Coldsmith, by all accounts a good man. I'd like to go talk to him."

"The best. I've known him for years but haven't seen him for more than a year. Years ago, he was a Missouri lawyer. Left that and ended up in the Sandhills. He was a deputy sheriff in North Platte for a spell and then was Custer County deputy some ten years back before the county had a sheriff and the law was handled by the North Platte sheriff. He was serving when Print Olive was raising hell in Sandhills country. I should have talked to Rance before now or sent you there. Yes, do it."

Maddie said, "I would like to ride with you."

Sam said, "It's a long day's ride when the weather is decent. With the heavy snow, I figured to stay over at a deserted soddy along the way."

"I've stayed worse places, I guarantee you."

Sam sighed. "I don't know how it would look, you spending the night someplace with a man." He looked at Gage for backup.

Gage smiled and shrugged.

Maddie said, "I don't think there's much of an audience out in these hills. And I sure don't give a damn anyhow. I'll have Pirate with me, sleeping right by my side. I want to hear what this Coldsmith's got to say, ask a few questions myself, maybe start earning my pay. I am going to take offense if you won't let me ride with you. For that matter, maybe I'll just go on my own."

"Alright, darn it. But you're going to freeze your behind out there at night. You don't know how easy you've got it here."

"I do know how easy I've got it. But I'm not getting paid for sitting in front of a fireplace, and I want to see more of this country."

Gage interceded. "I think that's settled. One more thing, then I'm headed for bed."

Sam said, "I'm listening."

"I'm trying to convince Chloe to combine the ranch operations. If she decides to go along, I promised her you would take charge of handling that and working out the details with her. Don't say you can't do it. You were the bait."

Blizzard

"I don't know what you mean about me being bait, but I've always thought we should move in that direction. She's a smart woman and knows ranching, but she's always been too tight to hire enough help, and we're doing more than a neighbor's share already. I'll talk to her as soon as we get back. I want to pull out by midmorning tomorrow for Coldsmith's. Do you and Grams have the wedding date settled yet?"

"New Year's Day or next April. She says April."

"Then April it will be. All I can say is, it's about time."

Gage stood. "I won't argue that."

Chapter 22

SAM AND MADDIE rode away from the K Bar K, Sam astride his muscular Appaloosa stallion and leading a pack mule, and Maddie mounted on the spirited sorrel gelding she had taken a liking to. Hands were already calling the mount "Maddie's critter." Sam knew that as far as the men were concerned, she was welcome to the horse. It tended to be rebellious and contrary and was a biter, but the horse seemed to reciprocate Maddie's affection and gave her no trouble. She had dubbed him "Outlaw."

Monique had seen that they were well supplied with foodstuffs and dug out one of her grown son Ben's sheepskin coats, a few flannel shirts, extra denims, and even long underwear. Ben had been about Maddie's height and a strapping young man when he finished school, but she swam in some of the garments, especially the britches at the waist. When she decided to change from her own, she would need some rawhide strips or rope to cinch the denims snug.

Pirate moved away from the riders, sticking to the higher ground where the heaviest snow had been swept away by the wind but keeping Maddie within sight. The sun shone brightly, casting near-blinding light on some of the white surfaces of the surrounding hills, and Sam guessed the temperature was significantly above freezing from the softening and shrinking of the snow crust. He led the way with his stallion, turning and twisting between the dunes and hillocks over hidden paths where experience had taught him the horses would find solid footing and would not sink into near bottomless drifts.

Neither had spoken to the other since departing the ranch, mostly because conversation was hampered when riding single file with a pack mule separating the leader from the tail rider. Finally, Maddie broke the silence and hollered, "Sam, why don't you let me lead the pack mule? It would be easier for you to break the trail, and we might even be able to speak to each other sometimes."

He reined in his mount. "You can manage the lead rope and that critter of yours at the same time?"

"Of course. Why couldn't I?"

He was not going to get into trouble by giving the wrong answer. "Well, sure you can, and it would help." He took the lead rope, led the mule behind the sorrel gelding, and handed her the rope end. "Thank you. This will help me, and I think I can get us moving a little faster. I would like to reach the soddy with some sunlight to let us do any patchwork that's needed and find some firewood if the last user didn't leave any behind."

"I hadn't thought about firewood."

He mounted his gelding and nudged the horse ahead. "That's why I brought the big axe along. Most folks are good about leaving firewood behind after a stay, but you never know. Regardless, before we pull out in the morning, I'll replenish the supply. Fox Creek passes within twenty yards of the place, and there's a fair stand of hardwoods there, always some dead stuff fit for burning."

Maddie said, "There aren't many trees in the hills."

"About the only place you find a natural growth of trees out here is along the creeks and rivers. Of course, settlement farmers and ranchers started planting trees."

"I saw the stand of trees south of the ranch house, maybe ten acres or more."

"Yep, Gramps planted those over thirty years ago, mostly oak and ash and other hardwoods. Grams has a smaller stand. They plant new for any they harvest. We'll count on wood for heat and cooking for some years yet. Towns with railroad connections are going to coal. Farmers near town, too. Not efficient to haul coal out this way yet, but I suppose it will happen someday."

They rode on, and he found she was seriously interested in the countryside and how folks survived in the Sandhills. He enjoyed pointing out the landmarks and talking about the history of locations they passed.

The soddy came into sight midafternoon, much sooner than Sam had anticipated. They could easily put more miles behind them before dark, but he did not want to construct a shelter in the woods along a creekbank someplace. If they got an early morning start, they could reach Rance Coldsmith's Rising Sun Ranch by noon tomorrow, talk to him about their concerns, and return to the soddy by evening, cutting a night's stay off the trip.

They rode into the yard of what had once been a farm home and dismounted. "We'll unload the mule and take our stuff inside," he said, "then we'll put the critters up in the barn. It's in decent shape, and there is hay stored there. The Slash Q owns this place now and everything surrounding the original quarter section. Pete Quinn's outfit makes use of the barn, and hands stay in the house during roundup. Folks are welcome to stay when passing by, and there's a tin on the table inside for contributions for those that see fit. I'll leave an eagle for the two nights' lodging and hay."

She helped him unhitch the mule's load, and they started carrying their food, cook gear, and other supplies inside. It did not take long considering they had packed for no more than a three-day journey. He noticed that Pirate was racing over the hill now. Maddie had not seemed worried about the wolfdog's disappearance.

Maddie said, "This is sort of an honor hotel? Anybody can stay and pay what they want?"

"Yep. Old Pete Quinn's kept the place going for almost ten years now. Claims he's never picked up an empty tin. I'm betting a few outlaws have stayed here, maybe even added to the tin. A lot of garden produce is sold like that at the roadside farther east in the homesteading areas. Pay what's marked or what seems fair and leave your money. Folks don't have time to tend the tables, and they're making a few dollars, or they wouldn't do it. I'm told a person wouldn't dare do such things in the big cities. I don't aim to find out. I was born in the Sandhills, and I will die here."

"The Flint Hills are like that, too, and the villages scattered about. The cities change folks, I guess, or certain kinds gravitate there. They're not all bad, of course. Lots of good people, but just enough of the bad ones to make for a different life. I've lived in Denver and Kansas City, visited St. Louis, Chicago, and New York City with my father. No, thank you. I'll stay in the ranchlands of the west."

Sam pondered what Maddie had said as they led the mule and horses to the barn. "You meant that, didn't you?"

"What?"

"Your love of ranching country?"

"Of course. Why would I say it otherwise?"

"Sorry. Dumb question."

"That's okay. You barely know me."

"We don't know each other. Maybe it's time to get acquainted."

When they returned to the soddy, Sam started a fire in the fireplace. He was pleased to see a healthy pile of wood next to the fireplace and thought he had seen a snow-covered stack outside.

Maddie sorted through the food supplies while Sam got the fire roaring. "We may want to warm some things up, and we'll have to brew our own coffee, but Monique wrapped plenty of cooked foods to feed us. I don't think we're going to be living like primitives here. She even sent along several bags of meat scraps for Pirate. It will save him some hunting."

Blizzard

"And we'll be plenty warm enough. The sod walls are at least two feet thick, and they hold the heat in during winter and the cool during summer. The place is well-constructed, and you saw that the barn is, too. This part of the hills just isn't for dirt farming, and I was told the homesteader and his family just starved out—couldn't raise enough to feed themselves let alone market much of anything."

Maddie said, "I'm going to take that shovel next to the door and make a path to the privy and clear the snow around the pump. I hope the well's working."

"I'm betting it will, but I can do that."

"You said you wanted to cut some firewood to replenish what we use. If you want that early start tomorrow, you'd better tend to that. I don't care to swing that monster axe you brought along. Besides, the snow didn't drift that much around the buildings, and it shouldn't take me that long. I'm sending Pirate with you. He'll be bored with my tasks."

"Well, I suppose you're right. I just don't . . ."

"Darn right, I'm right." She walked over and claimed the shovel.

He trudged through the snow to the creek where he found ample downed tree branches and a toppled ash.

Pirate had followed him but separated now, heading up the creek to investigate.

He dragged the longer branches back to the house where he found that Maddie had already cleared the snow from the nearly hidden woodpile and the nearby sawhorses. She had even put the big bowsaw that had been hanging on the inside wall out for him, making clear that the wood was his exclusive assignment.

There was a nice path to the privy and the area around the pump had been scooped. When he figured he had added more wood than they would burn in two nights, the sun was disappearing in the west, and he went back into the soddy, which was now toasty warm.

He was greeted by the inviting smell of brewing coffee and something cooking in the small pot they had brought. Maddie had let one end of fireplace burn down to coals, so she could use it for cooking. He was taken aback when he saw a mattress stretched out in front of the fireplace with both their bedrolls stretched out on it.

She evidently saw him staring at it. "No blankets on the bed in that other room, so I just drug the straw mattress out and put it down here. The dirt floor's packed hard like Chloe's, so I didn't think it would do any harm. I suppose I should have let you lay your own bedroll out, but I wanted to see how they would fit. We should be fine. The mattress came off a double bed."

"Uh, no, that's alright. You've been busy."

"Beats cutting wood. I've done that. Dodge the job when I can. We can eat if you're ready. Only thing missing in the soddy is a kerosene lamp, but the fireplace will give us a bit of light. Besides the bedroom being cold as sin, it would be dark as a coal mine. I did find a chamber pot under the bed, and I left it next to the wall just inside the doorway. I closed the door, though—thought it would stay warmer in here."

He had assumed she would take the bedroom, and he would bed down by the fire. The way she put it would not have made him seem very chivalrous, however. "Is there anything I can help with here?"

"Nope. Just sit down and eat. Starvation is not going to be a problem on this journey. I've got a kettle of ham and beans, a loaf of bread I warmed up near the fire, and some of Monique's apple cobbler for dessert. Breakfast, you'll have to settle for some tasty-looking pastries she sent along with the coffee. I can warm the pastries, though."

"A feast. I usually don't eat breakfast unless I've stayed over at Gramps's house. Of course, when I was growing up, Monique insisted I eat breakfast."

"I never miss breakfast. I'll eat your pastries if you want to pass on breakfast."

"Now I didn't say I wouldn't eat breakfast if it was there. I'm just too dang lazy to fix my own in the morning."

Chapter 23

"NOW TELL ME about yourself," Maddie said, after they finished supper and were still sitting at the small, rickety table.

"What do you want, the story of my life?"

"Not more than twenty minutes worth. I'm tired and we've got to clean up the supper things. That shouldn't take long."

"Do I get your story?"

"Twenty minutes of it."

"Okay. I was born at the ranch house twenty-five years ago last month. My mother died giving birth to me. No doctor nearby, of course, but Monique did all she could. She mothered me after that, suckled me with the son she had given birth to just a week earlier. He died when he was eleven."

"Your father?"

"Never knew him. He never even learned about my birth. His name was Dalton and he died with Grams's son Robert at Gettysburg."

"I'm so sorry."

"My father and Robert were best friends. Gramps took over raising me after that. Grams became my unofficial grandmother, and I spent a lot of time at her place. I've had a good life here. I did the equivalent of ten grades schooling at Cedar Creek, but I refused to go all the way to North Platte to earn a high school diploma—about the only time Gramps and I ever had a big fuss. Broken Bow wasn't even a town then, so high school there wasn't an option. But I learned my reading, writing, and numbers. I've read everything in Gramps's library and hope to double it someday. I'm doing what I want to do, but I admit now that a bit more schooling wouldn't have killed me. I've never been outside the state of Nebraska. With railroads spreading out like spiderwebs, I'll likely see more of the country someday, but like I told you, this is where I want to live out my days however many they might be. There, that's the story of my life."

Maddie said, "I'm guessing there's a lot more there, but that's a start for now. I'm pretty good at squeezing information out of folks."

"You being a detective, that doesn't surprise me. But you promised your story."

Maddie sighed. "Mine is different and more complicated. I was born in Colorado, and I'll soon be twenty-one. My father was and is a vice-president and shareholder with the Atcheson, Topeka and Santa Fe Railroad, but he was raised on a ranch in Missouri and purchased a ranching property in southeastern Colorado where I was raised and lived till I was nearly fifteen. My mother hated the place. She loved the city and finally left my father and divorced him. She forced sale of the ranch, and I moved in with her, but we never did get along, and it wasn't much fun for either of us. After a few months she sent me off to live with my father, who by then had moved to Kansas City."

"So by age fifteen, you had already traveled more than I have."

"That's not all. Before I reached my father, the train I was on was robbed and the outlaws abducted me and took me for ransom when they somehow learned I was a railroad official's daughter. They took me to a place called 'No Man's Land' squeezed between Texas, Kansas, New Mexico, Colorado, and Oklahoma Territory—rugged country, believe me. A prostitute helped me escape and gave her life for me—since then, I'm not quick to judge folks." She was not going to tell Sam about the rapes—not now, probably never.

Maddie said, "That's when I met Pirate, and he led me to a cabin on a plateau, where I found and buried his long dead master. I found food there, and Pirate adopted me that day. Eventually, I was found by folks from the Crockett Detective Agency, who had been hired by the railroad to recover me and the money. That's when my connection there started."

"So you joined your father in Kansas City finally?"

"For a year or so. Poor Pirate had to be penned, and I hated the private school. My father remarried, and looking back I think she was a nice enough woman, but I did not give her a chance. I didn't want to live in the city, so I ran off with Pirate to Trace and Darby Crockett's in Manhattan, Kansas, and they took me in after contacting my father and obtaining his approval with certain conditions, one being that I finish high school. They operated the detective agency offices in town but lived on a Flint Hills ranch."

Sam said, "So you were a ranch girl again?"

"Pirate was free, and we were happy there. I helped with the ranch whenever I wasn't in school and took a few agency assignments when a younger person was needed—nothing dangerous. I still wanted to be in ranching, so I attended Kansas State Agricultural College for two years before I decided I'd had enough of school and started working more for the agency. And that's how I came to be here. End of story."

Maddie had his head spinning. He suspected that her story fleshed out would be mind-boggling. He truly did not know what to make of her.

Maddie said, "You can help me with cleanup, then I'm catching some shuteye. I could fall asleep standing up, I think."

"Sure, do we need water to boil? I can take a container out to the pump."

"Just find a spot in the fireplace for that big kettle next to the cupboard. I found it inside and already filled it with water."

"You are always a step ahead of me."

"That's my aim."

Later, stretched out in his bedroll on the mattress, Sam could not be oblivious to the young woman lying only a few feet distant snuggled and apparently sound asleep in her own cocoon. He had volunteered to tend to the fire during the night, and she had not objected, but he suspected she would take care of it if he slept through his responsibility. The fact that she would remind him of it, however, made him vow to awaken and check the fire several times. She certainly had been anything but the burden he had anticipated on this journey. On the contrary, she was carrying more than her share of the load. Moreover, he was starting to like her—a lot.

He dropped off to sleep, but an hour later he felt a body pressing against his back. Did she want him? This would be too much luck. He rolled over to show his willingness and faced a dog's belly. Pirate was sleeping between them, gradually crowding him off the mattress. He got up to throw another log on the fire, and when he started to crawl back into his blankets, Sam found that the wolfdog had claimed the remainder of his side of the mattress and lay upon half his blankets. He was not about to fight the creature for the spot, but he did tug his bedroll from beneath Pirate, and put it next to the mattress. It would not be the first time he had bedded down on hard ground.

He woke up when sunlight began to creep through the only window to find that Maddie already had coffee brewing. He threw off the blankets and started the search for his boots.

"Next to the fireplace," Maddie said. "I thought I'd warm them a bit for you. Are you still going to eat breakfast?"

"Yeah, I am."

"I'll warm the pastries while you head for the outhouse. I'll warn you, it's cold out there."

She even read his bladder for him. He grabbed his boots and started to pull them on.

Maddie said, "I'm sorry about Pirate. I forgot to tell you he likes to sleep next to me, and I guess it was only natural for him to take the space between us. I didn't intend for you to sleep on the bare floor."

Sam shrugged and went outside with Pirate close behind. They didn't go to the privy, however. Instead, both man and dog went to the side of the soddy and made their marks in the snow.

Chapter 24

RANCE COLDSMITH WAS a handsome devil, Maddie thought. He could give Sam Kraft a run for his money. Coldsmith, though, was probably into his forties, with crows' feet starting to extend from his eyes and a few wrinkles engraved on his forehead. But she thought he was going to age well like Gage Kraft. He was almost as tall as Sam, and she could not remember the last time she had been with two men who were so much taller than herself. It was more common for her to tower over others of the opposite sex. Not that it mattered. She had learned, sometimes the hard way, that good and bad men came in all sizes.

They sat in the parlor of a nice two-story home perched on a hillside above a collection of farm buildings below. Besides the usual barn and stable, corrals, chicken house and other outbuildings, the Rising Sun Ranch included a large swine structure and hog pens with small A-shaped huts spread over a slope no more than thirty yards east of the house. Coldsmith and his eldest son, Morgan, had been feeding hogs from a grain wagon when she and Sam rode into the yard late morning.

Morgan and his mother, Lisbeth, sat in the parlor with them now after a delicious dinner featuring ham chunks, potatoes, and assorted vegetables cooked together in a pot, topped off with several choices of fruit pies. Coldsmith had insisted they join the family for dinner, and his wife had been unfazed by the surprise guests. Maddie liked her instantly, and Lisbeth had ample scraps to share with Pirate and the family's shepherd on the enclosed porch off the kitchen.

Maddie guessed that the pretty, auburn-haired Lisbeth was five or six years younger than her husband. Morgan was not far from her own age, so she must have been young when he was born, not unusual. Most women that Maddie knew had borne their first child, possibly several, before age twenty.

There had been five children at the dinner table. Sam had told her that Morgan and Marissa, a seventeen-year-old beauty, were Lisbeth's by a first marriage, and that Rance had adopted the widow's children. The three younger ones, one boy and two girls ranged from ten to five years in age. It was obvious that every family member had chore assignments on the ranch.

Coldsmith disappointed Maddie when he broke up the chatter between the two women who sat side by side on the couch. She was finding Lisbeth a fascinating and knowledgeable woman and wanted to hear more.

Coldsmith said, "Sam, we're all delighted you came to visit today, but I know you didn't ride this far to make a social call. What can I help you with?"

"Well, first off, are you still heading up the West-Central Cattlemen's Association?"

"Yeah, I'm president until they can find some other fool to take the job. I know the K Bar K is a member, but I haven't seen Gage for more than a year, I'd say. Do you have association business?"

"I don't know if you would call it business but we're looking for information. We've got a serious cattle rustling problem up our way."

"You've got company. All the ranchers have been after the association to do something about it. We can't turn up a clue so far."

"We've had a ten percent herd depletion, our neighbor, Chloe Downs of the Circle D, probably twice that figure."

"You do have a problem. Nobody else I know approaches those numbers. For what it's worth, the association has employed the Pinkerton agency to investigate the situation. Calvin Holiday, one of their agents, visited my place a few weeks ago. He was to stop at the sheriff's office in Broken Bow to discuss the situation and then head north to talk to ranchers. I even gave him a sketch of where to find folks. The K Bar K was on it."

"He never got to our place. I suspect that he's the dead man that Maddie and her dog turned up between Broken Bow and our place. She was with Gramps, and they found a Pinkerton badge on him. One of our hands took the body to the sheriff in Broken Bow just before the snowstorm hit. He should be home by now."

"We can't count on Wally Barnes to deal with this, but I suppose I should take a day and ride up to have a talk with him—be certain he met the man earlier and has his name. The agency needs to be notified."

Sam said, "We'll leave that to you. I should tell you that Maddie here is an agent for the Crockett Detective Agency out of Manhattan, Kansas. She was here to speak with Chloe about another matter and has agreed to stay on a few weeks to help with the rustling investigation. Chloe's been hit hardest, it appears, and has a big stake in this."

Coldsmith said, "If you will share any information you pick up with the association, we'll pay the Crockett people to extend your stay beyond that few weeks. Getting the Pinkerton folks here in the Sandhills is a challenge. I like that we've already got a detective in our midst."

He caught her by surprise. "I would need to contact the home office, but I think that could be arranged. Let's see if I can come up with anything helpful."

"Fair enough. If the weather's decent, maybe I'll take a ride up your way after the first of the year and get up to date on any progress—if I haven't heard from you before."

Morgan said, "I could do that for you, Dad. I haven't been off the place in weeks."

Coldsmith looked at his son quizzically, then smiled. "Yeah, I guess there's no reason why you couldn't handle it. We'll see when the time comes."

Maddie said nothing. She knew Morgan had been casting furtive glances at her during the conversation. She was flattered, not offended. He was quite handsome, sharing his mother's auburn hair and dark, brown eyes, a sprinkling of freckles under his eyes and across the bridge of his nose. He had not spoken much and appeared on the shy side, but his "aw shucks" grin made him instantly likeable.

They talked for another hour about the rustling problems at various ranches, and Maddie tried to map the locations in her head. She thought that with Sam's help she would sketch a crude map when they returned to the K

Bar K. Maddie said, "It sounds to me like the rustling is pretty much confined to three or four counties: northeast Lincoln, eastern Logan and most of Custer. Then, Chloe's ranch extends most north into Blaine. The Rising Sun in Custer seems to be the farthest south, is that right?"

Coldsmith said, "Yes, we're in the south part of the county. More homesteaders and farms as you move south. Most have cattle, some a good number, but they're mostly within sight of their home farmsteads. Our own herd is more north and west of the headquarters place, and we're not big operators compared to some, including Gage and Chloe. We raise corn and wheat along the lowlands, and you can see we've got a fair-sized hog operation. I think of myself as a cowman, and I hate to admit it, but Lisbeth's hog business carries the financial load for the ranch. That was all her idea, and she did most of the work early on, eased up some since the little ones came along, and we took on a few hired men from the farm families nearby."

Maddie had taken several classes in swine production at the ag college but had little direct experience with porkers. "I'd love to see your building and pen arrangements and hear about how you do this before we leave."

Lisbeth said, "And I would be honored to show you around."

Blizzard

She saw Sam roll his eyes. Like other ranchers she had known, he looked with disdain upon the lowly hog, and she figured he would rather starve than raise and feed the things. "That would be wonderful."

Sam said, "We'd better be moving on, Maddie, if we want to make the Slash Q soddy by nightfall."

"No more than an hour," Lisbeth said. "It's a nice day, no storms in sight, and I don't want to hold you up. Morg, why don't you come with us? You've taken over a lot of the day-to-day management. You can help answer questions."

Sam said, "I guess Rance and I can find plenty to palaver about, but I'm holding you to that hour. I'll have the horses saddled, and the mule ready to go."

Coldsmith said, "And I'll help you load some hams and bacon that Lisbeth wrapped for you to take along."

Sam sighed. "Well, I won't deny that I'll eat my share. I like good pork now and then, but I'll eat my hat if I ever see hogs being raised on the K Bar K."

Coldsmith said, "I remember saying that about the Rising Sun one time."

Chapter 25

COLETTE CHURCHILL WALTON squinted, momentarily blinded by the late afternoon sun, and paused on the last step off the train. She was already trailing her husband who had left the passenger car several steps ahead of her. A kind, booted, young man wearing a Stetson extended a hand and helped her onto the planked platform. She smiled and said, "Thank you, sir."

He grinned back and said, "My pleasure, ma'am. Can I help you further?"

"Not today, thank you. My husband's up ahead, and I must catch up to him." She scurried away, puzzled by the disappointed look on his face. The railroad station was a busy place, people coming and going, most loaded down with baggage, old people, young people, mothers leading children, making their ways through the maze.

She lost sight of Roscoe in the crowd. At no more than a few inches over five feet even in her heeled shoes, she simply could not catch sight of him over the melee of people. He had told her their bags would be brought to the side of the street on a big handcart and that someone would be waiting with a carriage to load the luggage and take them to the hotel where he had reservations. She wondered how he had made all these arrangements, but she dared not ask. She felt like a little puppy that was expected only to obey lest she be swatted.

She recognized an older couple from the passenger car not far ahead of her and decided to follow them. The husband was carrying a bag in each hand, and the wife had a carpet bag tucked under her arm. They would likely be headed toward the street where transportation presumably awaited. She kept her eyes on the pair, counting on them to blaze her trail.

Several minutes later, they arrived at the dirt street that was decorated with intermittent piles of horse dung and lined with wagons and buggies. The roadway was cleaner than most of the Omaha streets that appeared to have manure roadbeds. She looked up and down the street and saw Roscoe standing next to a buggy, arms folded across his chest. She could not see his face, but she could imagine the exasperated look frozen on it. She sucked in a deep breath and hurried up the streetside to meet up with her husband.

"Where the hell have you been?" Walton said, when she walked up to him.

"I lost sight of you and wasn't certain where to go for a spell."

She was saved further interrogation when a little man with a chest-length white beard and tattered, slouch hat came up carrying a bag in each hand and another tucked precariously under his arm. He dumped them in the back of the buggy. "Two more," he said, turned around and headed back to the baggage wagon.

Roscoe could have helped the man, she thought, but she supposed that men of his elite station did not handle their own bags. It occurred to her suddenly that she had likely not been much better over the years. When the man returned, he hefted the bags onto the two-seated buggy, forced to stack two bags next to the driver. This was obviously not a cargo wagon.

When he turned away, she extended her hand. "I'm Colette Walton. Thank you for taking care of the bags."

The man, obviously surprised at the introduction, grinned with a mouth that displayed seven or eight brown-stained teeth. He doffed his hat. "You're very welcome, ma'am. Let me help you onto the buggy." He took her hand and assisted her onto the step that allowed her to reach the second row of seats. He then claimed his own seat behind the horse and took the reins in his hands.

Roscoe was already seated by this time, and he would not have assisted her if she had asked. She had no notion of what was to become of her, but two encounters with gentlemen of contrasting appearances had made her less fearful of this place. She had not yet seen the crudeness and savagery of westerners that city dwellers of a certain class talked about.

They were soon settled in a room at a lodging place called the Cattlemen's Hotel. Reservations had been for a single room, and Roscoe was complaining that they did not have a suite of several rooms. It seemed clean enough, and Colette's only objection was that it offered no escape from Roscoe. She hoped he had other business that would take him away.

They had no sooner filled the small closet and the chest of drawers than there was a soft rapping on the door. "Who is it?" Walton said.

"Gar."

Walton opened the door, and a man of medium height and build stepped in and closed the door behind him. He had a somewhat pockmarked face, clean-shaven except for a thick mustache above his lips. His dark piercing eyes were fixed upon her. She was surprised to see a silver deputy sheriff's badge pinned to his leather vest.

He turned his gaze to Walton. "You going to introduce me to the lady?"

Walton shrugged. "Gar Ford. This is my wife, Colette."

Ford removed his wide brimmed hat. "Pleased to make your acquaintance, Missus Walton. You can just call me Gar."

She nodded but did not offer a smile.

"We should talk soon, Roscoe," Ford said. "Now, if you want."

Walton tossed a glance at Colette. "Not now. Where can we meet?"

"We don't want to seem like old friends or business partners. I slipped through the backdoor and up the staff stairway. Clerk don't know I'm here. You and the missus go ahead and have your dinner. They've got decent eats in the dining room downstairs. It'll be dark by the time you finish. Then you make your way over to the sheriff's office. I'm the only man on duty tonight, and no chance the sheriff will show up. He lives two miles from town and ain't inclined to extra hours anyhow. Not that it would matter much if he did. If you're perched in front of my desk, and you're seen, nobody'd give it a thought. Just another complainer or somebody asking for directions. Kind of like hiding out in the open, you might say."

"Makes sense. Just so we can talk privately."

"Nobody locked up in the jail right now. Most of our traffic is Saturday nights."

"And I hope you will explain just why you are wearing a lawman's badge."

"Yep. Turned into the smartest move I've made. Not inclined to give it up as long as we're doing business up this way. I'll tell you about it." He stepped toward the door and paused. "Best to come after eight o'clock. Except for the saloon crowds, the town gets dang sleepy by then." He peered out into the hallway, went through the doorway, and disappeared.

Obviously, Roscoe did not want her to hear his conversation with Gar Ford. She found him a sleezy man, confident just short of arrogant. Ford and Roscoe were a good match for whatever devilment they were up to. A wave of fear swept over her again, but it passed quickly this time. She hoped that she was starting to numb herself to all the changes that had suddenly been thrust upon her. She must bring calm to her thinking if she was to have any chance of escaping the mess she had made of her life.

She decided to risk a question. "You said we were coming to meet my grandmother. I know nothing about her except she lives on a ranch somewhere and that she is a terrible person. When do we visit the woman? And you still haven't told me why."

"I will know more after I talk with Gar tonight. And I will tell you when and why when the time is right. That will be soon, because you will need to prepare for your role."

"Role? Like I'm an actress or something?"

"That might be a good way of looking at it. An actress for an audience of one. Now, let's go eat."

She would not resist that order. Her fare had been skimpy all day and she was suddenly starved.

Chapter 26

ROSCOE WALTON ENTERED the sheriff's office and found Gar Ford planted behind the sheriff's desk, his feet propped on the desktop, a dying cigar stub between his lips. As Walton closed the door behind him, Gar tossed the stub in a bowl on the desk that was nearly overflowing with the remnants of cigar and cigarette butts.

"Good evening, Roscoe. Sit down and make yourself at home."

Walton sat down but was annoyed that Ford kept his feet in place, and he was forced to look over boot soles to see the man's face. He wondered if Ford remembered Walton was head of their enterprise and that the so-called deputy was a hired man, albeit a well-paid one.

"What's the deputy sheriff story?"

"Good fortune. I've been doing this for close to six months now. There's three of us, all part-timers. Sheriff never needs us all at once, not yet anyhow. If I want a week or two off, I just make sure somebody else will cover. Sheriff gets testy if he's got to put in extra hours."

"Rather like letting the fox in the henhouse, it appears to me."

"Call it what you want. I pick up lots of useful information here, some important to our business enterprises."

Walton flinched at his use of the word "our" but said nothing. "Such as?"

"Well, I seem to got me a knack for being here at the right time. Did you ever wonder what happened to Cougar Swanson, the gunman we hired to get rid of that old woman?"

"Figured the damn thief took the five hundred we gave him up front and skipped the country. Just as well. I've got a new idea anyhow."

"Well, the old biddy kilt him."

"You're serious?"

"Yep. A neighbor of hers—rancher named Kraft—stopped in to report it. Sheriff Barnes and me was both here that day and I didn't butt in, just listened. This Kraft feller even buried old Cougar. Seems Cougar was trying to break into her house one night, and she feeds him a shotgun load."

Walton had pictured grandma as a little wizened lady who spent her days in a rocking chair knitting. "Well, I assume they didn't have any idea how Cougar came to be there."

"Didn't seem to. Got to watch this Kraft, though. He's careful with his words and don't seem to like or trust Barnes too much. I don't think he expected much from the sheriff, them being so far out in the county and offering not many votes. I don't see how they could figure out who Cougar was working for anyhow."

"Well, I'm not interested in killing the woman just now. Changed plans."

"Another thing. The local cattlemen's association hired Pinkertons to look into the rustling hereabouts."

That information surprised and troubled him. "Not good."

"Took care of it. The Pinkerton agent stopped by here on his way to talk to ranchers northwest. He would have made his way sooner or later to the Downs and Kraft ranches. They've been our biggest suppliers, partly because you've got something against Downs, but they're also closer to the market. Anyhow, a young feller from the Kraft outfit brought his body in a week or so back. I didn't like that his badge was still on him."

Walton said, "So the sheriff knows now?"

Ford grinned. "Nope. It was luck I was the only one here when the cowhand showed up with the corpse. The badge disappeared, and I told the sheriff about a stranger's body coming in just in case Kraft would ask about it later. The man is buried in a nameless pauper's grave. A nasty snowstorm hit right after that and got everybody's attention for a few days, and the sheriff didn't ask no more questions."

"You hired somebody to take care of the problem."

"Well, you could see it that way, but your money paid for it. I got access to your account at the First National Bank here, and you signed the paperwork I sent you that gave me authority to draw money."

"You were only supposed to use that authority if I approved. It was for convenience only."

"This was convenient, I'd say, unless you wanted to hand the gunman the money personally. Cost five hundred dollars, and the killer got the horse and any money the man had on him."

"Too much killing. That draws attention."

"Speaking of killing, bundles of *The Omaha Daily Bee* from a few days back came in on the train this morning, and papers are being delivered to local customers. Most will go out in the morning, but downtown we get ours within an hour after they're dropped. Damnedest story in there."

Blizzard

He swung his legs off the desktop, opened a desk drawer, and pulled out a folded newspaper. "You might want to read this. Ain't much of a story, but they promise more next issue, which we might get tomorrow or days from now, never know."

Ford slid the newspaper across the desk, and Walton picked it up, noting that the story had been circled with a pencil. The headline read: "Prominent Lawyer Murdered." The story went on to say that lawyer Calvin Lockhart had been found dead of a gunshot wound at the residence of Lulu Perry, who also died as a result of brutal knife wounds. It continued, stating that Perry was an alleged prostitute but little else was known about her at this writing.

"Your hands are shaking, Roscoe."

Only then did Walton realize that his hands were trembling and the newspaper quivering. "It's shocking. Cal was a dear friend, and I counted on him to handle my legal matters. This is terrible."

"You had a woman named Lulu working in your office. Not a common name."

"Uh . . . Lulu's not a whore. And her last name is . . . Smith. She is still handling the Omaha office."

"You're sinking, ain't you?"

"What the hell does that mean?"

"I done a little checking of my own. Your house is being foreclosed. You got bank judgments against you and more on the way. Your back is against the wall, Roscoe, and I'm guessing the law in Omaha will start to make connections. It might take a few weeks, if you're lucky, maybe a month, but time's running out. Sooner or later, they will be looking for Mister Roscoe Walton."

"I don't know what you're talking about."

"I'm betting there ain't no Lulu Smith in Omaha, and somebody will figure out that Lulu Perry was working for you, maybe in several capacities. And then it will show up in public court filings that Calvin Lockhart was your law wrangler. First, they might just want to chat with you about it. Then they'll find you've skipped town. If you had nothing to do with the killings, I suggest you head back to Omaha and clear the air. But, of course, your train tickets here were just one-way."

"Are you accusing me of murder?"

"Let's quit playing games, Roscoe. We're fifty-fifty partners in Sandhills Cattle Company now. It's time we started to work together."

"Partners? You work for me, and you are damn well paid."

"I'm a full partner now, or I'm out."

Panic seized Walton, and he just wanted to run. But where? Ford was blackmailing his way into the business.

"You've got no proof of my connection with the Omaha killings. You just made up your own story."

"Then you ain't got no objection if I contact the Omaha law folks and inform them of your whereabouts?"

"You as much as admitted to me tonight that you killed that Pinkerton agent or ordered it done. How many have you shot down during the years you've been working for me? I hold some cards, too. If I go down, I'm not going alone."

"Then we got that in common, because I ain't neither. Who ordered them killings? I even came into Omaha to take care of that young brother-in-law for you, but you paid me damn good for it. I can't complain on that score. It didn't take you long to piss away the money your woman inherited from him, though, did it? She ain't got a clue that his death was your doing, does she?"

"She doesn't have a clue about anything. She grew up sheltered from real life. I married her for her money and a poke with a pretty girl now and then. Her mother was very fond of me and set things up so I would handle Colette's money. She is a nice trophy to display at parties and knows the social graces, but her brain is smaller than a grasshopper's."

"Partners or not?"

Walton sighed. He had no choice. He was trapped in a little oasis in what seemed like an endless desert. He dared not return to Omaha—ever. If he had the money, he would leave Colette behind and travel as far away from here as he could get and just disappear before he emerged again with a new name and identity. Yes, that is what he must do. The money. "Partners for one more venture. Obviously, I need to move on as soon as possible."

"We got the same goal in mind then. I ain't about to spend the rest of my days as a deputy sheriff in this Podunk town. No more fighting wind and snow, maybe south Texas or even Mexico."

Walton thought Ford's idea wasn't half bad, but he sure was not joining up with this snake after he departed Nebraska. "You had just as well know, my wife came with me to visit a relative."

"She's got family out here?"

"A rancher, Chloe Downs of the Circle D."

"The woman you wanted kilt? What kind of relative is she?"

"A grandmother. Colette has never met her, but she is the woman's only heir."

"And you figured your wife would inherit the ranch and livestock."

"Which we would immediately sell. The woman likely has some money, too."

"Sorry to tell you, that was a dumb notion. I ain't no lawyer, but I know that if this Downs woman has a will, it ain't likely she left her property to a grandchild she's never seen."

"It was a gamble. Calvin Lockhart told me three-fourths of the people who should have a will never get around to making one. And he said that those who do, no matter what's happened over the years, find it hard not to leave their estates to blood kin. There is no reason to think Chloe Downs even knows her daughter Darla is dead. Too bad I hadn't connected with the family earlier. Even if she's land-poor, this grandmother is worth some money, but I'm afraid I can't get to it fast enough."

"So where does the old lady fit in?"

"I've got to meet her, and then decide, but we can't hold up our other plans. I don't want to stay in Nebraska a day longer than I must, and the only quick money we can count on is cattle sales—if we've got a place to market the animals. Are you selling at the Sioux reservation?"

"Not directly. I did like you said, I found a go-between to take the cattle off our hands for twenty per cent off market. He's got a ranch up north, not more than ten miles south of the agency, but he can herd critters straight west to Fort Robinson or east to another agency. He's got markets, because so many ranchers are finding easier money at the rail connections now."

"I don't like the twenty-percent discount price."

"He won't do less. He's got to pay a commission to Indian agents or other government people to make the deals."

"Thieves. We're dealing with robbers."

"Well, the government crowd would want their share if we sold direct, and you said you wanted a layer between us so one of your companies didn't show in the government records. I wouldn't have thought of it, but I think that's smart, and it speeds up our job. Frank Bartek don't have much land, but he churns out a lot of cattle from that place—not sure he even owns it, might be a squatter. Anyhow, his place is the 'Box X' and they'll do some brand fixing if they got to. Guess that's not a problem going direct to the Sioux, but Army sales are another thing."

"How many men can you put together for a big rustling job? I'm talking as many as a thousand head."

"I got five men nearby I can count on. Frank could send me that many more if I sent somebody up to talk to him, but he wouldn't take that many cattle in one bunch. He'd likely do half that and take on another herd a few weeks later. We use Bobcat Canyon on government land as a holding place for the rustled cattle. If I can hire on a few more men, we can keep on collecting beeves while hands are driving the others to market."

"Can we get cash on delivery?"

"We can arrange that. I did that last time, and he took an extra two percent."

"Why am I not surprised? Well, I want to be there for the last delivery. Then, I want you to take me to North Platte to catch a train. There, we split and never see each other again. We'll work out the details. We can use the money in the bank for upfront payments, and what's left, I suppose you're planning to steal half."

"Yep. We're finally understanding each other."

"We should be able to walk away with more than ten thousand dollars apiece. That should be plenty to get me a fresh start someplace with a new name."

"We're thinking alike. What about your wife and any money you pick up from Grandma?"

"Grandma's money is mine if there is any. That's settled. Colette stays with Grandma, but she doesn't know it yet—unless I decide she knows too much."

"In which case?"

"She will be buried in the Sandhills alongside Grandma."

Ford shrugged. "I might buy her from you."

"I'm tempted, but I don't think so."

"You've got my offer of five hundred dollars. Just keep that in mind."

Walton did not reply, but it occurred to him that he should snatch any money he could for his new life. She'd go with Ford if he came up with the right kind of story, and Ford wouldn't chance her talking after he used her for a time. She would end up dead or in a Mexican whorehouse eventually.

Walton said, "I want to get to the Circle D Ranch by the day after tomorrow. Can you get me there?"

"Horseback? That's easy enough. I can get a guide for you. You'd be there in five or six hours. Does the lady ride?"

"Yes. She's a fair rider—does sidesaddle in a dress, but she can go like blazes wearing britches and astride. She can ride and play piano. That's about it." He thought a moment. "But I think she should arrive in a nice carriage."

"Sort of like a princess, huh?"

"Don't want to look like beggars."

"Or thieves."

Walton wished he could shoot the son-of-a-bitch right now. Maybe later, before they got to North Platte. He wasn't giving up on both shares of the money. What worried him was that Gar Ford might be thinking the same thing.

Chapter 27

WHEN SAM, MADDIE, and Pirate returned to K Bar K headquarters, Maddie found herself in a good mood. For some reason she wanted to stay around the ranch for a spell, and the cattlemen's association had given her good cause. She admitted that Sam was part of the reason. They had talked for hours at the Slash Q soddy last night, even with Pirate lying between them.

She could not believe how she had opened up to Sam, who may have been the least judgmental person she ever encountered. She had even recited the entire story of her abduction absent specifics concerning the rapes, but he knew now and had listened without interruption. His only comment was, "You've had a dang tough education, Maddie. Gramps always says that everything that happens to us adds to our education if we pay attention.

Life is school that never lets out, he says. Of course, some folks don't pay attention and don't learn anything. But I can tell you're not like that."

And Sam had confided to her about the sadness he felt sometimes because he had never known either his mother or his father, but the deep love he felt for Gramps and Grams was unshakable. He was obviously determined to be there whenever they needed him. She suggested to him that there was no way to tell how his story might have been written had his parents survived. Hers had not been an entirely a happy one. "Every day," she said, "I just try to count my blessings for the good things in my life."

It was midafternoon, and the snow cover seemed to sparkle from the sun's glow as they walked to the house from the stable. Maddie said, "At least the weather was with us. No wind or snowfall, and the temperature never more than a degree or two below freezing. The barn roof is even dripping water from the melt."

"Out here, that could change in less than an hour."

"Yeah, I know. I like winter best inside looking out."

When they entered the house, Rip limped over to greet Pirate, and the friends sniffed and nuzzled each other. Monique peered out of the kitchen and smiled and waved. "Rip, Pirate," she called, "come here. There's a snack in the laundry porch for you." The dogs understood the summons, because they swept past her in an instant, old Rip forgetting to limp for a few moments.

After escorting the dogs to the porch, Monique stepped out of the kitchen. "What about you two? I'm guessing you didn't have dinner."

"Jerky and a few stale biscuits," Sam said.

"Well, get those coats off and sit down at the table. You don't have to go to the porch. I'll have some leftovers warmed up in twenty minutes."

"No argument from me. Is Gramps here?"

"He's in his study, likely sleeping in his chair. He was looking for you today and said he wanted to see you as soon as you showed up. But you will eat first."

"Yes, ma'am."

Maddie looked around the room and realized that Monique and Vega had decorated for Christmas, and in one corner of the parlor a big cedar tree had been installed for the holiday, but the branches were still bare. She was obsessive about dates, and the calendar in her head told her this was the tenth of December, and Christmas was just two weeks distant. Happy snowmen danced on the walls along with countless Santas and the reindeer. Wreaths made of cedar branches, paper images of candy canes, everything a person thought of at Christmas time. The decorations were all handmade and painted, many obviously old and fashioned by children.

When Monique summoned them to the serving counter, Maddie said. "The decorations are beautiful. I've never seen anything to compare to this, and I love it."

"Smoky and Rick found the tree and set it up for me. I'm counting on you and Sam to help with decorating."

"I can't wait. When do we start?"

"Tonight, after supper. Smoky wants to help, too. I don't know about the other hands. Gage will need to be coaxed a bit, but he enjoys it once we get started."

After eating, Maddie and Sam went to the office, where as Monique predicted, they found Gage dozing at his desk, chin resting on chest. "Gramps," Sam said softly, "Monique said you wanted to see us when we got back."

Gage opened his eyes and lifted his head. "Sorry, I guess I nodded off. Doesn't look like I'm working too hard, does it?"

Sam said, "Looks to me like you're working *too* hard."

"I'm finding that old men wear down a mite faster than you kids, and then Chloe's got me running back and forth right now. She's having a fit about her rustled cattle, not that I blame her. I'm worried, too. We do need to get our operations combined and hire on a few more full-timers. I just worry about the cost. Can we gain enough to handle more salaries? Things are tight enough as it is with cattle prices down again and then losing a chunk of the herd we got. This is serious, Sam. I guess you know that."

Maddie suspected that her remark would not be taken well, but she decided to chance it. "Have you ever thought about raising hogs and cultivating more cropland to grow some grain? It appears to me that you've got some creek bottomland on the east end of the ranch that would grow crops."

Sam rolled his eyes, and Gage looked at her incredulously. Gage said, "We're ranchers, Maddie, not farmers."

"The Coldsmiths are doing very well with both, it seems. Lisbeth showed me the swine operation. She says you can get into the hog business cheap and expand fast because of litter size and at least two litters a year. Average is two and a half, my ag school professor said. If you raised enough grain, you could feed the hogs till butchering size. Build a smoke house, sell meat in town or take the hogs in and ship them out."

Sam said, "Farmers here are already raising enough hogs to satisfy most of the local market."

"Lisbeth said there will be buyers in Broken Bow soon to buy for Omaha and Chicago packers. Hogs are being shipped out from North Platte now—thousands of them. That's where they go with those they don't eat or sell locally. I don't know much about hogs except what I learned at ag school, but if I ever get located on a ranch, I'd like to give it a try sometime. They're calling that 'diversifying.' In other words, some are saying 'don't put all your eggs in one basket.'"

Gage was still staring at her. "Maybe that's something to chew on a spell. Nothing says our men have got to sit on their hands when they're not working cattle."

Sam said, "Gramps, no self-respecting cowhand is going to deal with hogs or walk behind a mule pulling a plow. Shucking corn and the like? Maddie means well, but this is cow country."

"Sam, I just said her idea was something to chew on. Let's chew. Now, besides learning about the hog business, tell me what you found out at Rance Coldsmith's."

"You were right. The West-Central Cattlemen's Association hired Pinkerton to investigate the rustling problem. Other ranchers have been losing cattle, too, but not at the high rates of the K Bar K and Circle D. The Pinkerton agent visited Coldsmith before he started working up this way. He was planning to make a stop in Broken Bow to talk with the sheriff before he eventually contacted you."

"That's strange. When Alex took the body to town, the deputy claimed he had never seen the man before.

The sheriff wasn't in the office that afternoon, though, so I suppose the deputy wasn't around when the agent stopped by to visit, and the man talked to the sheriff that time. Anyhow, the deputy said he would discuss it with the sheriff, and their office would contact the Pinkerton people. The deputy didn't give the corpse more than a glance before he told Alex to take it over to the undertaker. He did keep the Pinkerton badge, though. Alex thought he didn't seem all that interested."

"Who is the deputy?"

"Some fella named Ford. I met him at the sheriff's office when I was there. But he didn't say a word while I talked with Wally Barnes. Alex said he wasn't a very friendly sort."

"He must be new around here. Of course, I get to town even less than you do."

Gage said, "So what's the association going to do? Are they going to stay after the rustlers?"

"Well, they're not going to contact the Pinkertons for another agent right now. Coldsmith hired Maddie here to stay on for a time and see if she can come up with anything."

Maddie said, "If you can put up with a guest for a bit longer."

Gage grinned. "Maddie, you can just move in with us if you like. If you lose the detective work, we'll take you on as a cowhand."

She knew he was not serious but replied, "Be careful what you say. I might just take you up on that."

Sam chuckled. "You can be in charge of the hog pens."

She did not find his remark funny. "Then I'll order you to scoop out the hog shit. It makes good crop fertilizer, you know."

Gage interceded. "Maddie, I think you should head over to Chloe's tomorrow. She said she'd like to talk to you again soon."

"I'll do that. It's time I turn my attention to what I came here for and figure out if I'm working for her or the cattlemen's association. I may stay over if she'll let me bed down on the floor. I'm getting accustomed to that."

Gage said, "Push her to come over for Christmas Eve and stay over a day, maybe two if you need to."

"She doesn't usually come for Christmas?"

"For years she allowed Sam or me to bring her over Christmas day for dinner, but she's always got to milk that dang cow in the morning first and then get back home to do it again at night and, of course, her other chores. I'll give one of the men a bonus to take care of those things if she'll stay over a few nights. I want her to see how it could be here."

"I'll do my best."

They talked another fifteen minutes about the rustling plague before Sam said he had to head home with his horses and get resettled there. When he got up, he said, "I guess I'll be back over to help decorate the tree tonight. Monique will be hurt if I don't at least show up for a spell."

Maddie noted the lack of enthusiasm in his voice and manner. His mood had shifted decidedly downward during the conversation.

After Sam left, she and Gage sat silently for several minutes, and she supposed she should excuse herself.

Then Gage spoke. "Diversification. You know, Maddie, I take your suggestion seriously. I'm pondering what you said. Maybe we can talk more about it another time. I've been so fixed on the cattle business that I've never given much thought to other possible revenues. Maybe it's time."

"Sam didn't take to it."

"Oh, he's thinking about what you said. Take my word for it. He's generally cautious about his words, but you have got him tied in knots, young lady."

"I don't understand."

"He likes you . . . a lot, and his brains aren't working right just now."

"I still don't understand, but I like him a lot, too. I thought we were becoming good friends."

"Oh, you are. No doubt about it."

Chapter 28

MADDIE RODE PAST Sam's cabin on her way to Chloe's and considered stopping before she noticed the weak smoke plume rising from the metal pipe that stuck up from the wood-shingled roof and quickly feathering away into the stiff wind. The flames in the woodstove were obviously dying, and she figured he had probably departed for whatever task topped his work list today.

He had not appeared for supper last night, but he did ride over to help decorate the tree for several hours. Although he had been quiet most of the time, they shared some laughs and they both, because of their heights, had focused on hanging decorations on the tree's upper branches, and Sam stretched and placed the star at the top.

Monique and Vega ramrodded the festivities, but Bruce Potter, Gage and Smoky joined in, and Alex and Ricky showed up in time for punch and cookies. The ranch folks truly were family, she thought, but sadly, there were no children. The days when Sam and the Potter kids were growing up must have been great fun. Gage told her that Chloe used to come during those days although she never stayed over.

Her biggest surprise of the evening, however, had come when she and Sam ended up in a corner of the parlor together. Sam had turned to her and said, "I'm glad you are here to share this, and I want to apologize. I shouldn't have made light of your suggestion about the hogs. I think it's something worth looking into. We're going to be combining operations with the Circle D. Maybe it's a good time to step back and rethink some things."

He had been genuinely contrite and left her nearly speechless. "It's alright," she said. "I wasn't angry, and it is really none of my business." Her statement was true enough, but she admitted to herself that she had been a bit annoyed. Regardless, that was history now.

As she approached Chloe's dugout, she saw the woman walking from the barn with a milk bucket in each hand. The load didn't impede the spring in her step, however. Maddie met her at the front of the dugout and dismounted. "Good morning, Chloe. You've got a load there."

Blizzard

"Ain't that much. Not more than a gallon in each bucket. They'll hold over two apiece. I used to just need one. I've surrendered to old age, I fear. Rose is a four-gallon a day milker these days, so I'll get about the same at night. She used to do better, but what the hell? Mostly me and the cats use the milk. I throw too much milk away. Days when the hired man shows up, I send all I can home with him. Just makes his woman suspicious, though. She thinks he's poking me."

"I'm here for the day. Overnight, if you'll have me."

"Why not? Bring your bedroll in and wolfdog, too. Does he drink milk?"

"A little, but he'll throw it back up if he drinks too much."

"You can decide what he gets. Toss your bedroll and saddlebags on the porch and go ahead and put your critter up in the barn. Then come on up and we'll talk over coffee. You did eat breakfast before you came over?"

"I did, and I'll help with dinner at noon if you will let me."

"Let you? Girl, you are appointed head cook. I got plenty of foodstuffs, but I hate cooking."

Later they sat at the little kitchen table and talked, and Maddie told her about the visit they had made to the Coldsmith Rising Sun Ranch. "If you don't object, the cattlemen's association has asked me to stay on a while to see what I can turn up on the rustlings."

"If they'll pay the bill, I'm dang glad to have you here. Let's say I pay your firm for your work till Christmas. You'll give my needs priority till then, but you can work on the rustling at the same time. It appears I've got a bigger stake in that than anybody. They're going to clean me out if things keep going at this rate."

"That sounds more than fair. Speaking of Christmas, Gage really wants you to go over to the K Bar K for Christmas Eve and stay over for a few days. He will arrange for somebody to take care of your chores here while you're gone."

"I know. He asked me to come before he left. He even wants me to share his room. What would everybody think?"

Maddie laughed. "They wouldn't think anything. They would think it was strange if you didn't. Nobody thinks Gage has been coming over to your place to play checkers all these years. Besides, you're betrothed, about to be married. New Year's Day if you'll go along with Gage."

"Lordy, I don't know. I told him April."

"Why?"

"Because I feel deep inside there's a storm coming on soon. I saw the buzzards circling over the place. Things are going to change. Some folks, including me, might even die."

"Are you talking about a snowstorm?"

"Not necessarily. Just unexpected happenings."

"I am betting Gage would want to walk through this storm with you."

"Yeah, knowing him that's what he'd want for sure. If we're going to get hitched, I still want to wait for April. Spring's the time for fresh starts, and I'll have lots to do getting ready to move out of here and work out the new arrangements for the ranch with Sam."

Maddie said, "Maybe you could stay with Gage over Christmas as a compromise."

"Yeah, I suppose I could do that much. I know it would please him. Maybe I could even make more visits to the K Bar K, sort of get used to the way of living there."

"I'll tell him if you like. That would be the perfect Christmas gift for him, I know."

Later, Maddie prepared a simple lunch of corn dodgers, beans, and bacon chunks. "No dessert just yet, but I'll make an apple cobbler in the Dutch oven before suppertime."

After they ate, Maddie said, "The sun's bright, and it appears to be warming up some. Are you up for a ride? I'd like to see some of the north side of your range to get an idea of how the land fits together out here. Ranchers seem to be losing more cattle the farther north and west their pasturelands are located. That might be why you're suffering more losses, although I doubt if it is that simple."

"A ride would suit me fine. I'm itching to saddle a horse and go someplace."

Soon Maddie was astride Outlaw, the sorrel gelding she had claimed at the K Bar K, riding alongside Chloe, who was mounted on a nameless gray mare. Chloe obviously enjoyed conducting a tour, pointing out the fork of the Dismal and Loup rivers and a bluff that she said was a special place for her and Gage. Her mood was lighter when in the saddle, Maddie noticed, and she laughed more. Chloe talked a lot about the experiences she had shared with Gage over the years. She was seeing a different Chloe than she had seen before, and she understood. She also was a creature of the prairie lands.

Chloe mentioned that most of her land fell into Blaine County, which along with Loup County bordered Custer on the north. Maddie noticed some more rugged country across the fence line. "Who owns that land?"

"Government. We used to graze it, but the government folks decided we should pay outlandish rent. That's when we put the barbed wire fence in. Nobody's been pasturing it in recent years. Mostly canyons, but some have got good grass."

Maddie reined the sorrel nearer the fence to confirm what she thought she had seen. She dismounted and walked along the fence for more than a hundred feet. "Somebody's been crossing here, more than once I'd say. They've done a good job mending with wire bridges, but somebody's been running animals onto government land. But you haven't crossed since you did the fencing?"

"Nope. Not with cattle. I don't want government trouble."

"I would sure like to ride up there and look around, but with the snow cover, I don't know how much I'd find. I need to think about it."

Midafternoon, back at the dugout, Maddie got out the Dutch oven, flour, and canned apples from the supply room, while Chloe dozed in her ragged, stuffed chair in front of the fireplace. She heard Pirate stirring and tossed a glance at the dog.

Pirate's ears perked up, and he stood up from the buffalo hide rug he had been snoozing on at Chloe's feet. Inky let out a meowed complaint because he had been curled up against the wolfdog's back. Pirate walked over to the door and emitted a low growl. Chloe opened her eyes. "What is it?"

"We've got company," Maddie said and went to the window and peered out between the burlap curtains. "A one-horse carriage coming in from the road. I think the passenger is a woman. Besides the driver, there is a rider following behind the carriage."

"I don't want more visitors right now, least of all a woman showing up in a carriage."

"Well, they're pulling up right out front." Maddie was suddenly struck with the thought that Chloe's storm was moving in.

Chapter 29

COLETTE NEARLY PANICKED when she saw the stone and sod wall fronting what appeared to be a big cave. "She's a cave woman."

"You don't see many fancy mansions out this way," Walton said, tugging on the horse's reins and braking the carriage. "I'm sure the inside accommodations will be fine."

"And you think we're going to stay overnight here?"

"You are, my precious. I must return to Broken Bow to tend to business. I'm sure your grandmother will be delighted to have you as her guest."

"That's why you told me to pack my bags and bring all my belongings, and you didn't take a thing from the hotel. You plan to dump me here like garbage. You're running out on me."

"Now, don't be a silly goose. Of course, I am not. Remember, I need you to squeeze information out of the old woman. Find out if she's got any money, where she keeps it, that sort of thing. From the looks of this pigsty, I don't think we are going to find a treasure here, but I want you to be looking. I expect information when I come back in a few days. That's when I expect to do some fishing for a loan."

"Which you have no intention of paying back." The dilemma she faced had forced her to finally get a tenuous grip on the nature of Roscoe Walton's financial dealings. She had married nothing but a common thief who wandered through polite society to commit his robberies. Eventually, he would abandon her and seek out a monied woman. He did not love her, never had. Women were useful tools in his quest for riches, and she was on verge of being a useless one. She was learning quickly how naïve she had been about life, and she realized she had much yet to learn, and it was time to get started with her education.

"Remember, we need money fast or you won't have a roof over your head unless you want to take up whoring." Walton had already stepped off the carriage and was unloading her bags, dropping them on the ground in front of the dugout. He obviously did not intend to assist her down and neither was the rider who had acted as their guide. He remained in the saddle some ten paces behind the carriage, grinning with the leer that seemed frozen on his horseface. She climbed down, taking a certain pride in developing a technique that required no male assistance.

"We'll leave the bags out here," Walton said, "till we find out if she's lodging you in the house or barn."

"And what if she chooses not to lodge me?"

"She will. I intend to be here only long enough to introduce myself and to bait a hook if I can. Then I will be on my way."

"But you can't get back to Broken Bow before sundown."

"It would be pushing the horse to make that trip. Kruger knows a place—Anselmo, I think he calls it—where there is a lodging house, not more than two hours from here. We'll stay there tonight and return to Broken Bow tomorrow. Now move your ass up to the door and knock. Remember what I told you."

She could barely recall her name, she was so nervous. When she reached up to snatch the strap of her shoulder bag from under the seat, her hand was trembling so much she had difficulty clutching it. She could not remember being more frightened in her life. She stepped onto a porch that rose no more than six inches off the ground and had barely enough space to hold the bench and rocker there. She took a deep breath and rapped softly on the door.

She was startled when it opened instantly, and she was met by an elderly woman about her own size and might be considered pretty enough if not for the well-worn male costume that clothed her and the weathered skin of her face. The woman eyed her suspiciously with appraising, azure eyes.

The woman cast a look over Colette's shoulder, fixing her stare now on Roscoe who stood behind her. Disapproval was instant. The stare turned to glare. "What do you want?" Her voice was slightly raspy like she had a bit of sand in her throat.

Colette said, "Does . . . does Missus Chloe Downs live here?"

"Who's asking?"

"Her granddaughter. My name is Colette Walton. My mother was Darla Downs Churchill." The woman did not seem surprised or shocked as Colette expected she might be.

"I'm Chloe Downs. I guess you can come in. Who's the feller with you?"

"I'm sorry. This is my husband, Roscoe Walton."

"My pleasure, ma'am," Walton said.

Chloe did not respond. "And who's the gunslinger out there by the fancy carriage?"

Walton said, "Oh, that's Ozzie Kruger, ma'am. He is our guide. Ozzie's not a gunslinger."

"He's wearing a holstered shooting iron slung low on his hip. He fancies himself a gunslinger." She stepped back and pulled the heavy door open.

When they entered the dugout, Colette was startled to discover that her grandmother already had several guests. A young, striking woman with reddish hair, albeit also wearing britches, stood only a few steps to her grandmother's right. She was an unusually tall woman and standing beside her was the biggest dog Colette had ever seen. Off to her left, a black, three-legged cat sat on a pathetically small and ugly kitchen table. She had never been allowed pets in her life because her mother would never tolerate an animal in the house and had a disdain for cats and dogs in general. She remembered begging for a dog or cat to no avail when she was small.

With the door closed behind them, her grandmother broke the silence. "This is my friend Maddie Sanford and her partner Pirate." She nodded toward the cat. "That's Inky. He runs the house. Maddie, this young lady here is

Colette, claims to be my granddaughter. The sour-faced man is supposedly her husband, Rupert something."

Walton said, "Walton, and the first name's Roscoe, not Rupert."

Colette wondered if her grandmother had intentionally butchered Roscoe's name. She could tell from the tight set of his mouth that he was seething. "Could we sit down?" Colette said.

"Room for three in the parlor. Maybe Rupert could sit at the kitchen table, and the ladies can sit in there."

Why was her grandmother tormenting Roscoe so?

Chloe claimed her stuffed chair in the parlor, and Colette and Maddie sat down on the wobbly settee. The furniture faced the fireplace, and Colette welcomed the warmth. The sun might be shining, but it was teasing. A brisk breeze reminded folks that winter had settled in. Roscoe sat down at the near side of the table and turned the chair around, so he faced the parlor area.

Chloe said, "Okay, young lady. Tell me what makes you think you are my granddaughter."

"Like I said, my mother said she was born Darla Downs. She always told me that Chloe Downs was her mother and Henry Downs was her father. She told me you lived in the Sandhills country. We lived most of my growing-up years in Omaha, and I had no idea till I was older where the Sandhills was located."

"And where is your mother now?"

"I am sorry to inform you that she died a little over five years ago." Colette thought it strange that her grandmother showed no emotion at the news.

"I never saw her again after she left here. We sent her away to boarding school, and she never returned. We paid the fees and sent her money till she finished high school. Of course, we didn't have the railroad in those early years, so travel was nearly impossible. Maybe it was lucky she left. Her father was killed in a Sioux raid on the farmstead. They might have killed or taken her, too, if she had been outside. I was here in the dugout with Robert—he was your uncle—and we were able to hold the devils off."

From the way Chloe spoke, Colette assumed her grandmother was not seriously challenging her identity. "I didn't know I had an uncle."

"Robert died at Gettysburg. He's been gone a long time, but it seems like yesterday." Her voice cracked a bit when she said that, suggesting to Colette that her grandmother might not be the totally calloused soul she at first appeared to be.

"I'm sorry," she said. "I lost two brothers. George was just a baby, so I never really knew him. Grover was murdered three years ago. I still can hardly think about it without bursting into tears."

Colette felt Maddie's hand softly clutch her shoulder and squeeze it gently. The young woman could have no idea how much that could mean to a person who felt she was sinking into a swirling river.

Chloe said, "Your mother never answered my letters but a few times after she married your father. She lived in Boston then. I wrote all these years but never heard back. I don't know if she ever received them. I figured she must have moved, but I had no notion where to. But I kept writing every three months or so, last wrote in October. I had no idea she lived in Omaha. She must have hated me. Maybe she had cause."

"She never said that."

Suddenly, Chloe turned her attention to Roscoe Walton, who sat in the straight-back chair with his eyes half-closed, obviously bored with the conversation. "What about you, Rupert. How did you come to catch a pretty thing half your age?"

The remark grabbed his full attention. Colette feared he might explode into one of his tirades, but his eyes just smoldered. It was obvious that he and grandmother had taken an instant dislike to each other. She was nervous about the day still in front of her, but she was glad she would not be spending the night with Roscoe who would have taken his rage out on her.

"Many women marry older men, Missus Downs, not just because they might prefer a more mature husband but because of the financial stability they offer."

"Marry for money, huh?"

"A rather crude way to put it, I think."

"How do you make your money, Rupert?"

"Roscoe, please. I have many investments and enterprises. Those in Nebraska generally are cattle enterprises."

"You've got a ranch someplace?"

"No, no, I don't ranch. I let others do that. My investors are granted the opportunity to buy, hold, and sell cattle through my companies. We find bargains in cattle offered for sale by ranchers and farmers, send them by train to Omaha where we feed and fatten till the Omaha and Chicago markets are high and then sell for a tidy profit. My investors do quite well. If you would be interested in the venture, I could make arrangements."

Roscoe was turning on his charm now, Colette thought. He thought grandmother might be nibbling at the bait. She doubted it.

"I can barely make ends meet here. What gives you the notion I might have money to invest?"

"Perhaps you would like to sell your herd and lease out your land, retire, and relax in a more civilized area. I trust your land and cattle are not mortgaged."

"That ain't your business, but, no, Hank and me never borrowed a penny, not in the worst of times even when we first settled here. Sell my herd? What are you offering?"

"I would need to check the current markets, but for you, I would buy five percent under Omaha price. I would absorb all costs of getting them to market."

"In Omaha?"

"Maybe. We have markets all over the country, Army forts, Indian reservations, and small slaughterhouses. These places pay a premium. That's how we can pay our sellers so well and still turn a profit."

"Do you pay cash when you pick up the cattle?"

"We give you our note payable in thirty days."

"And what if you ain't got the money in thirty days?"

"Never happened."

"I guess it would be a way for me to unload the whole caboodle."

"You're interested?"

"Ain't saying right now. Talk to me the first of the year if you're still interested."

"I will certainly do that." He stood. "But now I must take my leave."

"Ain't staying for supper?"

"I would love to, ma'am, but my guide out there wants to reach Anselmo before dark."

"No bank to rob there. Not even much of a general store. And what about your wife? She just found her grandma, and now you're going to drag her away."

"Oh, no. She will stay if you will have her for a short visit. We just assumed your hospitality."

Colette was mortified. She hoped her face had not turned scarlet. "I'm sorry, Grandmother, I know we had no right . . ."

"Hush, girl." Speaking to Walton again, "Of course, Colette is welcome here. You just git. She'll be fine."

Chapter 30

MADDIE COULD NOT help but empathize with Colette. She guessed that the young woman was somewhere between twenty-five and thirty years old, although she could pass for some years younger. The sun had not had a chance to do its work on her fair complexion.

Chloe had followed Walton outside, evidently to confirm that he was leaving the property. She decided to make the visitor know she was welcome. She turned toward Colette. "It's going to be fine, Colette. I'm glad to meet you, and don't worry about Chloe. She may seem at first to be gruff as a grizzly, but there is a kind, caring heart in there, I promise. It means a lot that you came here. You'll see. And if you need a friend, count on me."

Tears trickled down Colette's cheeks. "So much has happened the past several days. I feel overwhelmed, and

I let myself become an incompetent fool, always doing what mother said, and after her, Roscoe. And this world out here is so far away from people, it's scary in a way, yet beautiful. I can't imagine what the future has in store for me."

"Don't look at the future. Think today, and then tomorrow, do the same thing. Get through the day. A dear friend who gave her life for me—her name was Minnie—taught me that. I did that, and it was several years before I could look beyond that single day. Still, though, when life gets tough, I forget about the future and turn my attention to today."

"I sort of understand, but you are so young, I cannot imagine you have experienced anything too horrible."

Maddie laughed. "It doesn't seem so horrible now that it's behind me. I think of my experiences as a part of my education."

Pirate got up from his rug and placed his nose on Colette's lap. At first, she started and tensed. "He's not going to bite me?"

"No, rub him behind the ears. He likes you, wants to be your friend."

She tentatively placed her fingers on his head, and when Pirate did not flinch or bite, she began gently scratching behind his ears. He pressed his head farther onto her lap. Colette smiled. "I've never petted a dog before. Mother taught me to fear them."

"It is not bad to be wary, but most dogs are like people. They just want love."

Chloe came back into the house and broke up the conversation. "Well, they're gone. I'm sorry, Colette. I don't like your man much, and that varmint that rides with him spells trouble."

"That's alright. I understand."

"Come over here by the window, granddaughter, so I can get a better look at you." Colette got up from the settee and walked slowly over to Chloe, timid like a pup expecting to be swatted.

There was a long silence as they faced each other, Chloe studying the young woman like a horse she was thinking about purchasing. Finally, she spoke. "Danged if you ain't the spitting image of your ma as I last saw her. Gold spun hair, sky-blue eyes, perfect little shape, even Darla's button nose. It's like she's come home to me." Tears started streaming down her cheeks and she opened her arms and moved to Colette. They held each other for several minutes, both sobbing softly, and Maddie for that brief time felt like an intruder.

When Chloe stepped back, she collected herself and said, "When is that man of yours coming back for you?"

"I don't know. I'm not certain he will. Things have not been good between us, and I don't have a penny to my name. I have no idea where I go from here."

"You can stay put here as long as you want, dear. And if he does come for you, it's your choice to go or stay. We have a tough life compared to what you are used to, but we get plenty to eat and keep warm enough in winter."

Colette appeared more relaxed now. "It helps to know that."

"One condition."

"What's that?"

"You've got to pay your way by working, helping with chores and the like."

"I know nothing about living on a ranch."

"You'll learn, and fast. You won't have trouble sleeping nights. I guarantee it. You may hate my guts for the things I expect you to do, but every day, you will be learning something. Can you ride?"

"I'm a decent rider. The man who gave me lessons said I was a good rider."

"That's a start then. We'll make a cowgirl out of you. Now we got to figure out where we're going to put you up."

Maddie said, "I can ride back to the K Bar K later and help make room here."

"No, I'd like you to stay on an extra day or two if you would. I think Colette needs a younger woman to talk to for a spell. There may be things she wouldn't talk about with an old lady. Besides, I need your help with getting the dugout fixed up for a guest."

Was Chloe hinting that Maddie might want to have a chat with Colette about her husband? She didn't need a hint. She was itching to talk with the granddaughter about Roscoe Walton. There was something about him that piqued her curiosity. "Certainly, I'll stay. It appears there is work to be done. Where do we start?"

"Well, I'm thinking I am going to take part of the storeroom and turn it back into a bedroom, put a bed in there and a chest of drawers. I've got the old ones stored up in the barn loft. It's going to be a job getting them down, but we won't need them till we get things restacked in the room. There may be some things that don't freeze that we can move out to the barn someplace. The cats keep us out of mouse and rat problems. It's going to take time, but we can make it work. Now, where do we start? The bunkhouse."

"The bunkhouse?"

"Yep. I've got six beds and a good woodstove in there. I'd like to have you and Colette bunk there for a few nights till you head back to Gage's. I think we can have things ready by day after tomorrow. You probably need firewood. Take some from the stack near the house. I've got plenty of blankets in the storeroom. I'll send you off with an armload. Of course, you've got your own bedroll, too. Ain't as warm in the bunkhouse as here, though. You'll need to keep the fire going through the night. It just doesn't hold the heat in like the dugout."

"Okay. Dig out the blankets, and I'll get started."

"You do that. I need to outfit Colette in some work duds. She sure can't wear those fancy heeled shoes to work in around here. I'll see if any of my old boots might fit. If not, I've got some Sioux-made moccasins she can wear for now. They give you some leeway on size. As soon as I've got her fixed up, she'll be coming down to help you. After you got the bunkhouse ready and a fire going, it will be getting along toward milking time."

She looked at Colette. "Have you ever milked a cow, young lady?"

"No ma'am, and I'm scared of cows."

"You will start getting over scared at milking time, and Maddie will give you your first lesson at squeezing cow tits. Maddie, if you and Colette will do the milking, I'll study the storeroom a bit and figure out what needs doing, and then I'll see if I can do supper. Maybe hotcakes and eggs tonight. I got more eggs than I know what to do with. We may be eating lots of eggs around here for a few days. And I think I'll put Colette in charge of harvesting eggs while she's here. I'll show her what's to be done."

"Suits me," Maddie said.

Colette looked bewildered by the pace of decisions being made. "One question. What should I call you? Missus Downs doesn't sound right, and Chloe wouldn't be polite."

Chloe thought a moment and rubbed her chin. "Grams. That's what I'd like you to call me. Grams."

Chapter 31

"I HAVEN'T EVEN had time to think," Colette told Maddie in the little six-bed bunkhouse, as she opened the woodstove door and fed another log to the flames. "There is so much happening, so much to learn."

Maddie smiled. She liked Colette better in the tattered blue jeans and flannel shirt. She even had taken to a pair of Chloe's scuffed, worn boots once an extra pair of socks had been added to her feet to compensate for size difference. Lord, the woman's small feet would swim in Maddie's boots. Chloe's garments adapted well to Colette's small frame, and the granddaughter seemed to be enjoying the novelty. But how many days before the newness of her adventure wore off and she yearned for her old, pampered life? That life was finished. There was no retreat. She hoped Colette would accept that truth.

"That should be enough wood for a spell," Maddie said. "We don't want to fetch more firewood in from outside during the middle of the night. It's cozy in here now."

Colette sat down on the side of her bed and faced Maddie who had claimed the adjacent one, both with the foot of the beds nearest the fire. Pirate seemed to be satisfied with the bed on the other side of Maddie's and was sleeping soundly already.

Colette said, "I know I put too much wood in, but I've never done this before. In Omaha, we used coal in recent years, and the heat came from a big furnace in the basement that piped warm air to most of the rooms in the big house. We did have a fireplace in the living room, but it wasn't depended upon for heat until a few weeks ago when we lost the last of the servants and didn't have anyone to scoop coal into the furnace. Of course, we didn't have much coal left anyhow, and not more than a few days' supply of cut wood."

"You lost your servants?"

"Roscoe would be outraged to know I was talking about this, but what the heck, I don't know if he is going to come for me, and I'm afraid to go with him."

"I promise you will not be forced to go with him. Chloe and I will see to that. And you have no idea of the friends you are going to have here."

Blizzard

"Seriously? Well, anyway, we lost the servants because they were not getting paid. The mansion was being sold at foreclosure a day or two after we left Omaha. Roscoe lost all my mother's money on his investments. I suppose he had a little cash money stashed somewhere, but we came to Broken Bow to escape creditors. I can't imagine what he planned to do there. I think he had some hope that Grams has lots of money to throw away, but when we came here and he saw where she lived, I think that hope withered."

"So what is he doing back in Broken Bow now?"

"Scheming, I suppose, but I don't know what he's got in mind. He does have a friend there."

"Really? May I ask who this friend is?"

"I only met him once. He sneaked up to our hotel room, came in the back way, he said. Startled me at first, and then I saw he was wearing a deputy sheriff's star. Roscoe introduced him to me. Gar Ford was his name. Simple, easy to remember. I didn't like him. They did not want to talk much in front of me and agreed to meet at the sheriff's office later. When Roscoe went out, he didn't come back for a long time, which suited me fine. I wanted to run, but I didn't know where to. I had no money, and I had no notion of how to get here or whether Grams would even take me in. I feel safe for the first time in months. Isn't that strange?"

"No, I don't think so." Maddie sensed there was more, but she opted for patience. She would earn Colette's trust before she pressed further. She did, however, need to get back to the K Bar K and speak with Gage and Sam before she headed for Broken Bow. She would stay over one more night and be on her way. Chloe wouldn't like it, but she was going to see if Gage could spare a hand to stay in the bunkhouse once they got Maddie moved into the dugout with Chloe. She did not like the thought of the two staying on the place without at least another person as an extra lookout.

Chapter 32

BY THE TIME Maddie and Pirate departed the Circle D after a two-night stay, Colette had moved into the dugout with Chloe. They put in a long day's work the previous day, moving the Spartan bedroom furnishings down from the barn loft, hauling some of the supplies from the former storeroom to new locations and handling chores that could not be neglected. Fortunately, Chloe's hired hand Mort Boone had shown up to tend to much of the ranch chores and to assist with furniture moving.

Colette was obviously tiring and a bit overwhelmed by it all, but Maddie had been amazed at her resilience. The sober, almost frightened, face that had appeared at the ranch a few days earlier was now surrendering a smile now and then, even an occasional laugh when something struck her funny. And Chloe had become a strict but loving mother hen. She was obviously relishing her new role as grandma.

Maddie had left before breakfast at the Circle D, telling Chloe that it was time for her to earn her pay and received no objection. She suspected that the rancher was ready for some alone time with her granddaughter. Her only remark had been, "You learned some things worthwhile, didn't you?"

Maddie had just nodded affirmatively, and she realized now that Chloe had deliberately lodged the two young women together for a few days so that Maddie might mine some information. That made sense. It would not be good for the new grandmother to be asking too many questions, and the family relationship could have made this touchy. Maddie felt a bit of guilt about using a friendship with Colette to elicit information that might help her do the job she was hired for, but she convinced herself that she could help Colette with this knowledge as well.

She put up her gelding in the K Bar K stable and was glad to see that Sam's horse was there. He needed to be in on her conversation with Gage, and it would be nice to see him. She was on her way to the house now. Smoky and Alex were coming off the porch and gave her "howdies." Nobody seemed to think much about her coming and going at the ranch now, and she liked that. Sam walked out of the house with Jim Hunter.

They met on the veranda, and Sam smiled when he saw her. "Maddie, Gramps thought I should ride over to Grams's place and be sure things were okay if you didn't show up by noon. Jim's got news to report, and we were hoping you might show up."

"I'm glad we're meeting up again, Jim. I'm eager to hear what you've learned."

Sam said, "Jim's learned a lot. We keep picking up pieces, but I can't quite put them together."

"Well, I've got some more pieces or a whole new puzzle. I'm not certain which."

"Now, you've got me curious. Gramps is still at the breakfast table. Let's all go inside and talk a spell."

"That's got my vote. I wouldn't mind if there would be some breakfast left for me."

"I can't imagine Monique not having something for you."

A few minutes later they were seated with Gage at the breakfast table, and Maddie had a plate of hotcakes smothered with maple syrup and fried eggs and sausages on a second plate in front of her. Of course, a steaming cup of coffee was within easy reach. Pirate had disappeared, following Monique who would give him breakfast in the mudroom. Creatures were welcome in the house, but they were not allowed to dine with the human guests.

Gage finished his own breakfast before he spoke. "Well, Maddie, you've got me itching to hear what you've got to say, but I'll let you eat first, while you listen to the gist of Jim's report. Jim, why don't you give us a short version of what you picked up?"

Jim Hunter was a poised man, obviously educated and anything but the Indian stereotype found in countless dime novels. "I had a hunch we should check the Sioux reservation and Army posts first to see if rustled cattle were being marketed there. I'm sure the cattle are being sold several places, but I learned what I needed to know a from my friend Lone Elk not far from an agency office near Fort Niobrara. He happens to manage the herds allocated by the government until animals are needed for slaughter."

Maddie said, "So they hold the cattle for a time after they receive them?"

"They've got to. There are no icehouses or any place to store the meat until it's ready to eat, so they graze the herd till cattle are cut out for butchering. Also, the government never delivers what is promised, so they must ration what they do get to avoid total starvation. Lone Elk says that most of the time there are not many cattle to herd, sometimes none. What angers him is that the agency won't allow them to keep breeding animals so they can raise their own beeves."

Maddie said, "Who makes the purchases?"

"Officially, the Indian Agent, but he has an assistant who handles everything and negotiates the purchases. The agent just signs the contracts. Lone Elk isn't certain the agent knows a cow from a deer, but he probably takes a share of the so-called commission collected from the seller."

"What did he say about rustled animals?"

"There have been K Bar K brands, Circle D, Rising Sun and a dozen others, but Circle D and K Bar K make up nearly half, he thought. He took me out on the prairie range near the reservation to look at what they were holding now. No more than fifty head, which made him uneasy with so much winter remaining. There were a lot of K Bar K and Circle D brands in the bunch. They're pushing the agent for more cattle right now so there's a market up there if you want to sell."

"And a market for rustled stock," Sam said.

"Now the most important question," Maddie said. "Who are they buying the beeves from?"

"I've got a part answer. A ranch not far south of the reservation. The owner is a man named Frank Bartek, not a man of high reputation. His acres wouldn't carry more than a hundred cows with calves year around. Lone Elk doubts that he runs any of his own herd. He seems to mostly buy cattle, hold them a spell, and then sell to the reservations and Army posts along the Nebraska and Dakota border. He doesn't know who Bartek buys the beeves from. He could be buying them from the original owners, but he wouldn't rule out rustlers. He figures it's none of his concern. They just need beeves. He's not going to lose a minute's sleep about where they are coming from."

Maddie said, "It's obvious that the cattle aren't coming directly from the ranches that branded them. Bartek needs to be put out of business, but we should stop his sellers first. This is progress though, and we might want to let Bartek know soon that we are onto his game. He might shut off the rustlers if he fears the law is watching. If the right person inquires of the Indian Agent, he might just back off dealing with Bartek."

Chapter 33

GAGE HAD ALREADY heard Jim Hunter's story, and, if the weather held, he was planning to call on Bartek and the Indian Agent. He would get the agent's attention by mentioning his friendship with United States Senator Charles Manderson, failing to mention that the relationship consisted of shaking the Senator's hand at a political dinner in North Platte several years earlier.

Gage said, "Jim's done a good job for us. We at least have a starting place now. I thought we would likely have a break in the rustling till spring, but with the cattle demand up north, I'm not so sure we can wait long to follow up on this."

Maddie said, "I agree, and I have stumbled on to something—or I should say, something has stumbled onto me—that has sent my head spinning like a top. There's been a lot going on over at the Circle D."

"Chloe's alright?"

"Chloe is fine, but she has had some sudden changes in her life."

Gage said, "I'm listening."

Maddie recited the story of Colette's experience at Chloe's, taking care to omit personal details that she felt the newfound granddaughter might have been telling her woman to woman in confidence. She also touched only lightly on the visitor's inexperience and coddled upbringing for fear that the others might prejudge harshly. "Colette will be staying with Chloe for now, possibly for a long time. She does not expect her husband to return. I agree. I think he made a fishing trip and concluded that Chloe was a poverty-stricken old woman. He was looking for quick, easy money and found no prospect."

Sam said, "You mentioned that he buys and sells cattle. I wonder if he deals in rustled stock."

"We should find out—and soon. My sniffer says he's a skunk, and I intend to follow his scent. I'll be headed to Broken Bow tomorrow. Oh, and there is something else. Roscoe Walton has a friend there. A deputy sheriff by the name of Gar Ford."

Gage said, "I've seen the guy. He was in the sheriff's office when I reported the killing over at Chloe's house. I spoke to Sheriff Barnes that day, but I was introduced to Ford, who was sitting at the corner desk, looking bored and sleepy. We said 'howdy' to each other and that was about it. Maybe he was more interested than he appeared. Come to think of it, he was the fella Alex said he dealt with when he took the Pinkerton's body in."

Maddie said, "I intend to meet Deputy Ford when I'm in town and track down the whereabouts of Roscoe Walton. I'm thinking I should speak with Sheriff Barnes as well."

Sam said, "And I'll be going with you."

She turned toward Sam, and her eyes narrowed. Gage thought his grandson was about to receive some cutting words, but she spoke very slowly and deliberately. "I will be wearing my detective hat, doing the job I'm being paid to do. I don't need any help, thank you."

Sam said, "And I'll be wearing my ranching hat, riding alongside you—or behind, if you prefer."

She did not reply, and Gage broke an awkward silence. "I'm thinking that if the weather holds, Jim and me will be heading up to the Sioux reservation and Box X Ranch tomorrow. How long will it take us, Jim?"

"The better part of two days each way, allowing for rests for the horses and riders, and a fair amount of sleep for us. We'll need to get food and gear together today so we can be on our way right after breakfast tomorrow. I found an abandoned soddy about midway, and a few line shacks, too. We won't need to set up a tent—probably just use the places I stayed riding up and back. I left a wood supply behind each place."

"I'll tell Monique what we're up to, and she'll help us with food." He looked at Sam and Maddie. "You two will have to work out your own plans. You should be able to make Broken Bow and still tend to some of your business, but I expect you will be spending the night there."

Sam said, "You and Jim worry about your job, Gramps, and we'll see to ours. We'll beat you home easy enough, that's for sure."

Maddie did not comment. Gage figured she might bend Sam's ear a bit later. "I guess that's about it for now, folks. Maddie, I wonder if I might have a moment with you in my office before you get on with your day."

After Jim Hunter and Sam left to find Bruce Potter for work assignments, Maddie and Gage sat down in his office. "Well, Maddie, I have a few more personal concerns about Chloe I wanted to ask about. How is she handling this granddaughter showing up?"

"At first, I thought she was going to boot Colette out of the dugout, and she was sure looking for a fight with the husband, but after he left, she softened, and in no time at all she was as happy and excited as I've seen her. And the granddaughter changed, too. When they showed up at the ranch, Colette was a frightened, cornered mouse, but when Chloe finally welcomed her, she changed, and when I rode away, she was an eager child wanting to learn everything."

"Chloe will be more than willing to teach her."

"Colette and I shared the bunkhouse for two nights while we were getting the old bedroom in the dugout back in business. I came to like her. She's never had a chance to prove what she can do, but she's qualified to teach school and smarter than her mother or husband ever gave her credit for. I'm sure she is penniless, but she will survive with Chloe's help."

"Chloe will make her earn her keep."

"Yes, Colette will be a different woman a year from now. Most of us have things happen in our lives that change us. If we're lucky, it's for the better."

"Do you think I should ride over and meet this young woman?"

"Chloe said you should give her four or five days. She thought she might even bring Colette over to the K Bar K to meet you and Monique and the others."

"Well, if I don't go today, it will wait till Jim Hunter and I return from up north."

"When I get back from Broken Bow, I'll ride over and see how everything is working out and let Chloe know what you're up to. She is entitled to know what I am doing since she's paying part of the bill, which reminds me that I must wire my employers when I'm in town and let them know I'm still on the job."

Gage was silent a moment before he spoke. "I might as well spit it out. I've got selfish concerns here. I can forget about a New Year's Day wedding, can't I?"

"I would say so, but it's not for me to say."

"I wonder if April is off, too. Now that the granddaughter is there, I can probably forget about marriage."

"I never saw you as a man who gave up without a fight."

Gage smiled. "You know how to prod a fella, don't you?"

"I don't think you need much prodding. I'm just saying, Chloe promised. I don't see her breaking her word."

"No, but I'd release her from the promise. It wouldn't be much of a marriage if she didn't want it. I don't suppose we have a chance of getting her and the granddaughter over for Christmas Eve and Christmas."

"I will take responsibility for getting them over here. You have a spare room for Colette, and I assume Chloe will . . . uh . . ."

"Yes, Chloe will share my room if it doesn't shock her granddaughter too much."

Maddie laughed. "I told Colette that you and Chloe are betrothed and have been seeing each other for years. I don't think she will be too surprised."

"I guess I'll just put the mission in your hands. It would make my Christmas."

"And I think it would help Colette to see that there are others who care about her."

"Maddie, you're always a step ahead of me. If you tire of the detective work, I'd hire you on as a hand in a minute. I've told you that before."

"I'm going to remember what you said. I always wanted to be a cowhand."

Darned if she didn't sound like she was serious. Well, she was full of surprises, that young lady.

Chapter 34

SAM HAD EXPECTED to be riding alone following a hostile Maddie who was likely on her way to Broken Bow by now and was surprised to find her waiting for him outside the stable when he rode into K Bar K headquarters. He was leading his mare for care at the ranch while he was gone. "Sorry, I'm late. Ginny was out in the lot and didn't want to leave. I'll put her up in a stall and be right with you."

"She's a pretty thing. Her belly says she'll be foaling late spring, May probably."

"Yep. King was the stud, of course. I'm leaving him here. He seems to be favoring a foot this morning. I've got a gelding that's stabled here that I'll take for this trip. King won't like it much, but the gelding needs work, too."

She hitched Outlaw to a post outside and followed Sam into the stable. "Are you planning to build a horse herd?"

"Not necessarily. I just love the critters. What happens, happens, as far as a herd goes. I just take each day as it comes."

"You're not a planner then?"

"Selective planner, you might say. Some things I figure out ahead of time, but I don't worry much about what I can't change."

"I plan all the time. My dad taught me to play chess when I was a tyke. I sometimes think of life as a chess game, and I don't like it when my plan gets derailed."

"Like when you get checkmated by surprise."

"I hate that."

"It happens. I enjoy chess, but I don't take it that seriously. It's just a game, something to while away a little time when you're with somebody you like to be with."

"I play for blood."

"You can be kind of scary sometimes."

Later, on the wagon-rutted trail to town, he noticed Maddie did not object to his riding his bay gelding alongside her. "You've sort of put a claim on Outlaw, haven't you?"

"I love the horse. You ride a fine critter, too. I've never heard this one's name. I meant to ask."

"Bay."

"That's his color."

"Yep. Easy to remember."

"Very imaginative."

Sam smiled at her sarcasm. "Thank you."

She looked at and eyed him suspiciously. "Anyway, I hope I can make a deal with your grandfather to buy Outlaw before I leave."

"Gramps won't be that hard to deal with, especially for you."

"What do you mean?"

"You've got him wrapped around your little finger. He adores you—everybody does, you and that dang dog roaming in the hills behind us."

"Does that include you?"

He grinned. "I like you well enough, most of the time." He was not about to admit he was on the list of those who adored her. Maddie Sanford was spending too much time in his head of late, and he was having trouble shaking her out. He changed the subject. "Where do we go first when we get to Broken Bow?"

"The Grand Central Hotel, where we will get two rooms. I've stayed there and know the layout—and for a dollar the clerk will let Pirate in. I want a place to retreat to when my day is finished. Then the sheriff's office.

Hopefully, he will be in. If not, we will track him down. I want to speak with him before I approach the deputy. Obviously, I want to track Roscoe Walton down, but he's last on my list."

"You have this all planned out, don't you?"

"As much as possible, but plans change with new information quite often."

"I gather you just want me to cover your back and keep my mouth shut."

"I wouldn't put it quite that bluntly."

"Not necessary. I understand, and I'm perfectly fine with that arrangement. You are the detective and have your plan."

They arrived in Broken Bow early afternoon, checked their mounts in at the livery, and went directly to the hotel. Maddie obviously was acquainted with Withers, the clerk, and obtained a main floor room near the rear door. She signed the register, gave the man three dollars, including a dollar for Pirate, and turned around to face Sam. "You will need to make your own arrangements. I'll meet you at the dining room in a half hour. I'm starved."

She headed down the hallway with Pirate trailing behind her and Withers's eyes not far behind. "Uh, sir, I would like to check in also."

He startled the gawking clerk, who turned back to the counter. "I'd like to register, too," he said. "A room next to the lady's, if possible."

"Sorry," Withers said, "the best I can do is second floor."

Sam did not believe him and was annoyed when he still got charged two dollars for his room. He was not inclined to fuss with folks over such things, though, and signed the register and paid his bill.

After he was settled in his room, he went to meet Maddie in the dining room, which they had to themselves since it was well past the noon rush. She had already claimed a table near the front window, and he joined her.

"I've already ordered for us," she said. "We should be served shortly. We don't have time to waste."

"I generally order for myself."

"Since the menu is limited after one-thirty, you had a choice between meatloaf, baked potato, and beans and meatloaf, baked potato, and beans. Dessert selection was between cherry pie and cherry pie."

"Oh, I guess I'll be fine with what you ordered then."

"I thought you would be. Let's talk about our visit to the sheriff's office. Are you acquainted with the sheriff?"

"I've met him several times, but I was always with Gramps. They were just office stops to report suspected rustling, that sort of thing. Gramps has known Wally

Barnes for years. Wally was a hand for the K Bar K for a year or two before my time but didn't take to the hard work and hours, Gramps told me. Gramps calls Wally a slow thinker. He's more reluctant than most to use harsher words about folks."

"Like stupid?"

"I suppose that would be one. And Wally needs more rest than some, Gramps says."

"Meaning he is lazy?"

Sam shrugged. "I suppose."

"Is he honest?"

"I couldn't say. He left the K Bar K for a deputy's job. Some years later, when the sheriff died, the county board appointed Wally sheriff until the next election. Wally ran and got elected and has been reelected several times since, always unopposed. Nobody else wants the job because it pays so little, but Wally has been able to live well enough on a small farm he bought near town. He has a wife and three boys, all in their teens. The boys do most of the farming and care for a herd of ten cows or so. He doesn't appear wealthy, but it seems they're far from hungry."

"Bribes?"

"Rumors of that, but nobody much cares. Small stuff, I guess. He would likely take care in a publicized case. I really couldn't say if any of that is true. I don't like even suggesting it."

Blizzard

A big man wearing an apron appeared with a tray loaded with dinner plates. Sam assumed he was the cook.

"Short-handed today, folks. You got the cook wearing a waiter's hat. I'm dishwasher, too. If you're looking for work, we can fix you up with a job. More jobs than people in this town right now." He set the food-filled plates and a coffee pot on the table. "When you're finished, you will have to come back to the kitchen and find me. I'm the cashier, too."

They thanked the man and he disappeared. The meatloaf was excellent, Sam thought. He enjoyed good meatloaf every bit as much as a steak. Monique knew that and catered to him a bit, always reminding him when meatloaf was on the headquarters menu.

"I'll cover the meal this noon," Sam said.

"Best idea you've had today."

"I don't think we're going to have any scraps for Pirate. I suppose he's in your room."

"No. He's across the street at Schwartz's Butcher Shop. He's a friend of Hans Schwartz's, and Hans said Pirate could stay with him till I came back. He won't starve, I guarantee you."

"That wolfdog knows how to pick his friends."

"Better Pirate's friend than his enemy."

Chapter 35

MADDIE ENTERED THE sheriff's office, which looked like most others she had seen, drab, minimally furnished and smelling of tobacco smoke. Sam and Pirate followed her, and Sam closed the heavy door. A man with a pendulous belly and porcine jowls stood up, crushing a cigarette butt in an overflowing bowl as he got to his feet. Maddie towered over him, and he had to look up to speak to her.

He spoke in a voice that was higher pitched than she expected. "Ma'am, are you wanting something?" He doffed his Stetson as an afterthought, revealing shaggy, unruly hair that was getting a good start on gray.

"My name is Maddie Sanford. My friends here are Sam Kraft and Pirate. From the star on your vest, I assume you are Sheriff Wally Barnes."

The sheriff looked at Sam and fixed his eyes warily on the wolfdog. "Yeah, I'm Wally Barnes. I've met Sam more than once. Remember him from when he was a pup. Now, with all due respect, Miss Sanford, I don't usually allow no dogs in here."

"Pirate wouldn't take it kindly to be booted."

She could see that the sheriff was nervous about Pirate, rubbing a three-day growth of whiskers on an otherwise beardless face and searching for the right words. He obviously did not want a fuss. "Over there in the corner's one of my deputies, Gar Ford."

She looked behind her and saw a man with a black mustache and dark reptilian eyes, who had been hidden by the door when she entered. He nodded but did not stand or remove his hat. She figured that any smile the man might offer would come with a snarl. "Pleased to meet you, Deputy Ford," she said just to annoy him.

She turned back to the sheriff. "May I have a seat, Sheriff?" She went ahead and sat down.

"Uh, yeah. That would be good." He sat back down in his own chair.

Sam went to a straight back chair sitting with several along the wall opposite the door, which Maddie realized would allow him to watch both sheriff and deputy. Pirate moved up beside her and sat, resting his jaw on the edge of the sheriff's desk.

Maddie reached into the inner pocket of her wool-lined coat and pulled out her bronze detective badge. She handed the badge to the sheriff who examined it before passing it back. "I am a detective with the Crockett Detective Agency," she said.

"I ain't never heard of the Crockett outfit."

"The firm is headquartered in Manhattan, Kansas. They focus their business in the Midwest and near western states like Wyoming and Colorado. We often contract with the Pinkerton Detective Agency for special assignments."

"But you ain't the law."

"That's true, but we try to work with local law enforcement folks so they aren't surprised or embarrassed by not previously uncovering something we have come across. We try to cooperate with local law whenever they are receptive to it, but if you prefer not, I'll certainly leave right now and work the case on my own."

She started to rise, but as she expected, the sheriff stopped her.

"Just hold up, Miss Sanford. Of course, I'd be glad to help you where I can. Just let me know what I can do."

"You are entitled to know who my clients are. I was first employed by Chloe Downs. Are you acquainted?"

He chuckled. "Yep. When I was working at the K Bar K years ago, Gage sent me over to help her out once in a while. And since I been sheriff, she's been in and gave me hell more than once. But I still sort of like the old gal. Ain't seen her for a few years, though. Gage was in to report on some poor bas—fella that got gutted by her shotgun when he tried to break into her house—or whatever you'd call that dang cave she lives in. Figure justice got done, so nothing for me to do about it."

"Weren't you curious about why he tried to break in?"

"Not too much. Maybe he thought she had money squirreled away in there. Lord knows she never spent it from what I hear. When I last saw her, she was still a good-looking woman for her years. Maybe the feller got the itch. Unattached women are few and far between out there in them hills. And we don't got any whorehouses in Broken Bow, that I know of anyhow. Ain't legal here, so the church ladies probably would've let me know."

Maddie tried to remain patient, but the man was testing her. "Since my arrival here, I have also been employed by the cattlemen's association to investigate rustling problems that have reached a critical stage for some. They intend to stop it."

"Well, there's always been some of that."

"Sheriff, they're talking about a petition to remove you from office, or at the least, putting up their own candidate at the next election, which I understand is less than two years away."

"You got my full cooperation, Miss Sanford, but I'm shorthanded and this is a big county."

She knew that she had his attention now. "Do you remember speaking with the Pinkerton agent maybe a month or so back about a rustling problem he was here to investigate for the cattlemen's association?"

The sheriff's brow furrowed. "Don't know what you're talking about. I never met no Pinkerton agent."

"Rance Coldsmith told me the man was going to Broken Bow to talk to the sheriff."

"Seems he changed his mind. He never got here. Leastways, I never seen hide nor hair of him." He looked at Gar Ford. "What about you, Gar? Did you talk to a Pinkerton?"

"Nope. I'd remember that for sure."

The sheriff said, "Archie Cox handles our night shift, mostly sleeps in my chair, but I'll ask him when he comes on tonight, or Gar can if I've gone home, but it appears unlikely the detective would've stopped by late at night. If I find out anything, where do I find you?"

"Main floor, Grand Central Hotel, Room 110, but I'll try to check in here again in the morning to see if you learned anything. I hope to talk to a man named Roscoe Walton who is staying here in town."

"Name has a familiar ring, but don't think I've ever met the feller."

"What about the body Alex from the K Bar K brought in a week or so ago. Gage Kraft sent the Pinkerton badge along. Did you contact the Pinkerton Agency to identify him?"

"Lady, you're talking in riddles. I don't know about no dead body, and I ain't seen no Pinkerton, dead or alive."

"Alex told us he showed Deputy Ford the body and was told to drop it off at the undertaker's." She turned to Ford, who had tensed now and had a twitchy eye but otherwise showed no emotion. "Deputy, do you remember the body?"

"Yeah, I do. I mentioned it to you next day. But the kid didn't give me no badge. Probably kept it as a souvenir or lost it if there was one."

"I found the body and the badge, Deputy."

"But you don't know that the kid gave me the badge, and I'm saying he didn't." His demeanor and voice had turned outright hostile now, Maddie thought, verifying to her that he had received the badge.

"So the dead man was buried in an unmarked grave?"

Ford said, "I guess so. Not that uncommon out this way."

She turned back to the sheriff, who was visibly shaken now. "Sheriff, I intend to investigate a few things while I'm in town, I will stop by to speak with you tomorrow before we leave. I will want to talk to you privately at that time. Perhaps you want to review everything with Mister Ford in the meantime."

"I surely will."

Maddie stood to leave. "Let's go, Sam. I've got work to do."

Before Sam opened the door, she glanced at Ford who was glaring daggers at her. He was like a rattlesnake coiled to strike. When he did, not if, he would not rattle warning.

Chapter 36

SAM HAD SEEN another side of Maddie in the sheriff's office, and he did not know what to make of it. She was a tough young woman, seemingly fearless. He wondered if she had ever played poker. Sheriff Barnes turned to soft clay in her hands, and it was clear that she was in charge when they left the office.

They strolled down the street together until they came to a bench that was adjacent to a span of vacant lots that were apparently the site of a new park and bandstand. "Why don't we sit down a minute and talk about what's next on your agenda?" Sam said.

"Let's do."

When they were seated, Sam said, "I think you got the sheriff's attention. I would be curious to hear the conversation between old Wally and Gar Ford after we left."

"If Sheriff Barnes has any backbone at all, our Mister Ford will soon be an ex-deputy. I don't think Ford likes me very much."

"His eyes were drilling bullet holes in the back of your head. He's a man to take seriously. Why in blazes did you give them your room number at the hotel? It was almost an invitation."

"It was intended to be. It might be interesting to see who shows up."

"I guarantee it won't be a social call if a visitor comes by."

"Of course not, but Pirate will let me know if somebody tries to get in. If Ford or anybody else does show up, it will confirm my suspicions about the so-called deputy. If Pirate doesn't take any would-be killer down, I assure you I can handle the Smith & Wesson tucked in my saddlebags quite well."

"I'd worry less if you would let me stay with you."

"I intend to get a good night's sleep, and there is only one bed. Now is not the time for us to be sharing a room or bed."

Sam thought, at least she said "now," not never. "But you think Ford is a part of the rustling operation, don't you?"

"I'm almost certain of it, and I suspect Roscoe Walton sees himself as the mastermind. He is one of those persons who has convinced himself he is brilliant, but, of course, he is really a bumbling fool. One of my bosses, Darby Crocket, told me that most criminals are more stupid than evil. They overestimate their own intelligence, and most end up in prison or an early grave."

"It doesn't make sense for him to show up here. He's not the type to get his hands dirty working cattle. He's obviously been keeping a healthy distance between himself and the cattle stealing. He's got to be desperate."

"Colette says they are broke. No money that she knows of. Their house was being sold out from under them. She is totally in the dark about their financial situation, but she has figured out that they have nothing except perhaps some cash Walton has squirreled away someplace. She doesn't expect to see him again. And she told me something else that she hasn't mentioned to Chloe."

"I'm listening."

"The night before they left Omaha, Walton came home with his clothes all covered with blood. He would not explain it, but he ordered her to burn every item in their fireplace. She obeyed. That was the life she lived, obedience, like a well-trained dog, first her mother, and then Roscoe Walton. She even suspects Walton might have been responsible for the murder of her brother. Her mind is opening, and she is starting to put the puzzle together. I like her. I think Chloe may be just the right teacher for her."

"Sounds like Walton might be running from more than money problems."

"That seems likely. I am going to track down some recent newspapers and see if I can find out what's happening in Omaha."

"I could check with Sunny at Bright's Barn. The old devil might not look like a reader, but he subscribes to the *Omaha Daily Bee* and saves the issues till they're used for the privy. He would have issues of the Broken Bow Republican, too, but they're the first ones to the outhouse. I could stop by the local paper, too, if I don't find anything in the Bee, but if it is to be found, I'm guessing the best bet is the Omaha newspaper. I'll bet if I tell Sunny I'm looking for some stories about Omaha killings, he can point me right to them."

"That sounds perfect. Only I would like you to take on another task. I'll talk to Mister Bright. Can he keep his mouth shut if I ask him some other questions?"

"If you give him a few dollars. Show him your bronze detective badge. He would like being part of solving a mystery. Of course, he will want to brag about it later if arrests are made. Now, what have you got in mind for me?"

"I can see the front door of the sheriff's office from here. I've got a hunch Ford will be leaving soon. I'd like for you to keep an eye out and follow him if you can. If Roscoe Walton is in town, it's very likely Ford will be headed for him. If so, it would be nice if you could find out where Walton is holed up. I know Ford would recognize you, but Walton would not. Walton would know me in an instant, so it improves our chances. Also, a man loitering about doesn't attract much attention, a woman in boots and blue jeans doesn't blend in so well."

Especially a gorgeous woman, Sam thought. "We're both a little on the tall side to hide in a crowd, but I'll see what I can do. I'll try to find you at the hotel later, hopefully in time for supper."

"I suppose you're expecting me to buy."

"Whatever the lady wants. After watching you deal with that poor sheriff today, I just want to stay as near as I can to your good side."

Chapter 37

GAR FORD SAT quietly at his desk, staring at Sheriff Wally Barnes, whose head rested between the palms of his hands, elbows propped on the desk. His gaze was fixed on the desktop like the words he was seeking would appear there. Ford bided his time, knowing what was likely coming his way.

Finally, Barnes spoke, still refusing to meet Ford's eyes. "You made me look like a damn fool, Gar. You didn't keep me on top of the happenings here. I don't know why. Just a mention of this Pinkerton. We could have contacted the agency at least. You knew who he was when the body came in. That woman made it look like you was a part of this rustling outfit." He finally looked up. "Are you?"

"Of course not. I ain't never stolen a cow."

"I wouldn't expect you to say you did, but I can't make sense of how things come down this way. I just know my job's at stake here, and I ain't taking no chances. I want your badge, Gar, and I want you out of here. You're done."

Ford thought he would like to put the son-of-a-bitch out of his misery, but this would not be the time. He stood, unpinned the badge from his shirt, walked over to the gunrack, and took his personal Winchester. On his way to the door, he dropped the badge on the sheriff's desk. Outside, he looked up and down the street. The boardwalk was busy as usual.

Many on the other side were walking on the manure-cluttered street, because a cement sidewalk was being constructed to replace the decaying boards. The town council was even talking about bricking some of the major streets. Yeah, this was an up-and-coming town, and he would not have minded sticking around for a spell. Too bad. He needed to get the hell out—and soon.

He had not hitched his horse at the sheriff's office because he didn't figure to leave the office for more than a stroll about downtown that afternoon. He decided it would be faster to walk to the boarding house, where he had arranged to lodge Roscoe in a room adjacent to his own. He was getting tired of his partner's whining about the lack of amenities at the "Like Home Boarding House." Three meals a day and the food was decent, rooms clean enough. Well, Roscoe was on his way to getting something to really whine about.

He took a route through alleys and side streets that required him to double back later to the boarding house at the far end of Main Street. He doubted anyone would be trailing him, but he decided to be on the safe side. When he reached the rectangular-shaped, two-story house, he entered and went directly upstairs to their second-floor rooms. He rapped softly on Walton's room door.

A sleepy-sounding voice replied. "Yeah, who is it?"

"Gar."

The door opened, and a droopy-eyed, unshaven Roscoe Walton appeared. "What do you want?"

"We need to talk. Now." He pushed the door open and stepped in, closing it behind him.

"Hell, I was getting a nap in."

"That's all you've done since you got here. Sleep and drink."

"You keep me here like one of your damn prisoners, what else do I do?"

"Well, you're getting out of here tomorrow first thing."

"That soon?"

"Yeah, we got trouble."

"What kind of trouble?"

"Some female detective showed up at the sheriff's office this afternoon, and she's on our trail. She's working for your wife's grandmother and the cattlemen's association. Damned good-looking bitch, tall, built like a snake on stilts with the biggest dog I've ever seen."

"And her name's Maddie something."

"Yeah. How did you know."

"She was at the old woman's cave when I dumped Colette there. She didn't say much. Grandma did most of the talking that day. I'd have never thought of a woman detective. What will they think of next?"

"She's got me tied to the rustling. You, too. I got fired by the sheriff, and if he finds some solid evidence, he'll come after me. I could kill him easy enough, but I don't need killing a lawman on my record. That puts a fella at the top of the target list."

"And the detective started all this? A woman?"

"Don't make light of her. This woman could cause more problems yet. I ain't sure about the man with her. He said nary a word, but I didn't like his look. He was taking in every word. His name was Sam Kraft, so I guess he's with the ranching family."

"Yeah, the K Bar K. You've taken a fair number of cattle with that brand, I think you said."

"I'm inclined to leave him alone, but I want to be rid of that detective. I've got two men in town who are going to ride with us to meet up with my five drovers at Bobcat Canyon. I hired these men for their guns. They're the ones that took care of the Pinkerton. Tonight, they'll put Miss Maddie to sleep."

"Do you mean, kill her?"

"You put it so crudely. We won't stop the law from looking, but we'll buy time. She mentioned your name. She's got this figured out. You're in the middle of it all, like it or not. Something else I was going to tell you about. The *Omaha Daily Bee* from a few days ago came in on the morning's train. The Omaha law people are looking for you. Right now, they're just concerned you might be dead. They've figured out that Lulu Perry worked for you and that Calvin Lockhart was your lawyer, so you've been connected. You ain't been charged or accused yet, but when you turn up alive, they will be wanting to talk with you. Hope you got some good answers."

"They can't prove a thing."

"Can you count on your wife to back you up?" From the look on Walton's face, the man would not be counting on his wife.

Walton said, "It doesn't matter, I plan to disappear."

"It's time for us both to disappear fast. I'm pulling out in the morning, and unless your brain's dead, you'd better ride with me."

"I wasn't wanting to go this soon."

"If you don't, especially if this detective lives, you'll be in the county jail in a couple of days. They'll find cause to hold you for questioning by the Omaha police, if nothing else. The sheriff ain't so dumb he won't pick up the news they're looking for you, and I'm damn sure the detective will if she's still alive."

Walton sighed. "So what do we do?"

"Get your things together. Get rid of what you can't carry on your horse. Put yourself together a bedroll."

"What's a bedroll?"

"Oh, Lord. I'll do it We go to the bank first thing and draw out all the money."

"I want gold."

"You ain't going to get it. Just be glad if we can get the paper without a hassle. Then we buy you a horse and saddle. We'll meet up with our gunslingers and head for Bobcat Canyon."

"There's a hotel up there?"

"Nope, not quite that fancy, I fear."

"A big house?"

"A one room cabin that will be sleeping nine men."

"You're not serious."

"You'll see how serious I am." He thought Walton was going to faint. It occurred to him that it might be best to kill him, too, but he was needed to withdraw the money, and he might yet be useful in some way. No, Walton would live for a spell but not long enough to get away with his share of the money.

Chapter 38

IT WAS NEARLY seven o'clock and dark under a starless sky when Sam returned to the hotel. He went through the lobby past a night clerk, who was dozing at his desk, and down the hall to Maddie's room at the far end. He heard Pirate's low growl before he even rapped on the door. Maddie's muffled voice said, "Who is it?"

"Sam."

She opened the door a crack and peered out before she stepped back and admitted him. When he closed the door, he saw that she gripped her pistol in her left hand. Thankfully, the barrel pointed downward. "You might control that weapon better in your right hand," he said.

"I shoot mostly with my left hand. I eat with my right, because it works better at most tables, unless I've got a lefty with me, then I switch. I'm what's called ambidextrous. I don't know if that makes me a freak or not."

Sam laughed. "I wouldn't go that far, but you are . . . an unusual woman. I'm getting so I'm not surprised at anything I learn about you. Have you eaten yet?"

"No. I wouldn't mind a good sandwich, maybe a beer."

"A sandwich would do me fine, too." He wasn't much of a beer drinker and didn't care much for liquors he had encountered. Gramps was a near teetotaler, conceding to a glass of wine on occasion. Sam assumed that this was probably because Gramps's own father had been a drunk, and he supposed his grandfather had influenced his own tastes. Unsurprisingly, Chloe liked her spirits now and then and produced much of her own brew in the barn still she and her deceased husband had contrived.

In the hotel dining room, they enjoyed roasted beef sandwiches and fried potatoes and looked forward to bowls of freshly churned ice cream for dessert. Sam observed, "The cook has help tonight, a bartender and a waiter. He should be happier."

"They're busy. They need it." She took a sip of her second beer while Sam continued to nurse his first.

"I assume you would like to hear what became of Deputy Ford."

"I almost forgot what we were here for. Yes, by all means, go ahead." There wasn't a chance she had forgotten their mission.

"I followed him to a boarding house, a place called 'Like Home,' a respectable place on the edge of town. He took the long way, so I gather he was concerned about being followed. I waited for several hours across the road and about froze my tail off. I was about to leave when Joe Clouse, a bartender friend of mine, came out of the house. I intercepted him and asked him if the deputy lived there, and he confirmed it. He didn't like Gar Ford much and mentioned that Ford had brought a snobbish friend to take a vacant room several days ago. He didn't know the man's last name, but at supper last night he had heard Ford call him Roscoe. We've got both nested at the same place, it appears. I headed for a warm place after I picked up that information."

"Your friend Sunny Bright was very helpful once I told him I was a detective. You were right, he wants to be a part of the team. He knows everything that's happening in this town, and I told him where we are staying in case he gets any new information. I told him just enough to keep him curious." She plucked a newspaper clipping from her leather bag and passed it to him. "*Omaha Daily Bee* two days ago. Arrived on the train this morning, Sunny said." She reached for her beer glass again and took a healthy gulp while he read the short article.

Sam read the clipping. "They're looking for your friend Roscoe. The police seem more concerned about his wellbeing than anything. I suppose they would like to question him about ties between the two victims."

"He has ties. I told you about the bloody clothes he ordered Colette to burn. It is very likely he killed them. He certainly is not going to come forth. More likely, he will try to disappear. He looked like a man who could order killings but not one who would dirty his own hands with such matters, but as the saying goes, appearances can be deceiving."

The waiter appeared with two bowls of vanilla ice cream and another smaller bowl of melted chocolate with a dipping spoon in it and placed them on the table. "Anything else for you folks?"

Maddie said, "I'm fine, thank you. We will have the table for you shortly. The bill is mine tonight."

When the waiter walked away, Sam said, "Maddie, the woman does not pay. You embarrassed me."

"Sorry, but this woman pays on occasion." She reached for his half-full beer glass. "It appears you are not a connoisseur of fine beers. If you are not going to drink this, I can finish it for you." The glass was emptied before he had a chance to reply.

"You first," she said, nodding at the chocolate dish.

Blizzard

Sam took a small dip of the chocolate and put it on one side of the creamy top. He preferred some of the ice cream plain. He might not know beers, but he appreciated good ice cream. Maddie poured the remaining chocolate sauce over her ice cream, covering the top so the white disappeared. He hoped she would not be sick tonight. All that beer and chocolate. He did not think that would set too well with his stomach.

They ate quietly for a spell, before he spoke. "What next?"

"I'm tired. Thank the Almighty there's a water closet across the hall from me next to the back door. I need to get rid of some water soon."

"I am thinking of tomorrow."

"I would like to visit with the sheriff again to be certain he knows about the Omaha police seeking Roscoe Walton and inform him of Walton's whereabouts. I'm confident that if Ford knew he would not have told the sheriff. After that, I want to do a bit of Christmas shopping."

"Christmas shopping? We don't do much about gifts at the ranch. Gramps gives generous bonuses to all the ranch hands. We used to do things for Bruce and Monique's kids when they were little but that's sort of been phased out now. Monique does a lot of homemade things, boxes of candy and cookies and such, sometimes a quilt or two."

"I'm buying clothes for Colette, working and riding shirts and britches, maybe a pair of decent boots since I know her size. She's got nothing but Chloe's hand-me-downs, and some go back thirty years."

"Quite a change for a little rich girl."

"She needs friends more than money. I'm trying to be one."

"I'll find something else to do while you're shopping."

"Good. You would just be in the way."

Later that night, after Sam figured Maddie would be in bed, he buckled on his gun belt. He slipped the Colt from the holster, checking the cylinder to confirm the weapon was ready. There were exceptions, but most men did not walk the town with pistols on their hips these days. Even at the ranch, he preferred his rifle and was inconsistent about wearing his sidearm.

He went downstairs and woke the night clerk, who had dropped off to sleep again. He startled the little old man who had seen his best years and probably handled the job for a dollar or two a night. "I'll be staying in your lobby a good part of the night. I can't sleep, and it beats looking at four walls."

"Uh, well, I guess that's alright. You're a paying customer. You can sleep on the hall floor if you want, if you stay out of the way of other guests."

Sam claimed a rocking chair that faced the hallway that led to Maddie's room. His angle did not allow him to see her room or the back entrance, but he was confident he would hear any disturbance. Most important, he was no more than a minute or two from the room. The clerk took about ten minutes to nod off again. After that, Sam fought sleep for the better part of three hours before he heard the creak of a door open down the hallway. The Regulator clock on the lobby wall said it was almost one-thirty.

Of course, it could be a partying customer slipping in late or a nighttime guest of one of the occupants departing or entering. He got up from the rocker and crept nearer to the hallway before stopping and waiting. Then he heard Pirate barking frantically. He stepped into the hallway and saw one man enter Maddie's room and another waiting to follow. "Stop," he yelled, his Colt clutched in his hand now.

A tall, rail-thin man, his face covered with a black hood, spun around ready to fire. Sam instantly tagged him a professional and did not wait before he got off two shots with his Colt, the deafening blasts echoing through the narrow hallway. The man crumpled and dropped to the floor, his gun clattering in front of him.

Another gunshot erupted from Maddie's room, then another, and the wolfdog's racket sounded more like a lion's roar than a dog's vicious growling. Sam raced down the hall as a man's screaming sent chills down his spine. As he reached the open doorway, he heard Maddie call, "Down, Pirate, down." The dog's noise tapered off to a low threatening growl.

When Sam started to step into the room, he nearly stumbled over a bear-like man crawling toward the doorway, the coat and shirt covering his right arm and shoulder ripped off and the flesh underneath shredded. The side of his head was drenched with blood still flowing from where there had once been an ear. "Help me, help me," the man pleaded between moans and sobs.

Sam hollered down the hallway, hoping the night clerk could hear. "Doctor, we need a doctor here, and get somebody to roust the sheriff."

He squeezed past the injured would-be killer and found Maddie sitting on the edge of her bed, bootless but wearing britches and a blood-soaked shirt. Pirate sat on the floor, his muzzle resting on her knee. "Maddie, you're hit." He rushed to her side and saw that the source of the blood was from the left side under her arm. Maddie was pale as the white bed sheets and seemed to be in a dazed stupor.

Sam said, "Where's the wound?"

"I'm going to puke." She bent forward, spread her knees, and vomited, lifted her head a moment, leaned forward, and vomited some more.

He thought it would never end, but finally it turned to dry heaves, then stopped. During the process, he took his penknife and sliced her shirt and undergarment open on the left side, exposing part of her left breast. It appeared that a lead slug had passed through the flesh just above her ribs. He sliced away a piece of her shirt, folded it, and put in her right hand. "Hold that against the wound while I find something better."

Sam cut part of a bedsheet into several long, narrow strips and fashioned a better compress from another. When he returned to her side, he said, "We'll have to take your shirt and undershirt off so we can wrap this around your chest."

"You just want to see my little apples."

"I'll keep my eyes shut."

"Oh, who cares? I just want to die anyhow. Do what you got to do."

So he did and soon had a good compress against the wound secured by a cloth strip bound about her chest. "Do you have an extra shirt?"

"In the top drawer."

He retrieved the shirt and got her respectably covered again. "Now let's get your head back on a pillow, and I'll cover you up a bit. I want you to rest until a doctor shows up. I've got to see to the man on the floor now."

"Let him rot in hell." She dropped off instantly to sleep.

Pirate's growl caught his attention, and he turned toward the door, fingers instinctively feathering his pistol grip.

A young man with a silver deputy's star pinned to his shirtfront stood in the doorway next to the moaning man on the floor. His eyes were so wide, they appeared they were about to pop from his skull, and he wore a Stetson several sizes too large, so it rested on his ear tops. His skinny face exhibited a mustache and chin whiskers of blond peach fuzz.

"I'm Deputy Archie Cox," he said, his voice shaky.

"Well, Deputy, I guess you're in charge. How do you want to handle this?"

"Good question. I sent somebody out with word for the sheriff, but I don't look for him anytime soon, maybe not till after breakfast. I was told somebody's tracking down Doc Svenson. His office is at his house, but he's out someplace that's got a cow with calving trouble. The new doc ain't to be found, either. Anyhow his wife's not telling where he's at. Them two doctors don't get much sleep, but young Doc Biederman don't do four-legged creatures."

Sam sighed. "We want Doc Svenson anyhow. I'll see what I can do for the guy on the floor. He's quit his moaning all at once. He's either dead or fainted away. I'll tell you what happened while I tend to him."

Chapter 39

MADDIE WOKE AT sunrise to find Pirate on one side of her and Sam on the other. She sat up in bed and looked around the room, trying to recall what had happened just hours ago. She remembered puking her guts out, a man just opening the door and entering the room, gunshots, the burning in her side. More gunshots in the hallway. Sam appearing and taking charge.

She was mortified by the way she had handled things. Nausea had come on shortly after she first went to bed, and she struggled to sleep, but she had finally succumbed just before the man came in and triggered Pirate's reaction. If not for her wolfdog, she would be dead, of course. If not for Sam, it appeared they both might be.

"Feeling better?" It was Sam, swinging his legs out of bed and pulling on his boots.

"Yes. I'm just confused and hungry. How can the room be so tidy?"

"Different room. You left the other quite a mess. I think I got all your things, but they won't be putting anybody in the other one for a spell, and this one is just two doors down."

"You've been through all my personals? And you've seen my bosoms. I'm so embarrassed." She suddenly realized she was wearing a long-sleeved, flannel nightgown. "And somebody brought me a gown and took off my clothes and put it on me. You did that, didn't you? Now, I am really mortified."

"Don't be. I didn't look."

"Liar. Now tell me what happened last night."

He told her about his sentry duty in the lobby and altercation with the man he killed. "Of course, I could only guess what was going on in the room. There were two gunshots, but your gun wasn't fired. I'm guessing they'll find a hole in the wall. I think the guy was trying to get off a shot at Pirate. The slug that went through you was found on the floor with a bit of your tough hide attached."

Maddie said, "A doctor hasn't been here?"

"Doc Svenson will be over to visit you midmorning and try to do what patching is needed. He'll decide then if we need to haul you to his office. I like Doc Svenson. I lived with him and his wife five days a week and made calls with him for almost a year when Gage sent me over for some vet training from Doc. It was that or go to North Platte to high school."

"I've got things to do."

"No, you don't, and I've taken your boots to guarantee it. I promised to go talk with the sheriff. I dealt with his deputy through the night. He may want to talk to you later, but I've got a hunch he'd rather not."

"How did that man get in the room so easily?"

"Master key. The sheriff's office has them for some of the lodging places. They can be handy if there are problems the hotel people don't want to deal with."

"And Gar Ford helped himself to the master key for the rooms here?"

"It appears so. It confirms what we already knew when you gave him the invitation yesterday."

"And I wasn't prepared for his acceptance."

Sam's shrug told her his thinking. What a fool she had been.

"Can you eat?"

"I'm starving."

"Withers will be on duty soon. He will act as a monitor of comings and goings today. The back entrance will be locked down with an iron bar across the door. You will be served breakfast at eight o'clock. I will be here till then, grab something to eat on my way out before heading for the sheriff's office. We will be staying here at least tonight, longer if the doctor thinks we should. I will be moving my things down here. We are sharing this room tonight. I don't give a dang what people think or say."

She guessed it wasn't any different than their sharing the cabin on the Coldsmith trip, and they were comfortable enough with each other. With her wound and Pirate, she doubted he would try to get more comfortable. "Yes, I suppose that's alright. We have a lot to talk about anyhow."

"I'm going to take Pirate out to water the trees out back, and then we'll go across the street and visit the butcher. Maybe I can bring something back, and you two can have breakfast together."

"What about my water?"

"I'm sorry. There is a chamber pot under the bed."

"I'm not going to try straddling one of those dang things. I'm heading for the water closet across the hall." She started to get out of bed, but a wave of dizziness struck, and she plopped back down.

"Dizzy?"

"Yeah, and now I've got to go bad."

Sam stepped back to the bed. "Do you want me to carry you?"

"I don't doubt you can do it, but I'm hurting too much to be tossed around like a sack of flour. Get on my right side and help me up. I'll anchor my arm about your neck, and you can help me across the hall and into the little room. I'll rap on the door when I'm finished, and we'll come back. I just need steadying."

"You lost a lot of blood, and then you tossed last night's meal. You'll feel better when you eat. I'll ask for a pitcher of water with your breakfast. Drink as much as you can today—and I mean water."

"I don't need my nose rubbed in my bad judgment, thank you."

After he got her back in bed and placed her Smith and Wesson on the lamp table next to the bed within arm's reach, Sam left with Pirate, and she found she could not fight off sleep. She had no idea how long she slept before she heard Sam's voice again.

"Maddie. Maddie, wake up."

She opened her eyes and saw Sam on a chair, shaking her right arm gently. "Breakfast is here. Eggs and biscuits with honey. A cup of coffee and a pitcher of water. Can you hold a tray on your lap without spilling it?"

"I . . . I think so."

She scooted into a sitting position next to the headboard, and Sam propped pillows behind her back. With the tray in her lap, she was ready to eat and did not hesitate.

Sam said, "I don't look for more trouble, but Pirate will be at your bedside. Three taps on the door, tell him to stand down. Someone will be by to pick up the plates and see if you need anything. Withers will escort the doctor in. He does vet work, too, in case you want Pirate checked over."

"A vet. You're having me treated by a vet? You weren't just joshing when you said you trained with this man?"

"He's the best, animals or people."

Sam walked out the door, and she tore into her breakfast, pleased to find out that her stomach was not rebelling. She washed it down with coffee and was feeling much better now, except for the throbbing pain on her left side. She guessed she should just be thankful that the slug was not planted a few inches to the right. The no-good Sam had shot was feeling no pain, and the shooter Pirate worked over likely knew real suffering.

She maneuvered the tray onto the bedside table, fell back on her pillows, and dozed a spell before she heard three distinct raps on the door. "Stand down, Pirate," she said softly when the dog scrambled to his feet and faced the door. She reached for her gun and slipped it under the blankets. Her left side was disabled, but she could make-do fine with the right hand. "Come in."

The door opened slowly, and a fair-skinned blonde girl who could not be more than sixteen-years-old stepped in. When she saw Pirate, she froze. "Will he bite?"

"Yes, but not you. Did you come for the dishes? They're over here." She pointed to the tray on the lamp table.

"Yes, ma'am. I will have to go past the dog. You are certain it's safe?"

"Lie down, Pirate." The wolfdog obeyed.

"I promise. You can just step on by."

"Thank you, ma'am." She picked up the tray and started to leave the room but turned around before she exited. "Is there anything else I can help with?"

"Not at the moment, but you might check back in an hour or two. Please call me Maddie, and my hound is Pirate. May I ask your name?"

"I am Lorelei. Lorelei Schoenbeck."

German, she assumed. Germans and Scandinavians seemed to comprise most of the surrounding citizenry. "Thank you for taking care of this, Lorelei. Perhaps we can talk more later."

"I would like that, ma'am—Maddie."

After Lorelei left, she drank a glass of water, knowing Sam would scold her if the contents of the pitcher were not reduced. She lay back again, but she could not sleep because the pain was increasing now. When she lifted the blankets to examine the source, she saw that blood was leaking through the compress. She figured that her trip to the water closet and shifting positions on the bed had opened the wound. Sam had not explained much about it, and she had seen nothing before he dressed it. She hoped the doctor arrived soon.

As if on cue, there were three raps on the door again. This time it was Withers with a stocky, white-haired man with a brushy mustache nearly dropping over his lips, which were formed in a big smile. Withers introduced Doctor Hakon Svenson and departed, but Lorelei slipped in behind him.

"Your newly recruited nurse. She says you have met," the doctor said.

The doctor wasted no time, and after handing his big black bag to Lorelei, went directly to Maddie's side and yanked back the covers, pulling them down to her waist.

He turned to Lorelei. "Set my bag on the floor on the other side of the bed. Our patient leaves no room at the foot." He smiled and winked at Maddie. Again, speaking to Lorelei. "Can you find me some clean towels, dear, maybe four or five, and a pot of boiled water from the kitchen? Clean rags would be nice, too."

Lorelei nodded, took the bag to the other side of the bed, and disappeared.

The doctor turned back to Maddie. "Can you scoot to the other side of the bed, so I can examine the left side more thoroughly, then slip your gown down to the waist? We can wait for Lorelei if you prefer."

Doctor Svenson had just a touch of accent and a soft voice that was somehow reassuring. "Yes, I can do that, and no need to wait." She winced a time or two as she shifted but accomplished the task so that her left side was near the bed's edge and accessible to the physician.

He pulled Sam's crude dressing back and probed his fingers gently about the wound. He evidently sensed her pain and gave her a spoonful of laudanum while they waited for Lorelei's return. "This will make you sleepy and help the pain some. I will likely do some stitching. I don't see any sign of infection in the surrounding flesh, but I will be doing some cleaning. Your friend, Sam Kraft, said he does not think a slug is lodged anyplace because there is an entry and exit wound. He likely knows. He's probably a better vet than I am."

"You are a veterinary surgeon?"

He chuckled. "Don't worry, young lady. I graduated medical school years ago. My vet work is because I don't like to see animals suffer. I was a Union surgeon during the Civil War, so I've dealt with a few gunshot wounds and worse."

She was getting drowsy by the time Lorelei came back into the room with towels and hot water. She heard Doctor Svenson ask, "Lorelei, does blood bother you?"

Lorelei said, "I help my folks butcher chickens and hogs. I cut up the meat all the time."

"Well, we don't need to butcher Maddie, but you are officially appointed my surgical nurse."

Those were the last words she remembered when she woke an hour later with Lorelei at her bedside. She felt groggy, and the girl was fuzzy in her vision. Lorelei had pulled the straight-back chair over and was holding her hand.

"I'm right here, Maddie, if you need me. Doc arranged for me to stay with you today. He left enough laudanum for two days. If you need more, you will have to talk to him."

"I'll try not to use any. I don't like it. What time is it?"

"Almost noon. You probably don't feel much like eating yet, but Doc says you can when you feel like it. I'll run and grab a plate from the kitchen."

Blizzard

She tried to move so she could sit up but stopped when a jolt of pain struck the side of her chest.

"I'll help you," Lorelei said. "Doc expects you to be sore for a few days. He left a salve to put on when I change dressings later. He said the wound seemed clean, but he did some more cleaning to be sure before he did his stitching. You are to see him again in a week or ten days to remove the stiches unless you want to have Sam Kraft do it. He thinks a lot of Sam."

"He's turned you into quite the nurse, it seems."

"He offered me a job at his office after school's out in May. I think I'll take it. I graduate high school this spring. Of course, I'm missing school today. My folks need the money, so I only make classes two or three days a week. A lot of kids have got to do that when they're needed on the farm. I've got three brothers for that."

Lorelei helped Maddie sit up and put the pillows behind her back for support, then poured a glass of water from the pitcher. "Doc said I should keep you taking water. Can you drink?"

Maddie reached for the glass, but it trembled so much in her hands she almost spilled it. Lorelei took it and pressed it to her patient's lips. "Doc said just a little at a time until the laudanum's worn off."

Maddie took a few sips and nodded. "I'm dizzy, but I feel better sitting up. Sam hasn't been back, has he?"

"No, he hasn't been here. I've never met him, but I saw him in the hotel this morning. Hard to miss, he's so tall."

"I expected him back by noon."

Chapter 40

SAM WORRIED THAT Maddie would be upset at his tardiness, but his venture out had turned more complicated than anticipated, and then he had stopped at Doc Svenson's house to ask Doc about Maddie. He had been relieved to learn that she should be fine in a week's time, but that did not ease his concern about her reaction to the news he was delivering.

It was closing in on three o'clock when he rapped on the door to Maddie's room. "It's Sam," he said.

A teenage girl opened the door. "Hi, Mister Kraft. Come on in."

"You must be Lorelei. Doc Svenson spoke very highly of you. He said the patient was in good hands."

Maddie interrupted from her bed. "Yes, thankfully, I had her and wasn't counting on you to show up."

Sam winked at Lorelei. "It sounds like she's recovering quickly."

The girl smiled. "I'll take a break now."

"Take an hour, if you like. I'll be talking to Maddie a spell."

Lorelei left, and Sam took the chair next to the bed. "Hardly room for both you and Pirate." The dog didn't look too threating stretched on his side beside Maddie.

"He's bored. Withers came and took him out for fifteen minutes, but he's ready to run again. I promised him we'd be in the saddle tomorrow."

"I was thinking we might stay a couple more days."

"Only if I decide I can accomplish something more here. Lorelei said there's talk about town that the Weather Bureau Office in Lincoln is predicting a major snowstorm in a few days. I don't want to get trapped here."

"I told Doc you were stubborn as blazes, and I wouldn't be able to hold you short of a hogtying. He just laughed. Have you eaten anything?"

"Beef stew and a biscuit. I left dessert alone. I've lost my taste for sweets for a meal or two, I guess. Now, are you going to tell me what you've been up to?"

He sighed. "You're not going to like it."

"Just give me your story, and I'll decide."

"Well, I spent most of the morning with Sheriff Barnes. He's had a remarkable change of attitude. Mister Cooperation now wants to do his job."

"I'm afraid his best is none too great."

"Better than him getting in our way." He reached into the pocket of his quilted vest and plucked out a silver star. "I feel funny wearing this around town, but I am now a duly sworn deputy sheriff of Custer County. The law now extends to the northwest corner of the county. I even get a salary of one dollar a year."

"I trust you will work with a private detective."

"If I'm treated with proper respect."

"Anyhow, I don't see the development as bad news. I have a feeling you gave me the good news first."

"The man Pirate took on last night died, so we won't be able to question him. His name was Ozzie Kruger. The fella I took down was known as 'Tater.'" That's all anybody knows right now. I guess it doesn't matter. I doubt if Kruger was going by a birth name."

"I was hoping to interrogate Kruger—with the sheriff's approval, of course."

"Of course, now you just need the deputy's approval if we get an opportunity."

"I wonder if we should go ahead and confront Roscoe Walton."

"Too late."

"What do you mean?"

"He and Gar Ford pulled out this morning."

"I assume they didn't catch a train."

"Nope. I told the sheriff what we had learned about the Omaha alert regarding Walton, and he decided to bring him in and hold him for questioning, maybe Ford, too. He wanted to hold them at the jail till he talked to the county attorney about legal grounds. That was when he swore me in to go help him. We no sooner got out the door than Sunny Bright caught up to me and told me Ford and Walton had been at the stable to pick up horses. Ford had his own there and helped himself to Tater's and Kruger's. He must have learned of their fates."

Maddie said, "Since he no doubt sent them here, I'm sure he kept tabs on what was happening."

"Anyway, he threatened to kill Sunny if he said a word to anybody. He let them clear out and then started looking for one of us. He was headed over here when he saw me with the sheriff. Sunny said the men were in a big rush, and he didn't see how they would take the time to come back and kill him. The sheriff and I saddled up but only went a few miles out. We saw no sign of where they went, and given our flimsy basis for holding them, decided to let them go."

Blizzard

"Yes, you could chase them forever in this country and never find them. I suppose the snow might help in tracking if they took off across country, but if they stick to established trails for a time, you would have no way of knowing who you were following."

"Well, we can talk more later. I told Withers my plans about staying in your room tonight. He didn't even lift an eyebrow. He's going to have a mattress and bedding moved in, so I can bunk on the floor."

"Then I shouldn't have to sic Pirate on you."

Chapter 41

GAGE KRAFT DECIDED that age was telling him to give up journeys of the kind they had made to the reservation. He hurt everyplace, and it seemed that when one ache eased another caught fire. And he had been cold since the day they departed the K Bar K. He prayed he would know what it was like to be warm again someday.

Gage and Jim Hunter had at least been granted lodging in a shack on the edge of agency grounds that was set aside for occasional visitors. It had a woodstove and a stack of wood outside the door, but cracks between the boards invited snow and wind, and he supposed rain in its season. It was just past sundown, but he intended to roll up in his blankets soon and hope he might find sleep quickly. He was not handling the journey well. Nights on dirt or wood floors no longer agreed with him, and it was a challenge to roll out and get to his feet each morning.

The two men sat on a wobbly bench in front of the woodstove that was putting off plenty of heat that was carried away quickly by the drafts that slipped through the walls. He did not complain, but he knew that Hunter recognized his misery and put himself out to improve conditions. The Sioux appeared unfazed by it all.

Hunter said, "I don't think you will have trouble with the Indian Agent here in the future. Cattle with brands on the list you gave him won't be purchased without decent documentation. He will be forced to figure out a new system for his commissions when cattle show up."

"Yeah, and there are plenty of cattle out there that don't come in from association members."

"The Sioux are worried there will be no cattle."

"Hell, association members will sell cattle. We'll just drive them here ourselves. We can sell for less than would be paid on other markets because we can cut out some middlemen. I may just have you do some dealing for us up here."

"I could do that. Of course, this won't necessarily keep your cattle from being rustled and sold at forts and agencies to the east and west of here."

"Nope. We've still got to put an end to the rustlers. I'm expecting Sam and Maddie to make some progress on that end. In the morning, we'll stop by the Box X and talk to this Frank Bartek, see if we can squeeze the rustlers even more on the buying end. After that, we head home as fast as we can."

"I know of a line shack we can bunk in tomorrow night. It will be better than this, but that's not saying much. I think we should swing by Bobcat Canyon on the government land while we're going home. It won't be more than an hour out of the way. There's a decent cabin there we could lodge in overnight, but I think we should see if there's anything going on. It's the perfect place to collect a cattle herd."

"I just want to get home before it snows again."

The next morning, they headed out early. The woodstove had allowed Gage to catch some shuteye, but he had left the cabin to piss twice, struggling to get back to sleep after each nocturnal call. Just before sunrise he had barely made it outside again and had not even tried to sleep after that. No more nighttime coffee next stopover. At least the horses had decent shelter in the agency stable and should be rested.

The agent was nowhere to be found before they pulled out, and Gage figured his absence was intentional. He didn't care. He didn't want talk to the snake again anyhow. His message had been delivered.

The Box X was only a bit over ten miles south, the sun was shining and there was a decent well-used trail between the reservation and the ranch. When they reached the ranch, they entered the trail to a run-down house, passing a wood sign that lay on the ground, half-buried in the snow. He could make out the faded brand burnt into the wood, though, that told him it was the right place.

Gage could see that the owner took no pride in the ranch's upkeep. It appeared nothing had ever seen a coat of paint or whitewash. A barn was leaning so far east, it appeared it might fall over if a man blew on it. How the structure endured the blasts of winter wind, he could not imagine. He doubted it would see spring and only hoped critters were not in the barn when it fell.

As they rode into the yard, two large Shepherd dogs raced out from under the porch, barking wildly. They charged toward the horses and then swerved away before repeating the action several times. Their mounts were nervous and dancing, but the riders brought them under control and reined them in. Gage judged the dogs as more barkers than biters, but he was not inclined to dismount.

Abruptly, the house door flew open, and a man clutching a shotgun stepped out. Another man, gun slung low on his hip, appeared in the doorway. The shotgun holder, an average-sized man with a short-cropped, gray beard, said, "You got business here?"

Gage said, "I'm looking for Frank Bartek. I was told he runs this spread."

"I'm Bartek, and you got that right. You got cattle to sell?"

Gage dismounted before he replied, the dogs having retreated under the porch. Hunter remained in the saddle. It was obvious they were not going to be invited in for a chat. "I don't have cattle to sell, but you've been buying my cattle and reselling to the Sioux agency."

"I don't know what the hell you're talking about."

"I'm Gage Kraft. K Bar K Ranch and brand. We've been visiting with Sioux at the reservation and the Indian agent. You've been selling cattle with our brand there, cattle that weren't for sale. Our neighbors' stock, too, a good number from the Circle D."

"I just sell whatever other folks bring here to sell to me. I buy, maybe hold a spell till the market will give me a profit and sell again. Lots of fellers do that. No law against it."

"Nope. But buying cattle you know are stolen pulls you in as a part of the rustling operation. My information is that you've made a living doing just that. I'm here to tell you that the Sioux agency won't be a part of your market anymore and that we're going to notify the Army and the Bureau of Indian Affairs of the rustling problem and furnish a list of all the brands for members of the West-Central Cattlemen's Association. We have a private detective agency hired, and if we get word of somebody trying to sell our cattle, we'll track down the source and help send anybody involved to prison."

The man glared at Gage with cold, gray eyes that were lusting for a kill, and the shotgun barrel inched higher. Gage was not carrying a sidearm, and his Winchester was sheathed in its scabbard.

"You're a dead man, Bartek, if you move that shotgun another inch, and you'll be next Mister Doorman." It was Hunter, who had a Colt in his hand aimed directly at Bartek.

The man standing in the doorway, evidently not a gunfighter, disappeared, and Bartek lowered the shotgun. "Get the hell off my place," Bartek said. "You show up here again, and the greeting will be a lead storm. I ain't taking no more from you."

Gage said, "I've delivered my message." He mounted and reined his horse back down toward the entrance. He tossed a look over his shoulder and saw that Jim Hunter was backing away slowly, putting some distance between himself and Bartek before he turned away.

After they headed away from the Box X and Hunter caught up with him, Gage said, "Thanks, Jim. I think you saved my hide back there. I'm getting careless in my old age."

"That's a bad man you were dealing with, Gage, but I think you just put him out of business—for a spell. That kind never looks to making an honest living."

"Yeah. There have always been folks like that and probably always will be, looking for the dollar they can steal from somebody else instead of an honest day's work."

Hunter took the lead, Gage insisting he wanted to get as near home as they could without overtaxing the horses. Hunter knew the country and had an instinct for picking the best paths and trails that wound through the dunes and hills. But midafternoon, the sun gradually disappeared under dark, billowy clouds, and snow began to fall. Gage cursed under his breath.

He was cold and sick of winter that was just getting started. He had never liked winter, and this had been milder than most, but he wasn't giving the weather gods any medals for it. Every winter in December for the past thirty some years he asked himself why he hadn't moved the operation south—as far south as a man could get without moving into Mexico. And then he would think of spring luring him to hang on and knew he could never leave the Sandhills.

Hunter reined in his gelding. "We'd better get out of the weather, Boss. The old line shack I mentioned is no more than a half hour away. There's a lean-to for the critters and a spring-fed stream nearby. I think there would be some grass amongst some tree cover along the bank, so we could graze them some before dark."

Gage had hoped to get a few hours closer to K Bar K but couldn't argue with Hunter's good sense. "Yeah, let's find the place and get settled. I'm just praying we don't get snowed in."

Later, when they arrived at the shack, Gage was encouraged to see a stack of wood outside and a decent three-sided shed for the horses. Somebody had even left a small stack of hay at one corner, an invitation to the mounts. He resolved to find out who owned the place and do them a good turn with some dollars, if nothing else. The people. That was why he could not abandon this land. There were none better, generally folks who worked hard and looked out for each other, cared about their friends and neighbors like family.

Blizzard

When they entered the line shack, Gage was glad to see a good woodstove, and he could hardly wait to get it going, but what pleased him most was the sealed cracks between the cedar wall boards. Somebody had used a tar-like substance to seal the winds out. Perhaps he would not freeze tonight after all. They dropped their bedrolls, possible bags, and the nearly empty gunnysack of foodstuffs on the floor and went back outside to unsaddle the horses and retrieve their saddlebags and rifles. The snow was heavier now, but they were spared serious wind so far.

They took the horses to the stream to drink, thankful that the fast-running water had not frozen over except along the edges. Gage was especially grateful for the hay now. Once the horses were settled in the lean-to shelter, they hauled the saddles and remaining gear into the line shack. By now, Gage was about tuckered out. This darn trip kept reminding him of the toll the years were taking on him.

Jim Hunter said, "If you will tend to starting a fire and think about some eats for supper, I'll head out and cut some replacement wood. I've got my axe, and I saw a bow saw hanging on one of the lean-to's side walls." Gage had a hunch he was being coddled by the Sioux cowhand, but he wasn't about to protest. He was cold and tired, ready for a fire, supper, and bed.

When Hunter returned, the shack was starting to warm. "Pickings are getting slim. I've got two stale biscuits, a good helping of ham slices and a can of beans. It hurts an old cattleman to be depending on pig meat to survive, but I'm glad for it tonight. I can warm the beans in the can on the stovetop. No skillet, but the ham is already baked. I suppose that's why Monique sent it along. Tomorrow, we've got mostly jerky to dine on, but I'm hoping to be home for supper."

Gage's hopes were dashed when a nasty wind came up and the snow was still coming on strong when they rose the next morning. When he saw the drifting outside, he resigned himself to staying on at least another night. Thankfully, Hunter took his rifle out in the morning and brought back two rabbits.

"I could have got a doe," he said, "but I figured we didn't want to try to carry the carcass with us, and too much would have gone to waste."

By noon, Gage was hungry enough that roasted rabbit tasted almost as good as a prime steak. He was restless, though, and hated the idea of spending more time trapped in the line shack. Still, it gave him a chance to get acquainted with the new hand and decided that this was a man with many skills and brains to strike out on his own someday if he chose. Sam had made a good pick, and they should give the Sioux, who was only twenty-eight years old, enough opportunities and money to keep him at the K Bar K.

The wind eased and the snow stopped early evening, and the next morning the riders were on their way again. They were slowed some by drifting snow, but Hunter always found a route to bypass the worst. Gage estimated that there must have been eight inches of snowfall, which would have been tolerable if not for the wind. Shortly after noon, they found themselves on the brink of a deep canyon, The country was becoming more familiar to him now, but at first, with the snow cover, Gage did not recognize the place.

Finally, it registered. "Bobcat Canyon. I haven't been here for seven or eight years, ever since the government put a stop to grazing."

Hunter said, "And we won't be staying in the cabin down there. There's smoke coming from the chimney, and I don't think we want to chance a visit."

"Outlaws?"

"I couldn't say, but I can't imagine somebody coming up for a fishing trip this time of year."

"I just want to get home. I don't care if it gets dark on us. I'm sleeping in my own bed tonight with old Rip to warm my back."

"We'll need to keep the horses rested, so I doubt if we can make it for supper but not too long after maybe. I'm thinking the critters wouldn't mind stalls in the stable tonight either."

Chapter 42

"GAGE RETURNED TWO nights ago," Maddie said. "I would have been here sooner, but we ran into trouble in town."

Chloe's brow furrowed. "What kind of trouble?"

They were sitting at the kitchen table with Colette, nursing coffee mugs midmorning. Colette seemed to be thriving, she thought. Her blonde hair was a bit tangled, but her face was prettier without all the paint and powder, and the dirt smudge on her nose was somehow becoming. Her eyes looked a bit tired, but the changes in her life seemed to be far from breaking her down.

"I assume you and Chloe have talked about the reason I'm here."

Colette brightened. "You're a detective. Grams told me all about you. It sounds so exciting."

"Some days more than others. I'll pass on taking a bullet anytime."

Colette's eyes widened. "You were shot?"

"I wasn't badly wounded. The slug went through the flesh in my chest under my left arm, just above the ribs. Slug went in and out. A few more inches to the right, and I likely wouldn't be sitting here. I was lucky. Sam was there right away to patch me until Doc Svenson could see me. It's been nearly six days now and no sign of infection. Doc said Sam can take the stitches out in a few days. I learned that he's handy with cattle and horse injuries and ailments."

"Yeah, I get him over here for calving troubles a couple of times every spring, other stock problems in between. But tell me about that trip to town."

Maddie told the two women about the meeting with the sheriff and Ford, the attempted killing and the disappearance of Gar Ford and Roscoe Walton from Broken Bow. "Gage and Jim Hunter think they may be hiding out in Bobcat Canyon with some other men, probably the rustling crew. I'm sorry, Colette. I have doubts that your husband is coming back."

"A blessing, I guarantee you. I might kill him. Grams has taught me how to use and clean a shotgun. She says I should get started with a rifle, but she thought maybe you would be best to help with that. I want to learn about pistols, too. I knew of Omaha women who carried derringers in their bags."

Pity the man who might try to get rough with her in the future, Maddie thought. "It would be my pleasure."

"There's something else I should tell you. I haven't said anything to Grams about this, but when you told us about the Omaha police looking for Roscoe, I decided it was time for me to talk. I think Roscoe killed the lawyer and his so-called office clerk. I told you he left the house for several hours that night and returned home with his clothes soaked with blood. It was ghastly. I almost vomited. When he made me burn the clothes in the fireplace, I knew he had done something terrible. That's when he informed me we were leaving town immediately."

"I'll pass that information on to Sam. He is an acting deputy sheriff now. He can decide if the sheriff needs to be notified immediately. It appears to me, though, that we likely know the whereabouts of your husband and that there would be no urgency."

"He's not my husband anymore, and Grams says I can go by Colette Downs now if I want. When I know where I go from here, I'll see a lawyer and take care of the legalities of it all."

Chloe said, "I've told you, girl, you've got a place here as long you want. You're more than earning your keep. I hadn't realized just how much help I needed around here. Mort Boone's not close to getting things done that need doing, and he won't work any extra. I hate to admit it, but Gage is right about the K Bar K taking over running this show. I'm thinking that I'll just look after the horse side of things—me and Colette, if she sticks around."

Maddie noticed that Colette was nodding her head enthusiastically. "Gage is anxious to meet Colette. Christmas Eve is less than a week off. He's still expecting you for a few days."

"Well, I don't know. I can't just go off and leave Colette here."

"Don't be silly. She's invited. A room is already set aside for her."

"Well, I just don't rightly know if we can be gone that long. Maybe we could just stop by Christmas day to say hello."

"Gage is digging out the carriage that's stored in the barn. He's sending someone with it Christmas Eve morning to pick you both up. He said to tell you he'd come himself and pick you up and toss you in it if you turned him down."

"I'd like to see him try."

"You will, if you refuse to come. Now, I am going to empty that bag I brought over." She got up and walked over to the big gunnysack she dropped when she came in the door. She bent over and started pulling out plain-wrapped packages. "These are pre-Christmas gifts, and I am Santa Claus come early."

Chloe said, "I don't understand what in the devil is going on."

"You will." She held out a package. "Chloe, this one is yours. The other is at the bottom of the sack."

Chloe abandoned her chair and walked toward her, eyeing Maddie suspiciously. She accepted the package and returned to the table. "I just don't know about this, Maddie."

"Colette, I've got five for you. I'll just put them on the couch."

Colette bounded out of her chair and scurried to the couch like a little girl, a smile spread across her face.

Finally, Maddie took the last package and placed it on the table in front of Chloe. "You are not going to be all that happy with these, but I hope you will listen to me."

Colette squealed, holding up two pair of blue jeans in one arm and flannel shirts in the other. "Oh, my own shirts and britches. I can't thank you enough, Maddie."

Chloe frowned when she spread a pale blue, satiny dress out on the table. "Oh, my Lord. A gown. I ain't worn a dress in years. If I've got any, they're stored in the barn loft. It's very generous of you Maddie, but I don't know what I'd do with it."

"You will take it with you when the carriage picks you up and at least wear it Christmas Eve. There is a pair of shoes in the small bag. They might be a bit large, but I'll help you with some padding if need be. You could get two of your feet in one of mine."

"I ain't dolled up like that since before I married Hank. I'd feel like somebody in a freak show."

"Do it for Gage. One night. That's all I'm asking. Monique and Vega are planning to help you and Colette with your hair and maybe a few extras."

"I suppose, but you're crowding me into a corner, young lady."

When Maddie turned back to Colette, she found her new friend with her hat perched on her head and clutching the new boots to her chest, tears slowly trickling down her cheeks. She joined the granddaughter on the couch and wrapped her good arm about her shoulders. "What is it, Colette?"

"I love them so much. I'll wear them till they fall off."

"You were wearing a nice dress and pair of shoes when you came here, nicer than anything in the general store. I thought you might wear those Christmas Eve and that these things would be more practical."

"You are right, absolutely right. It is so strange. I came here with nothing, beyond destitute, and I have never been happier in my life, thanks to you and Grams." She turned and hugged Maddie and then grabbed her new possessions and headed to her bedroom. "I've got to try these on. I'll be out to show you."

Maddie returned to the table and sat down with Chloe. "You love having her here, don't you?"

"I won't deny it, but there is a complication."

"Gage?"

"You nailed it."

"You haven't told her about you and Gage, have you?"

"No. I was afraid it would upset things."

"Why should it? And I have already hinted to Colette that you and Gage are beyond mere friendship."

"Well, I can't stay here if I marry him."

"If it helps, he's dropped any notion of a New Year's wedding. He understands that you need a little time alone with Colette. He's not giving up on April."

"Yeah, he would. If he wasn't so danged understanding, we'd probably been married years ago. My one regret. I do love the ornery cuss, you know."

"You are far wiser than I am, but I'm going give you my opinion anyhow."

"I ain't been so wise. I've left behind a trail of mistakes and foolishness during this life. But go ahead, have your say."

"First, tell your granddaughter about you and Gage, that you are betrothed and plan to marry in April—if that's your intention. If not, Gage is entitled to know. I would not say anything about you and Gage sharing a room Christmas Eve. Just do it. She may be naïve about some things, but she's quick to figure things out. She won't be horrified. Talk about Gage and your past."

"I'm afraid I'll scare her off if I tell her about the marriage coming up."

"Gage says she's welcome to move over to the K Bar K headquarters house with you. She will have a home there if that's what she wants. You've got time to prepare her for those choices. Have you ever considered she might want to stay here on her own?"

"I can't imagine."

Colette came out of her room and interrupted the conversation. "I love everything and it all fits perfectly."

She did a little turn to show the new garments. "How did you know the sizes?"

"There aren't that many choices at the store, so I just went for the smallest. You and Chloe are almost the same size, so I took the same approach with her dress and shoes—went small."

Maddie felt Chloe's hand on her arm, and she turned and swore the crusty woman was fighting to hold back a few tears.

"Thank you, Maddie—for everything," Chloe said.

Chapter 43

"THIS HAS BEEN a wonderful Christmas Eve," Maddie said, as she approached Sam, who stood in the double doorway that separated the parlor from the dining room. "I can't remember one so special. I suppose there were a few when I was small before my parents started warring, but I seem to have blocked those memories from my head."

Sam had been standing there for fifteen minutes or more waiting for her to pass by and pause a moment. He had never seen her in a dress before, and she looked stunning with the chestnut hair flowing onto her shoulders and tied back with a light green ribbon matching the dress and complementing her aqua green eyes. He was nervous about what he had planned but was committed to his mission.

Sam said, "I'm glad you could share this Christmas with us."

"Even music. I wondered about the piano. Vega is an accomplished pianist. I took lessons when I was small and hated them, possibly because my mother nagged me so much. Anyway, I rebelled and refused to continue. Who taught her out here in the hills?"

"Her mother. Monique is unbelievable on the keyboard. Mother and daughter might perform a duet before the evening is finished."

"And I never would have dreamt that Smoky is a violinist."

"Yes, when it's warm out and the windows are open, you will hear him several nights a week, usually melancholy songs like Stephen Foster's *Jeanie with the Light Brown Hair* or *My Old Kentucky Home*. Smoky hails from Kentucky, you know. That's about all his back story anybody knows."

"That's not unusual in the west. You know more of mine than about anybody. You got my mouth running like a mountain stream when we made that visit south to Rance Coldsmith's. Of course, there are some things I didn't let loose—and never will."

"We're all entitled to a few secrets. I've held back a few of mine."

"Well, I'd better circulate a bit and catch up with Colette, although she seems to be having a good time."

"Sorry, you can't leave yet."

Her brow furrowed. "What do you mean?"

He looked upward and pointed to the top of the doorway. "Mistletoe."

"Are you suggesting—"

He stepped forward and wrapped his arms around her, lowering his head a bit. She raised hers, and their lips met for what he had intended to be a chaste kiss, but he found his mouth pressing hungrily to hers, and she responded in kind. He pulled back a moment. Their eyes met, and there was no one at the celebration but the two of them. Their lips came together again, and this time lingered.

He did not know how long it might have continued had the clapping not started. They stepped apart. Everyone was applauding now.

Maddie smiled at him and rolled her eyes. "I think I'd better circulate."

"Uh, yeah, me too." Maddie did not seem embarrassed, but he could feel the heat on his flushed cheeks.

Later, Maddie slipped in beside him at the dining table where he was eating a piece of Monique's special Christmas chocolate cake and sipping on a cup of punch.

The only others at the table were Colette and Monique who were seated at the opposite end engaged in animated conversation broken up with frequent laughter.

Maddie said, "I needed a place to eat my cake, and I saw Mister Lonely sitting here, so I thought I would join him."

"I welcome your company—always."

"Thank you. I checked the ceiling for mistletoe before I sat down. None here. I was disappointed."

"It's a custom, not a requirement, you know."

"I know." She changed the subject. "I loved the caroling this evening. This has been a special Christmas Eve. Any gifts have changed hands very subtly without a big fuss. I saw your grandfather passing out envelopes to the hands."

"Yeah, bonuses, I'm sure. We don't make a big ceremony of such things here. Monique will have a box of baked treats for each of the hands, but nothing is expected." He hesitated and turned his chair toward her. "I have something for you."

"Are you serious?"

"I was hoping for a more private moment, but I don't think privacy is on tonight's menu. Everybody seems huddled in their own little groups right now. It's not wrapped, and it's not store-bought." He reached into the pocket of his doeskin jacket and plucked out the item and held it out to her.

"I've never seen you wear jewelry, not even tonight, so you may have no use for it."

She took the gift in her hand and studied it, her face a mask of bewilderment. "A pendant; it's beautiful. The stone almost looks like an emerald."

"That's what I've been told. It was my mother's. My father gave it to her before he went off to war, Gramps said. He wasn't sure, but he thought it came from the Navajo. They do a lot of silver craftsmanship." The oval stone was encased in a simple silver setting attached to a silver chain.

"Like most women, I love jewelry. I wore a lot of it as a young girl, but my mother kept all of that, and I don't spend money on myself for such things. It nearly takes my breath away. I love it. But it's an heirloom, a treasure. I don't think I—"

"No obligations come with it. I don't know what the future holds for you and me, but if you move on, I want you to have this so you have something to remember me by even if I become just a short chapter of your life's story."

"You are a strange man, Samuel Kraft, but I'm honored to wear your mother's pendant." She handed him the pendant and bent her head forward. "Can you fasten the chain clip in back of my neck?"

He obliged with fingers that trembled slightly. "I've never done this before."

"Good." When he finished and she lifted her head, she straightened the chain about her neck. "It feels like it belongs there."

"It's perfect. Matches your eyes. Merry Christmas."

She leaned toward him, pressed a hand behind his neck and pulled his head down, pressing her lips to his for a quick kiss. "Thank you. I will treasure this always. Merry Christmas."

She was beaming, and he could not have been more pleased. He almost felt it was his mission to make Maddie Sanford happy. "I will be leaving for my cabin soon, so I may not get another chance to say goodnight. I'm doing chores at Grams's tomorrow morning, but I'll show up here for noon dinner. I'll see you then."

"You will see me shortly after sunrise. I'll swing by your place, and we can ride over together if you like. I'm harvesting chicken eggs tomorrow morning. Monique wants all I can collect, so I will need to do some packing, I guess. I may need to turn Pirate into a pack animal."

"I can carry some."

"I thought you would pick up the hint. You're hired."

Blizzard

It would be easier if she would spend the night, Sam thought, but he was not going to press Maddie and spoil things between this woman and himself. She was like a darn cat. You needed to give her room to make up her own mind about how things were going to be.

Chapter 44

GAGE AND CHLOE were in his bedroom preparing for bed. "I've never slept in your bedroom," Chloe said as she wriggled out of her dress. "Seems strange."

"It's not because you haven't been invited many, many times."

"I know. I just felt funny, didn't want folks to know we were sharing a bed. It was more private at my place, not all those people around like you've got here."

This was the Chloe he loved, a maze of contradictions to wade through, sometimes prim and proper, others rough-hewed and not giving a damn about what folks said. "Chloe, you don't really think folks didn't figure us out a long time ago, me being gone overnight or even two or three nights running?"

"Well, I suppose, but I didn't have to climb out of bed and look them in the eye in the morning, like I will tomorrow."

Gage chuckled. He finished stripping off his clothes and crawled in bed. "You coming to bed?"

She stood naked at the foot of the bed. "You ain't wearing anything?"

"Not yet. I thought maybe we could do for a Christmas poke. It's after midnight, you know."

She tossed her long-sleeved flannel nightgown on a chair. "Well, Merry Christmas to you, too." She joined him in bed, buried herself under the blankets and inched herself against him and then moved on top, pressing her lips to his and kissing him as passionately as any he could remember during their years as friends and lovers. It was plenty good enough to stoke his fire.

Later, with pajamas and nightgown on and after building up the fire in the fireplace, they lay snuggled in bed, Chloe's head cradled on his shoulder. "You know what I like best about your place—besides the bossman, of course?"

"Nope."

"The water closets—especially the one across the hall. No chamber pot hassle or a trip to the outhouse in the snow. I think I could get used to that."

"I think once you live here, you will get used to a lot of things."

"I'll marry you New Year's Day, if you still want."

He could not believe what he was hearing. "You're not joshing? It's not because you're drunk on the poke we just had?"

She giggled. "No, Sweetheart. I thought this out before Colette and me came over. We don't know how much time we've got left. We've waited too many years already. My fault. But before you agree, I want you to understand some conditions. Colette and I would still live mostly at my place till as long as April, but we would come for overnight visits sometimes, and you could come to my place when it suited you. But at both places we'd be sharing a bed respectably. I've got to be a good example for my granddaughter. I even gave up my smokes and shut down my still."

"A twenty-seven-year-old woman needs an example?"

"She does. She has been so sheltered. That's why I want to stay at my place with her a spell. I can teach her better what honest work means and what it's like not to have everything you want. But did you see how happy she was tonight? She'll be fine with a little time. I love her dearly, and I think she's coming to love me. It's like a second chance for me. Somehow, I failed her mother. Maybe I can make up for it with the next generation."

"Colette and Monique seemed to take to each other."

"Monique is going to teach her about cooking and running a house and proper bookkeeping. She works on your ledgers, I know."

"And Monique works too hard. Colette could be handy in the kitchen or help with the books, ease the load for Monique."

"We'll just see how it all plays out. I've got a hunch that Colette has a lot of surprises in store for us—good ones."

Gage said, "Now about the wedding. The judge lives in Broken Bow. That's a long trip out. I guess we could get married in town."

"I thought we'd get married here. That new Methodist Church ain't more than six or seven miles east. I'm thinking he might do the job for a fee. I'd like to tie the knot in the parlor downstairs. Just you, me, Sam and Colette. And Maddie, of course. We'd add Monique and hers, since they live in the house, and, knowing her, she'd insist on doing something special. That's it."

"Whatever you want. I just can't believe this is happening."

"We'll do it in the afternoon, because I'll have to get back home for chores. But first we've got to talk to the preacher. I thought we might go to church Sunday, if the weather holds, and make the arrangements. You'll be paying him, I assume."

"Yes, of course." It appeared the tight side of Chloe wasn't going to loosen up with marriage. "When was the last time you were in church? Have you ever met Reverand Harper?"

"We lived in St. Louis when the kids were born and got the kids baptized by Presbyterians there and went to church a few times when the kids were baptized. Hank, crooked as snake, insisted they be baptized. I guess he was dunked by a Baptist when he was a kid, but it didn't take as near as I ever knew. As you know, there wasn't a church anywhere near when we first settled here, only a circuit preacher now and then."

"Well, you don't need to worry about chores on the wedding day. Jim Hunter and Alex Paul will be living in your bunkhouse by that time. They've agreed to headquarter there now that we're combining the operations. I'll be taking on a few more new hands here."

"I don't think I'm set up to feed regular hands."

"Monique will send some things over, and Jim can cook. He'll see if we might need a cookstove in the bunkhouse, but I think he'll be happy to do with a fire ring outside. When it works out, they'll try to ride over here for supper so they can get work assignments for the next day."

"You are sending us protection, too, ain't you?"

"I don't deny it. Think of your granddaughter with that crazy husband out there. Don't you want help for her if it's needed? Outlaws won't be so quick to come around if they see the bunkhouse is occupied and there are gun-toting men in the vicinity."

"I guess you're right. I've got to get accustomed to lots of changes, it appears."

They were both silent for a spell, lost in their thoughts. Gage turned his head to look at Chloe. Her eyes were closed, and her head still rested on his shoulder, her arm tossed over his chest. For an instant he feared she had died, but then he saw her chest rise and fall. The woman he loved asleep beside him. This is the way it should be. He vowed that they would be together most nights once they were married.

Chapter 45

January 12, 1888

GAGE AND HIS bride of a dozen days sat at the K Bar K dining table enjoying a seven o'clock breakfast. All the others had departed before their arrival at the breakfast counter. "I feel lazy as a cow tick," Chloe said, "doing nothing but eating off everybody else's back."

"You're going over to your place to milk and see to the chickens and eggs this morning. You'll find other work while you're there. Do you need my help with anything?"

"Nope. You'd just be in the way. I suppose I'll be back for supper and stay over again. Now that Colette's teaching at the school, it works nice for her to ride over to Cedar Creek with Vega till she heads to Broken Bow for high school in a few weeks. She wants her weekends at the dugout, though, and still plans to stay there fulltime after Vega leaves. She says she'll be fine over there on her own, but I'm not so sure."

"Chloe, she's a grown woman, and we've got two hands staying in the bunkhouse if she needs help of any kind. It's not like she's totally alone on the place."

"I know, but she's still my grandbaby. It's funny, when she first showed up, I figured I was going to end up Colette's slave to wait on her, and I vowed I wasn't going to let her do that to me. Well, I was dead wrong. She's taken to work like a duck to water. Monique's teaching her to cook, and she loves it. I've yet to find a ranch chore she doesn't dive right in to, and now Vega recruited her to teach, and she loves that and the kids. And she's thrilled to be earning her own money even though it's a pittance. I'm proud as can be of that girl."

With Colette's arrival, Gage was seeing a softer side to Chloe than he had witnessed before, and he rather liked it. He thought they might both be learning to take life a bit more slowly. Perhaps it was time. "Well, I've got some chores of my own to see to around the place. I promised to do that, since most of the men are checking cattle totals on the place. I don't think we're losing many to rustling lately since we started the boundary patrolling. Taking on a few extra hands may be worth it, but I don't think we've seen the last of rustlers."

"Maddie said she and Sam are headed up to Bobcat Canyon today to see what's happening up that way. If they find a herd with our brands, Sam plans to collect some men and go in tomorrow with a posse to clean things up, hopefully make some arrests."

"Yeah, it makes me nervous when there's possible gunplay coming on. But if they're going to make a move, they need to do it while there's a break in the weather. It's been nothing but snow and cold since Christmas up till a few days ago. We were lucky to get that preacher over to do the vows for us. I don't think he'd have done it if Sam hadn't escorted him here and back. The twenty-dollar gold piece didn't hurt any, either, I suppose."

"A double eagle was too much. If you had let me handle it, I'd have hired him for an eagle, maybe less."

"It was our wedding day, Chloe, and preachers get paid starvation wages. Special occasions like ours help keep the wolf from the door."

"Nobody's making him preach."

"He's called to do it, Sweetheart. He's God's messenger."

"Then God ought to pay the bill."

Gage sighed. Chloe always had an answer, and she was a little crazy sometimes, but he loved that crazy side, always had. He also knew when to end an argument with her. He got up.

Chloe said, "You're leaving me?"

He bent over and kissed her on the forehead. "We've both got work to do. The sun's out, we've got that warm southerly wind today, the snow's melting away. A perfect day to go out and get things done."

"I hope you're going to pick up your own plate and eat ware."

"I am. I wouldn't dare do otherwise."

She stood, "Well, before you go, I expect a real man's kiss." She pressed against him and squeezed him with a bear hug that he swore was stronger than anything he could muster. She lifted her chin upward waiting for his kiss, and he obliged.

Chapter 46

ROSCOE WALTON MORE than once had thought about taking the short-barreled Colt he secreted in his coat pocket, pressing it to his head and squeezing the trigger. He hated this place and these worthless pigs that shared the single-room shack. He had slept on the sagging, broken wood floor for over three weeks now, slapping away the rats and other vermin that came up between the shattered boards at night to scavenge. One creature, he was not certain what, had bitten him on the hand a week ago, and the appendage was painful and swollen now.

Seven men cramped into the space, and the nights seemed endless. He could not sleep for the belching and snoring and farting. Several moaned and cussed in their sleep. He had never even ventured into an environment like this. And now food was running short. No flour for biscuits or breads, no beans. A few rabbits and occasional deer kept them from starving.

The coffee had disappeared days ago, but somebody always came up with liquor. It was like they were mining that somewhere. He could not join the fools in their drunken stupors or daylong poker playing. He must think, plan a way out of this.

The five so-called drovers had departed a few hours earlier to see if they could bring in more cattle. Weather had been an obstacle for a long stretch of time, but the past few days had presented an opportunity to bring in a decent harvest. They were complaining, however, that they had to be wary of outriders now watching parts of the nearest herds, the Circle D and K Bar K. They could not cover the entire ranges at one time, but they shifted daily, and Gar Ford had told him they could kill a few easily enough, but that would trigger an army of ranchers coming after them.

Gar should be back this morning. He had headed north to make a deal with the Box X head man for the cattle—five hundred head. Of course, they only had fifty collected in the dead-end branch of the canyon. He got up and tossed another log on the fire in the fireplace. He only had three logs left, and the outside supply had been depleted several days ago. The worthless idiots had been too lazy to go up the canyon where there was a wooded area to cut more.

Of all things, the big hairy-faced man called "Ox" had suggested that he, Roscoe Walton, the man who paid their wages, go cut wood today if he didn't want to freeze tonight. The ugly creature had pointed to the axes and bow saws in the corner on his way out. They could go to hell. He was not about to spend his day cutting and sawing wood. Besides, it had warmed a lot this morning and would get warmer this afternoon. They could chop the wood like they were paid to do when they got back with a decent herd of cattle.

Walton heard the door open behind him and spun around to see a grim-faced Gar Ford standing in the doorway. "Gar, I was hoping you would show up this morning."

Ford stepped inside and shut the door. "I don't bring good news."

"What do you mean?"

"Nobody at the Box X. The place is deserted. So I went to the reservation thinking I would make a direct deal with the agent. This is our last sale, so who cares if he knows who we are. We just want our money and we're gone. He ain't buying. Gage Kraft was up there and warned him off. He's got a brand list he won't buy without talking to the owners. Kraft probably ran the Box X crowd off. I think they was just squatting on a deserted place anyhow."

"Can't we go to another market?"

"It's a good bet that Kraft or the cattlemen's association sent warning to all Army posts and reservations we could get to. The law's likely waiting in any rail-connected towns in this part of Nebraska for us to show up."

Walton fought to control his panic. "So what do we do?"

"Split our money and run."

"But the cattle the drovers bring in—"

"They can keep the damned cattle. I don't care what they do with them. We should make our split now and get the hell out of here. We've got enough from what we took out of the bank to get out of this damn state and disappear—start over. Game's over. We didn't get rich, but we ain't broke neither."

Walton did not trust the greedy son-of-a-bitch. "We already split the money we took from the bank."

"But you got some other. I'm thinking I ought to share in that. Let me slip out of this big coat, and we'll just have a friendly talk."

Walton slipped the Colt from his coat pocket while Ford was tangled in his coat and the former deputy's back was turned to him. By the time the coat was dropped on the floor, the Colt was aimed and ready to fire. Walton squeezed the trigger, and his ears rang from the explosion. Ford turned around fumbling for the weapon holstered on his hip, his eyes wide in disbelief. Walton launched another slug into the gunman's chest for good measure, and Ford collapsed on the floor.

Ford must have thought he was a fool, Walton thought. He always knew the man never intended to split. It just was not Ford's nature and not his own either. He had just counted on a truce till they got closer to North Platte.

He tossed another log on the fire and sat down on the bench again. He had two concerns now. First, find Ford's share of the money. He figured there should be close to eighteen hundred dollars. When he added his extra, he would have better than a four-thousand-dollar stake, sufficient to get a new start someplace.

Then he must find his way to North Platte. It would be southwest someplace. He knew he could not move Ford's body so far from the cabin that the drovers would not find it upon their return. And Ford's horse. He did not know much about horseflesh, but he knew the man would not ride an inferior animal. The horse would come with him, and he would sell it someplace. The sky and south wind promised a nice day. Surely he would come across a ranch or farm where he could obtain a meal and lodging for a price.

As soon as he found Ford's money, he would saddle up and leave this godforsaken hellhole. Two hours later, as noon approached, he still had not turned up Ford's money. He had cleaned out the saddle bags, shook out the man's bedroll and pulled off his boots, looking for money hidden there. He found only a few coins in the pockets of his britches. The handling of the dead man did not faze him, nor did the thought that he had killed a man. He was learning that each killing came easier, and he would not hesitate to kill again.

He sat down again to think a bit. He would need to leave. He had no choice or remain and risk losing all he had to the no-good drovers, including his life, in all likelihood. He got up to begin collecting his gear, and the room turned gray. He peered out the only window which faced easterly and had offered the morning sunlight. The sun was hidden behind dark, roiling clouds now. The building shook like the earth was swallowing it. What was happening?

Chapter 47

"THE WIND SHIFTED to the north all at once," Maddie said to Sam, who was riding beside her. She saw the worried look on his face.

"And the sun's disappeared. I swear the temperature just dropped ten degrees. We'd better get out those fur-lined coats. We've got a storm moving in. I've never seen a change happen so fast. It's at least two more hours to Bobcat Canyon and we'd likely have to shoot our way into shelter there. I'm thinking we'd better turn back."

Suddenly, it began to snow so heavily that it formed a white curtain between the riders, and she could barely make out Sam's face. The wind screamed so loud as it tore through the hills it was nearly deafening. "Sam," she yelled, "is there a place nearby where we can hole up?"

"Dismount so that we can get our coats on and hear each other."

They reined in and dismounted, untied the thick coats that were hitched behind their saddles, and helped each other worm into the garments. "We can thank Monique for these," Maddie said. "Like a doting mother, she insisted we bring the coats."

"Yeah, she mothers the whole ranch. You asked about holing up someplace. We're well west and north of the Custer County line. The boundaries run together out here. We could be in either Blaine or Thomas—not that it matters now. I just don't know this country as well, and I can't see where we're going anyhow. Hopefully, this will ease up soon. I think we ought to lead the horses till we either find shelter or a better trail. The footing is treacherous here, and the ground is already covering up with snow. I think a lot of it is stuff already on the ground and being lifted up and moved. A wind like this could be bringing snow from miles away."

Maddie had been worrying about Pirate and was relieved when she saw him bounding down the hill toward them, seemingly unfazed by the snowstorm. He came up to her for his customary ear scratching and she pulled off a glove and accommodated him. After a few minutes, though, her hand was nearly frozen, and she slipped her fingers back into the comfort of the glove.

Blizzard

Sam said, "I've been thinking. The Dismal River can't be more than a mile or two north of here. We were going to cross it to get to Bobcat Canyon. The river joins up with the Middle Loup eventually, not far from Grams's ranch. If we follow the river east, we'll eventually get to familiar territory. The Willow School is on the south side of the Loup. It can't be all that far. There would be shelter there and we might be able to help some."

"That makes me think of the Cedar Creek School. Colette and Vega are there today with all those kids. The head teacher there, Harriet Galbraith, is a sweet young woman, but she's barely out of school herself, and I hope she can deal with this."

"Many of the kids are within several miles of the school, and I'm sure parents can get to them."

"Not all. I remember Vega and I escorting the Timmons twins home when a storm hit, and it was a good five miles out. And the three Gable children, the youngest girl about six, weren't much nearer."

"We can't get there to help them. We'll have to hope good sense takes over. These things are so dang unpredictable, and we can't do anybody else any good if we don't get out of this trap ourselves. I'm just hoping it doesn't get worse, and the storm blows over in a hurry."

A half hour later, as they trudged up a slope that overlooked the Dismal River, Maddie thought that neither of Sam's hopes showed signs of realization. The wind's force was like those of a tornado she had survived in Kansas, and it was twice as cold as the Manhattan icehouse where she and the Crocketts picked up ice blocks on occasion. It was impossible to estimate the snow in terms of inches because the wind was sweeping some of it away and building drifts now.

She edged closer to Sam, her mount's reins clutched in one freezing hand. Any warmth offered by the gloves seemed to have been sucked away. "How far to the school, Sam?"

"I don't know. I just don't recognize this place. With this snow, everything looks alike. And like I said, I don't know this part of the Sandhills as well. It could be three miles, or it might be six, but I'm hoping closer to three."

His hopes had not worked out so well so far. The wind was howling like a pack of wolves now, and the snow was not letting up. It was like the snow ghosts were up there dumping wheelbarrows of the white stuff from the clouds. For the first time, she considered the possibility they might die out here and that their frozen bodies would not be discovered till spring, if ever.

Blizzard

Sam said, "Now that we've found the river, we'll head back downslope. If it doesn't drift in too much, we'll work our way between the hills and take less wind. We've just got to keep the river in our sight. The Dismal River is our compass. Forget about riding. The horses are wearing down as it is. As I recall, the school has a lean-too stable since a lot of kids ride horses to school. We should be able to get a windbreak for the critters. Pirate seems to be holding up. And I'm getting back to country that I know better."

"I think it's the wolf side of him coming out, but I'm sure he'd prefer a snooze in front of a warm fireplace."

They trudged on. It felt like hours had passed, but she knew better. They were going to die here. She just felt it. She wondered what her life might have been like. She thought of the many others her age and younger who had died because of disease or disaster, leaving their stories unfinished. Was she so special that she should be spared that fate? Of course not. People always said life was not fair, and some folks were just shorted. But to die like this in the bitter cold and an ocean of snow? She would prefer a lead slug in the back of her skull, but she knew Sam would never do it no matter how she begged.

Sam pulled her back from the desperation pit she was sliding into. "Missus Norman will welcome Pirate at the heat stove in the school. She's a rancher's widow, pushing seventy, I suppose. She went back to teaching when they couldn't find a schoolmarm to come out this far to teach. She lives with her son and his family on the Double N Ranch and rides her horse three or four miles each way to teach. I doubt if they have more than ten students in a given school year, and this being pure ranch country, they all have got to make a long trip to get there. But they learn their reading and numbers, I guarantee you. Everybody loves her, and the parents see her as a godsend."

She knew he was talking to distract her from their dilemma. She appreciated that, but the strategy was not working, and she could see that Sam was tiring, too. Their boots were not made for long walks, and her feet had pained her earlier. No longer. They were numb now, oblivious to pain. She wondered if they were frostbitten or iced over. She had heard of amputations in such situations and pictured herself with two stumps at the end of her long legs. Would that repulse Sam? What did she care? She felt a few tears squeeze out of the corners of her eyes, but she would swear they froze before they hit her cheeks.

"Maddie. Maddie, are you alright?"

She stared at him blankly, unable to speak, wondering if her tongue was frozen in her mouth.

Blizzard

"Smoke. Smell it? It's got to be the school. The wind is bringing it in. We've got to angle north. I think we almost passed it, strayed too far from the river."

She smelled nothing. But perhaps she had lost her nose. More likely, Sam was hallucinating, and if that helped, she was glad for him.

He turned and headed over a low rise, walking face into the wind. Like an obedient dog, she followed, suddenly aware she could not close her eyes to the storm. Her eyelids were frozen open as if they had merged with the surrounding flesh. He stopped at the top of the rise and pointed. "The school, not more than fifty yards. Let's move." He turned to her. "Do you need help? We'll get you in the saddle."

She nodded, and he swept her into his arms and lifted her into the saddle. Where did the strength come from? She was not a petite woman by any means.

She clutched the saddle horn, and he led both horses now toward the school. Pirate was tiring, but he ran ahead. He knew that a warm fire awaited.

"I'll get you inside, and then I'll put up the horses. It looks like there are only four critters in the lean-to. Maybe they'll have hay to share." He helped her off the gelding. "Can you walk?"

"I think so. With your help."

He still half-carried her to the door. He opened it and led her into a vestibule where normally coats would hang. The schoolroom would be behind the next door.

When they entered, she saw seven wide-eyed children staring at them from near the stove that rested off to one side of the room's front. They all wore coats but not suitable for the storm that raged outside. It seemed warm to her here but probably not so much so for the children. A stove could only do so much against this icy blast.

The building trembled and windows rattled. The view outside was nothing but whiteness. If the windows held, they could survive here.

There were four girls and three boys. One of the boys was obviously the eldest, fourteen or fifteen years old, she guessed.

Sam said, "I'm Sam Kraft from the K Bar K, and this is my friend, Maddie Sanford. The big dog here is Pirate. Don't worry, he's not mean and won't bite."

Half true, Maddie thought. He was no danger to the children.

The eldest boy stepped forward. He was a handsome, freckle-faced youngster with rust-red hair. He stood two-or three inches under six feet, but Maddie figured he was not finished growing. "I'm Matt Johnson. My dad's got the Rocking J."

Sam said, "Where's Missus Norman?"

"She's gone after the Kleine girls. They snuck off when the storm hit, told Polly they were headed home." He placed his hand on the shoulder of a nine or ten-year-old, red-headed girl who stood beside him and stated the obvious. "Polly's my sister."

"I need to get Miss Sanford seated and then we'll talk."

Matt said, "She can have Missus Norman's chair. I'll move it closer to the stove."

When she was seated, Sam said, "Maddie, where is it worst? The feet?"

"Yes. My fingers are a little numb, but I can move them, and my cheeks and nose burn. But I feel nothing in my feet. It's like they're dead."

Sam knelt in front of her. "I'm going to tug your boots off." She could feel him pulling from the pressure on her knees, and there was a slight burning in the top of her right foot but no sensation in the left. She bit her lower lip, determined not to let the horrid images that flashed through her mind overwhelm her. She was not alone in this nightmare, and there were children who needed her to be strong.

With the boots tossed aside, she looked down at her bare feet. The right was colored reddish-purple and swollen, but it was the left that clutched her gut. The little toe and the one next to it appeared as if they had been charred in a fire. The others were almost white interspersed with bluish patches that extended to the ball of the foot. Beyond, the flesh was swollen and nearly scarlet to just above the ankle.

Sam turned to Matt Johnson. "Can we get water?"

"Yessir. There are buckets in the storage room. It's through that door behind the teacher's desk. There's another door from there to outside. The water pump is only ten feet from there. It hadn't frozen an hour ago. It's around the corner on the south side. I've brought in water twice for the kids to drink. There's a bucket on the desk with a dipper for anybody that's thirsty, a couple of steel chamber pots in back, too."

"Can you get me two half-full buckets of water? Then, I want you to heat water warm on the stove, not so hot it burns. Test it with your own fingers. Help Miss Sanford get one foot in each bucket for a half hour or so, then take them out. Find something to just cover her feet. Reheat the water again and do the same thing after another half hour. Repeat three or four times."

Matt left to retrieve the water, and Sam turned his attention back to Maddie. "You heard what I told Matt?"

"Yes."

"Please do what I say. Don't try to get around unless you just must. Matt seems like a responsible boy. You can't let any other children leave no matter what. You've seen what it's like out there. Hold everybody here even after the storm slows. The parents will be here eventually, and they can escort the kids home. One of them can help you get back to the K Bar K if I'm not here."

He was frightening her now. "You are talking like you are pulling out. I don't like that."

"I expect to be back. I just want you ready for anything."

"Where in the hell are you going? You are insane."

"After I get the horses sheltered, I've got to try to find the teacher and hopefully those kids."

"You don't have a chance out there. You don't even know which way they went."

"They didn't likely go north right away. They would have had to cross the Dismal, and there is no bridge until a good distance east. I need to find out where the girls live."

He noticed Polly was just a few feet away. She had apparently been hanging close to her brother. "Polly, what were the names of the girls that Missus Norman went after?"

"Alice and Mazie Kleine. Mazie's my age—ten. Alice is almost seven."

"Where do the Kleines live?"

"I heard Missus Norman say they'd have a three-mile trip to get home. It's east along the Dismal. We're neighbors almost, but there's a bridge across the river, and we're on the other side."

Maddie said, "Sam, they could be home already."

"Do you really believe that, Maddie, after what we've been through? Two little girls afoot? But maybe Mabel Norman got to them, and they found temporary cover someplace, but they won't last long."

She did not answer. He was right, of course, but the thought of him charging back into the storm sickened her.

"Can Pirate track by scent?"

"Yes, of course. But I don't know if he could in the snow cover and with all that wind." The building shook again, as if sending a reminder of the wind's force.

"Would you let him try?"

How could she deny him? "Yes, of course, if you think he might help."

"I need something that Mabel Norman or one of the girls has handled a lot or worn."

Blizzard

"Missus Norman has the canvas bag under her desk that she carries back and forth to school with books and school supplies." It was Matt Johnson, who had returned with water and was heating the buckets on the stovetop.

Pirate was standing not far from the stove basking in pets and hugs from his new school friends. Sam walked over to the desk and slid the bag out. "Pirate. Come here, boy." He lifted the bag and held it to the wolfdog's nose. Pirate stuck his nose in and seemed to be sniffing it out like there was something edible inside.

Sam put the bag down, buttoned his coat, wrapped a wool scarf around the lower part of his face and pulled the coat's hood over his head. He saw that Maddie was looking at him with sad eyes, and he stepped over to her and clutched her wrist. "We'll be back, I promise. Just don't worry if it takes a spell." He leaned down and pressed the side of his shrouded head to hers and spoke softly to her, "I love you, Maddie Sanford, always and forever."

The words caught her by surprise, and she was silent for a moment before she whispered, "And I love you, Sam Kraft." But Sam did not hear. He and Pirate were already headed for the door, her two best friends leaving on what could be their last journey.

Chapter 48

COLETTE DOWNS, AS she was now known, stood in a corner of the schoolroom talking with the head teacher at Cedar Creek School, Harriett Galbraith, and Vega. Harriet was insisting they should dismiss school and let the children go to their homes. She was near panic and appeared to want to be rid of the responsibility as soon as possible.

Two fathers residing within less than a mile from the school had appeared within an hour after commencement of the blizzard and claimed four children, leaving fifteen attendees in the school, not counting Vega, who was more teacher than pupil now as she awaited her move to high school in Broken Bow. Vega favored holding the children until the storm ended. Harriet feared decision-making, but the only way to evade the task was to remove the children from her hands. Colette judged the young lady a proficient teacher, but nearly ten years younger than herself, the schoolteacher's answer to serious problems was to run and hide.

Colette could not fault the head teacher. If not for Grams Downs, she might not have challenged Harriet, but her experiences of the past month were transforming her bit by bit, and she was embracing these changes. She finally intervened in the argument. "The children stay," she said.

"You are not in charge here."

"You are not showing common sense, Harriet. You are playing with small lives. I can't stand by and let you do this, and I will not," Colette said firmly.

Harriet stepped forward and slapped Colette sharply on the cheek, launching her a step backwards, but she stood her ground and declined to strike back. She just glared at the woman who struck her.

Harriet, even more flustered now, said, "I quit this job. I never wanted to teach out here in this desert where people are only a step ahead of savages. It was the only position I could find. I was leaving at the end of spring term anyway. I am going to my room at the Anderson house down the road and taking the two Anderson children with me."

Blizzard

Colette said, "You are not taking the Anderson children with you."

Vega chimed in. "The family lives only a half mile down the road. If the parents wanted them to leave school, they would have come for them."

Harriet said, "I guess I am outnumbered. Very well, but I refuse to stay here. I am getting my coat and leaving. I will inform the Andersons of your insubordination and that you refused to allow me to bring the children home." She turned away and opened the door to the vestibule where the few unused coats were hung.

Vega called after her, "Find the fence along the roadside, hang on to it. The fence will take you to the farmstead." Vega turned back to Colette. "I'm afraid for her."

"She has lost her head. There is no reasoning with her, but we must protect the children at all costs."

Vega said, "The coal is running low. It won't last the night. It is already nearly freezing in here, and it will be dark within a few hours. The children are still in danger if we lose the heat before the storm ends."

"Are there tools in the building?" Colette asked.

"There are tools in the storeroom. An axe for chopping firewood and a saw. I think I saw a hammer once."

"If the coal supply doesn't hold up, we will have the older children help us with tearing the desks and benches apart and cutting the wood down to fit in the stove. If we burn all that, window and door frames come next and anything else that burns. We will keep a fire going till daylight. And I think it would be good for all of us to pray together tonight. Divine intervention may be needed to see us through this blizzard."

No sooner had she spoken those words than a north window shattered, and wind whistled through the opening, bringing a blast of snow and bitter cold. Smaller children screamed and began to cry. Colette's heart raced, and fear gripped her. She was on the edge of panic.

Vega yanked her back. "Colette, what do we do?"

Somebody was asking her what to do. A first in her life. She looked about the room, and her eyes fixed on the storeroom door. She went among the clustered children. "Do not be afraid. We must fix the window." She looked at an eighth-grade boy. "Wesley, can you take the storeroom door off its hinges?"

Wesley said, "Yes, ma'am. That's easy."

"Get some friends to help. Vega, see if you can find a hammer. Maybe there are nails. If not, we will pull some from the woodwork. We will nail the door over the broken window. That will keep out the worst of the wind and snow. Maybe we can find rags or even scarves or other cloth items to stuff around the edges. I know nothing about such things, but it seems we should brace it some other way as well."

Wesley said, "I can make a brace from the top of one of the long benches, anchor it with another brace board nailed to the floor. Cooper, Jake, help me. We can do this. We'll need the small ladder from the storeroom. It will be easy enough to nail. It's holding it tight against the opening with the wind fighting us on the other side while we nail that will be the hardest."

Of course, Colette thought, farm and ranch boys dealt with such things all the time. They would get this done. Just turn them loose. "Wesley, you are in charge. If there is something I can do, tell me." She turned to the other children. "I want each of you to tell me your favorite thing to do."

The window was covered in a half hour, and in not much more time the door was anchored and braced solidly to the floor at its new location. She had not pounded a nail herself. The three boys and one of the girls along with Vega had carried the physical load while she calmed the other children, but somehow, she felt a sense of accomplishment.

Chapter 49

THE WIND AND snow had appeared not more than an hour earlier, and Gage was worried sick about the cowhands and Sam and Maddie out in the storm. He was worried most about his new wife, however. Chloe had gone to the Circle D farmstead earlier to take care of morning chores since Jim and Alex had been away overnight on outrider duties at the westernmost end of the ranches. A line shack there gave them a stove and shelter from the weather, but he feared they would be far from that by now.

He vowed that at the first break in the weather, the milk cow and chicken flock would be moved to the K Bar K. Chloe could do her morning and evening chores not far from the house. If Colette was going to be teaching school, she didn't need that responsibility, but if she insisted on chickens and something to milk, they'd leave a few laying hens behind and get her a goat to milk. The barn cats would be satisfied with that. Inky had taken a liking to her, so she could look after him if Chloe decided not to move the black cat.

Another hour passed, and the storm increased its force. He would bet it was raging at sixty or seventy miles an hour, and the snow was blinding. He had to get to Chloe. He went to the closet off the entryway, retrieved his heaviest coat, and started to slip into it, when Monique raced in from the kitchen.

"Gage, where in the devil do you think you are going?"

"I've got to get to Chloe's."

"Put that coat away. You are not going anyplace."

Monique never did understand who the boss was. "I want to be with my wife, be sure she's alright."

"Gage, you are for the most part the smartest man I ever met, and you've stood up with the years. Please don't make me think you are getting addled. Chloe would expect you to have better sense than to ride out into that storm. She'd be angry that you didn't think she could take care of herself and would give you what for. You know she would."

He sighed and put the coat back. "Alright, I surrender. I guess I'll go back to the office and twiddle my thumbs."

Blizzard

Rip came over and licked his hand as if consoling him. "You can come with me, Rip. Maybe we can talk a spell."

Monique said, "I know you are worried, Gage. I am, too. Bruce is out there riding the range with Smoky. Vega's at the school. I'm praying she doesn't try to get home—Colette, too. People are going to die today across our state and others nearby."

"Yeah, a little praying might not hurt."

Chapter 50

CHLOE SAT AT the table in the dugout and watched the snow blow by. She could hear only a muffled howling here, and because of the almost blinding whiteness, she was uncertain about the amount of accumulation. She got the milk cow in the barn when the storm first struck. There was hay aplenty in their pen, but she would not get milked this night. Better than freezing your tits off or dying in that merciless wind, she figured.

The cats wouldn't starve with their mousing always handy. They were well fed and could miss a night of extra. She would not risk her life to go out in this hell. She had almost blown away during her race from the barn after she got the cow and horses quartered in the barn lot. Inky was with her now, and he would not be asking to go out. The cat had good sense about the weather. She hoped

Gage had the same good sense and did not take a notion that he had to get to her. She thought if he stepped out in the storm for a few minutes he would see the foolishness of such an idea.

She lit the cigarette she had just rolled, maybe the third she had snatched since she married Gage. Her smokes were on the sneak these days. She did not want to smoke when Colette was around, and, although she knew he wouldn't say anything, she did not want Gage to see her smoke anymore. She would just give it up when she finally got settled in at the K Bar K. That would be soon. She and Gage were sharing a bed five days out of seven now, and she missed him when they were not together.

Her home was warm as toast even with the storm outside. She had plenty of wood inside to feed the fire for a day, if necessary, with more stacked just outside the door, and she still had a week's food stored in Colette's bedroom. She would soon surrender her room to Colette. She had been such a fool not to marry Gage years ago.

She inhaled the smoke from her cigarette and coughed and blew it out. It didn't taste as good as it used to. She stubbed the cigarette out in the dish. She was thinking tonight about all the foolish things she had done over the years. Marrying Hank when she was no more than an orphaned, near-starving kid in St. Louis came to mind.

They just were not a matched team, always pulling different ways. Yet they had some tolerable years before he made the mistake of selling home brew to the Indians that killed a few. That had brought the revenge strike. She never did figure out what he put in the stuff.

Still, Gage, ever the philosopher, always insisted that good often springs from the dumbest things we do, and she had Colette here now, and then, of course, Robert until the stupid war took him from her. She would have never known him, either, if not for her pairing with Hank. She may have had other kids with somebody else, but they would not have been the same, and that thought wiped out any regret. Maybe that's what was meant by the oft repeated statement "dumb luck."

Then there was Colette's mother. She failed Darla somehow. She could never forgive herself for that. Gage had told her that old folks had to take care. For some reason they tended to dredge up the wrongs they had done—or imagined they'd committed—through life and needed to remind themselves to tally the good occasionally. "I hope when I head for that last roundup," Gage said, "that friends and family won't judge me by the worst thing I have done. I hope they can find some good I did that evens up the score some."

Gage had ghosts, too, which he did not speak of. That was okay with her. We all have secrets, and most are nobody else's concern. They never asked each other about anything from their pasts that was not surrendered voluntarily. Darn, how she loved that man. She hoped more than anything that they had a few years together yet.

Inky jumped on the table and reflexively her hand went to his ears. That came first in the whimsical loving he demanded. Short one leg, she always wondered how he made that leap so gracefully.

"Let's put a few more logs on the fire, Inky, and cuddle up in bed. I'm tired tonight, feeling my years, I guess." The cat insisted that their ritual be finished and then leaped off the table. A half hour later they were buried in the blankets, oblivious to the devastation being inflicted upon the people, animals, and property elsewhere in the Sandhills and beyond.

Chapter 51

ROSCOE WALTON SAT on the floor in one corner of the Bobcat Canyon shack, shoulders and back braced against the joining walls and legs splayed in front of him. Darkness had settled in a few hours after the coals from the last log died in the stove, about the same time as the wind shattered the window and brought the storm inside.

His legs were buried under more than a foot of snow now, but there was no pain. The cold had left them for some time now, and he was glad for that. He felt nothing there. It was as if the feet and legs had separated from his body and blown away with the wind. Maybe they would come back when he needed them to walk out to his horse and leave this place. He would try once more to find Gar Ford's money before he left in the morning, though.

He clutched the leather bag that held his own money to his chest with his right hand, which was frozen to the ice on the bag. He could not raise the left, but the excruciating pain said it was still with him. His breathing was labored because the mucus that had been running from his nose had frozen and formed icicles that ran across his lips, nearly sealing off the mouth.

Somebody would return soon to seal the open window and start a fire. He was confident of that. He was an important man, and he had funds to buy their assistance to lead him from this purgatory so he could start over someplace warm. He was thinking southern Arizona now. He had never been there, but surely blizzards did not curse the place.

He needed sleep now but could not close his eyes. It did not matter. Blackness was descending.

Chapter 52

PIRATE SEEMED CONFUSED, Sam thought. The wolfdog turned right for fifty feet, then left for one hundred, before plunging ahead in one direction for a time. He lost sight of Pirate in the blinding storm several times, and about the time he decided he had lost him, black spots would appear against the whiteness.

He had lost track of time and could not get to his timepiece without removing the mackinaw, which he would not even consider. The sun, if there had been one, would have set by now, so he assumed they had been on the search for well over an hour. His freezing body was telling him he might be reaching a critical point for his own survival. It suddenly occurred to him that he had no idea where he was at. The twists and turns had disoriented him and there were no stars or a moon to seek out for guidance.

He had evidently wandered away from the river's course, or it was hidden by the driving snow, and now he had lost sight of Pirate again. He tensed when he heard a faint barking through the howling wind. He tried to pick up the location. The dog barked again, and he trudged toward the sound, the going getting slower now with the snow high as his knees even on leveler ground.

He changed course a bit whenever he heard Pirate bark, and he finally found the wolfdog by a snow-cloaked haystack. When he reached Pirate, he saw that his companion's nose was pointed at a shoed foot protruding from the hay. From the style, he guessed it to be an older woman's shoe, and he yelled, "Missus Norman, Mabel." He began to claw the hay back. As he worked his way in, burrowing like a badger, he found two forms, face down, side by side. He crept up so he could hover above the two.

He reached first for Missus Norman, and when he touched the side of her face, he knew instantly she was dead. He gently shook the shoulder of the other. No response. He was certain she had died also. He guessed her to be the ten-year-old Mazie Kleine. Then a moan startled him. Pirate must have heard it, too, because he

Blizzard

started barking again. Another moan. It came from beneath the bodies.

He carefully pushed the bodies of the schoolteacher and girl aside, and buried beneath in a pocket of hay, he found little Alice Kleine, like the others face downward, hers nearly buried in the matted hay. He reached down and pulled her free. She was unconscious, but there was shallow breathing. They could not wait out the storm here. It was still bitter cold, and the others had not been saved by this temporary shelter from the blizzard's vicious attack.

But what if they got lost out there? The girl could not endure two hours in the storm, and he doubted that he could, either. He was forced to chance an escape back to the schoolhouse. He checked again to be sure that his initial opinions about the condition of the older sister and teacher were accurate, brushing his fingers across their icy faces and seeking a pulse in their necks. There was nothing he could do now. Others would arrive to help retrieve the bodies when the storm ended. His mission now was to save little Alice.

He backed out of the haystack, dragging the little girl with him. Then he unbuttoned his coat and lifted her into his arms before he pulled her to his chest wrapping as much of the garment about her as possible. Her own wool coat was not nearly enough. Of course, nothing was this day.

He still could not figure out his location in relation to the school. There was one hope. "Pirate." The wolfdog's ears perked up. "Maddie. Take us to Maddie."

Pirate raced away like his tail was on fire. Sam followed, hoping he did not lose sight of the wolfdog. Thankfully, Pirate was on a straight line this time and stopped to wait for his followers periodically. Sam guessed it was not more than twenty minutes before he sighted the schoolhouse. If only Mabel Norman and the girls had turned back to the school, they would all be alive now. They no doubt were lost out there just as he was, but he had Pirate as his guardian angel.

When he staggered into the schoolroom with Alice cradled in his arms, he felt like he was walking into a furnace, although he suspected the temperature any distance from the stove was not much over freezing. It was dark save for a few lanterns near the front where the occupants were gathered. He carried Alice to the stove, and the other children parted to make room. "Matt, I need you to take Alice for a minute while I spread my coat out on the floor."

Matt obliged and then Polly and another girl came to him with a blanket that they had been sharing as they stood near the stove. "Thank you, girls," he said.

Polly nodded. "Where's . . ." She stopped, probably realizing that Mabel Norman and Mazie would not be joining them.

Matt helped him get Alice situated on the floor. She was a pretty, blonde girl who appeared in a restful sleep now. He would not attempt to awaken her yet to remember the nightmare she had just lived through. He was encouraged by her steady breathing. She must live, he thought, to honor the sacrifices made by her schoolteacher and older sister.

He looked up and saw Maddie, her feet in the buckets, sitting on the bench not more than five feet away, watching with sad, puppy eyes, as he tended to the girl. "Pirate saved our lives," he said.

She said, "We have something else in common then."

Sam, kneeling beside the unconscious girl, examined her as much as he could in the orange light offered by a kerosine lantern held by Matt, who had turned into a competent partner this day. Her face and hands displayed light frost bite burns, but he thought warmth and time would resolve those issues.

There had to be something else to put her in this state. He slipped off one shoe and stocking, footwear hardly suitable for snow. She had not been prepared for walking. Her parents probably delivered the girls to school in a wagon and planned to pick them up after dismissal. The right foot was terribly swollen, several toes dark purple, others turning bluish. They could try the warm water and see if that helped.

He had to struggle to remove the shoe from the left foot, and he found it strange that it was coated in ice. The shoe fought his efforts, and when he finally pulled it free, the girl screamed. And screamed, and screamed. That brought Maddie off the bench, removing her feet from the bucket, easing to the floor and half-crawling to the girl. She lifted little Alice's head onto her lap and gently raked the girl's long, tangled hair with her fingers.

Alice was conscious now, sobbing uncontrollably. "It's alright, Alice. We're friends, and we are here to help you," Maddie said.

"It hurts," Alice said, repeating the words between sobs.

"I know dear, but I will be here with you. My friend Sam Kraft is almost a doctor, and he must look at your foot."

Maddie's reassurance seemed to calm the girl, and Sam continued very tentatively. The stockinged foot was encased in a thin layer of ice, and it puzzled him. She must have stepped in a pool of water or the river's edge before it froze solid, perhaps when they were lost, and then the frigid temperatures did the rest while she battled through the snow. It was melting some now, and he began peeling the shards away. He dreaded removing the stocking for the pain it might cause the poor girl, but he could not leave the thing on her foot.

Sam pulled his penknife from his pocket and cut the stocking at the top, carefully lifting it away, tearing when he could, slicing with the blade when necessary. The girl's sobs told him when he was hurting her, and he was glad he could tell her when he had the cloth removed. He was not happy with what he discovered: a small foot twice its normal size almost to the ankle, raw and near black, like the worst of Maddie's toes. Dear God, what could he do to help this child? He was at a loss.

He finally decided to try the warm water ritual. Maddie told him that the pain was terrible at first but that it had eased the pain significantly after the first soaking. Alice sat with Maddie on a bench and clutched her new friend's arm, refusing to release her during the soakings, but after the third attempt the pain appeared to ease some.

Several hours later, Sam was pleased to see them lying on the blanket in front of the stove, snuggled together with Sam's coat covering Alice, whose hand clasped Maddie's. Pirate lay on the opposite side of the girl, pressed against her back, offering the warmth of his big body. All three slept.

Chapter 53

SAM WENT TO the east window that offered a faint sunrise the next morning. The wind had disappeared as quickly as its arrival the day before. Outside was an almost blinding scene of glowing whiteness. The deep snow had buried everything in sight, and drifts formed waves like stormy ocean waters. The scattered cedar trees revealed not a single branch, the snow having built up about them forming giant cones or tipis.

With the shovel from the storeroom, he dug his way out the back, hoping to make a path to the lean-to to check on the horses. Some places, the wind had swept a path here and there, but others it had constructed walls to break through. He got only far enough to snatch a view. A huge snow drift had climbed over the north side, nearly swallowing the structure. But most of the open south side was still visible, and he could see the rearends of the horses, so they were still standing. He supposed that the snow had eventually sealed any cracks in the walls and offered the animals more protection from the wind. He would get to them later, perhaps recruiting Matt and one of the other boys to help.

He had not been able to see the water pump at first, but a bit of digging had uncovered it, and he was pleased to find it working. The two privies were just mounds rising above the snow blanket. They had been abandoned early on anyhow for a bucket and back-up chamber pots.

Now what? He returned to the schoolroom to check on the occupants. He had seven hungry kids and another on the brink of death. Maddie did not look well, and he could tell that she was in pain, although uncomplaining with her attention focused on Alice, who still desperately clung to her friend. Somehow, he must get Maddie and Alice to a physician, but right now Broken Bow seemed hundreds of miles distant. Maddie might be able to ride, but her feet would be useless in the stirrups. A horse would have enough struggle breaking through the snow with a single rider. With Alice in his arms, they would not have a chance.

He walked over to the stove where Maddie and Pirate sat on the floor with Alice, who was stretched out on the blanket on the floor with his coat on top of her. "I think we're done with the snow. We've just got to dig out of here. Our best hope is for parents and maybe a few others to plow their way in here. I'm going to get you and Alice to Doc Svenson. I like his experience for these things. Of course, if Alice's parents show up, that's their choice. Until then, I guess I make decisions as deputy sheriff, although we're outside of Custer County and my jurisdiction."

Maddie said, "You've made good decisions, Sam, and you will get no arguments from me—for now, anyway." Maddie jerked her head around. "I heard a voice outside."

Sam walked over to the window and looked out and saw two men with shovels outside headed toward the school's front door which was snowed shut. He had tried it earlier and been unable to budge it, but they were on the way to being dug out. Then he saw a man reining a team of mules and sitting on a two-wheeled contraption with a wide, steel blade drawn behind it, attempting to clear a path from the schoolhouse to the hidden dirt road in front. He was making a dent in the surface but not much more.

He turned back to Maddie and the school children. "Help is here, everybody. It won't be long, and you will be back with your families."

A few cheers, some smiles, and a lot of chatter. There would be some happy reunions soon for some families but tragic news to greet others, and he still needed to get Maddie and Alice on the way to medical care. He took another look outside. Three more riders were arriving and a buckboard on steel runners drawn by double mule teams.

"Matt," he said, "I'd like to have you take a look at something."

Matt joined him. "What is it, Mister Kraft?"

"The wagon with the runners, who is that?"

"That's Alfred Kleine, Alice's and Mazie's pa."

Sam dreaded conveying the news he would be giving to this man shortly, but Kleine also brought the one chance to get his daughter to a doctor and yet save her life, and Maddie's, too. By the time the men cleared the doorway and entered the Willow School, there were nearly twenty-five people, several women but mostly men, in the schoolyard, including parents and cowhands who had arrived from nearby ranches to render aid. Snow around the pump and privies was now being shoved aside as well as drifts around the building entrances.

Several men were clearing the lean-to opening and tending to the horses. A second buckboard with snow runners was out front now, and four men went to retrieve the frozen bodies of Mabel Norman and Mazie Kleine.

Blizzard

Sam could not think of anything harder he had ever done than inform Alfred Kleine of his daughter's death and Alice's fragile condition. Matt and Polly Johnson's father, Lars, had eased his burden by intercepting the schoolteacher's son and telling him of the tragic death of his mother, who had died trying to save the lives of the Kleine children.

Alfred Kleine had regrouped some from the news and was kneeling by his daughter, who was in and out of consciousness now but had opened her eyes, offered a small smile, and whispered, "Help me, Papa." She still clung to Maddie as if she were her lifeline.

Kleine looked up at Sam who stood nearby. "What can we do?"

"We must get both Maddie and Alice to a doctor. I recommend Doctor Svenson in Broken Bow. The wisdom of his years is called for here. With the runners on your wagon and the double mule teams, you should be able to make it, but it will take most of the day."

"Someone must tell my wife about Mazie, and why I will be away. She stayed home with the little boys. We live just across the river from the Johnsons. Margaret Johnson is outside. I'll talk to her and Lars. I'm sure Lars and Matt will look after the ranch until I get home."

"We need more blankets for the wagon trip. I will ride with you, but it would be nice to have a few others in case you get bogged down along the way."

Kleine got up. "I will find help. Everybody brought blankets. That will not be a problem. I want Margaret Johnson to prepare my wife before they take Mazie's body home. Above all, we must try to save Alice now."

Sam stayed with Maddie and Alice. Pirate remained seated on his haunches beside his dearest friend. "We'll have you both on the way to real help soon, Maddie."

"And you are not going along. Neither is Pirate."

"But I want to be with you."

"I would like you with me, but you have the folks at the ranch, Gage and Chloe and the others. Colette and Vega would have been at the Cedar Creek School. Hands were out on patrol, and then the rustlers. We've got to find out how the storm affected them. This may even present an opportunity to put a stop to their thievery. It's my job to be on top of this, and I can't be right now. You're a deputy sheriff. Please, help me with this."

He knelt beside her on the floor where she sat and kissed her softly on the lips. "I'll do what you ask, but I cannot vouch for Pirate. I will be in town the instant I can shake loose from the ranch."

"I know you will. You can bring Pirate then."

Blizzard

Later, when the wagon glided away with the patients stretched out in the bed and three riders alongside or behind, Sam fought back the tears that threatened. He could not remember when he had felt more alone. Pirate did not help when he looked up and whined pitifully. The wolfdog at first had disobeyed Maddie's order to remain and commenced following the wagon. She had asked Kleine to rein the mules to a stop and then scolded Pirate harshly. The wolfdog had finally turned and walked to Sam, the usually curling tail drooping behind him.

There were still a dozen men and the crude snowplow clearing the snow and breaking down drifts about the school. He figured it would be a good three-hour ride to the K Bar K with the snow traps waiting along the way. He could follow the trail left by the wagon and riders for half the distance before they veered away to the currently invisible wagon road. He retrieved and saddled his mount and Maddie's sorrel gelding, thinking he could alternate horses if the critters were being pushed too hard. He waved to their rescuers and headed south, with Pirate bounding through and over the snow, roaming some but always within his sight.

Chapter 54

WHEN PARENTS BEGAN to arrive at the Cedar Creek School, Colette and Vega, with help from Wesley and his crew, had already dismantled half the benches and desks and fed the pieces to the fire. It had been a long night, and Colette had to put down several rebellions when some children insisted they were going home.

The Timmons twins had been especially difficult, but when Vega informed her that the boys' ranch home was over five miles distant from the school, Colette told the twins that if they tried to leave, she would have the several older boys help tie them to the desks. As the storm worsened the two seemed to lose interest in departure anyhow.

The first parent inside the door was James Anderson, coming to claim his seven-year-old son and nine-year-old daughter. He was a younger man in his early thirties, Colette guessed, and carried heavy coats for his children. Colette knew that the head teacher Harriet Galbraith boarded at the Anderson home.

Anderson was a gaunt, tall man with tired blue eyes that betrayed a sleepless night. "Thank you," he said, "for holding the kids here overnight. My wife and I have been worried sick that the kids left the school. I tried twice to come to the school and thought better of it after I got into the storm and couldn't see three feet in front of me. If my wife hadn't been screaming for me to come back, I likely would have got lost."

Colette said, "Harriet?"

"Dead. I found her just ten feet from the barn this morning, not more than a hundred feet from the house. That's what got me running down here to the school. We were afraid she tried to bring the children with her. Thank God . . . and you, that she did not."

"I'm so sorry about Harriet. She was a fine teacher and a good person. The storm just terrified her, and she wouldn't stay."

"She was no more than a kid herself. The family was fond of Harriet. I hate having to tell the kids. And we'll have to track her parents down. They lived in North

Platte. I'm afraid a lot of folks lost family yesterday and last night. It'll be spring before some are found."

It was several hours before all the children were turned over to their parents, and during that time Colette was steadfast in her denial of permission for any children to depart on their own. Stephen Timmons was the last to show up, and he thanked her profusely for holding the twins at the school. "The boys can be a handful," he said. "They don't know fear, and that gets in the way of good sense. We just prayed they'd stayed at the school."

After the children were gone, Colette and Vega began getting their own things together. The men had cleared the snow around the stable and made a path from the schoolhouse. Just before they departed, the schoolhouse door opened again, and a short, stocky man walked in and removed his hat. He was a middle-aged man with salt and pepper hair and a thick mustache.

"Miss Downs, could you spare me a minute?"

"Of course." He had a kindly face, but she had not seen him with any of the children.

"I'm Asa Wentworth, chairman of the school board here. My kids are pretty much growed up, but I've stayed on the board because nobody else wants the job. I've been talking to the two other members out front—Steve Timmons and Jimmy Anderson. You've met them. We need a head teacher now, and I'm authorized to offer you the job. One hundred dollars a month to finish off the school year. If you will stay on, we'll do better for you next school term."

She was struck nearly speechless. "I . . . don't know what to say."

"Just say 'yes.' We'll close for a week to get the window fixed and the school ready and the furnishings and such rebuilt." He turned to Vega. "And young lady, if you would put off your schooling in Broken Bow another term, we'll pay you sixty dollars a month to teach here till school lets out in summer."

Colette had never made as many decisions in a lifetime as she was being called upon to make the past few days. "I will accept the job, Mister Wentworth."

Vega said, "I will, too. You don't have to be sitting at the student's desk to keep on learning."

Chapter 55

SAM STOPPED BY the Circle D on his way to the K Bar K. Nobody was at the house, but he could see horse and human footprints in the snow outside the building. A visit to the barn confirmed that the cow had been milked this morning. The only visible damage was the chicken house that had been tipped over with dozens of dead hens scattered in the snow outside the structure. It didn't appear anyone would be gathering eggs here for a long time. There was no sign that hands had occupied the bunkhouse last night, and that worried him.

Following tracks that went to and from Gram's place, he stopped by his cabin and checked the stable to see if his mare survived the blizzard. He had expected to return last night and not taken her to the K Bar K. She was gone, but tracks in the snow indicated she had been led from the stable this morning, and an extra set of prints joined the others heading toward the K Bar K headquarters.

It was nearly one o'clock when he arrived at the headquarters house. He was starving, and he was counting on Monique to have something left to eat. He put up his and Maddie's mounts in the stable, noting that his mare was there. When he went into the house, he found diners still at the table.

Monique saw him and raced over and wrapped him in her arms. "The Lord has answered my prayers. I have been so worried." She stepped back. "But Maddie. Pirate is with you, but where's Maddie?"

"She's on her way to the doctor in Broken Bow. Let me fill my plate and grab a mug of coffee, and I'll tell you about it."

Gage got up from his chair and embraced his grandson. "I've been worried sick, Sam."

Chloe was next. "I never worried a minute. I knew you'd be fine," she lied.

Even Vega and Colette gave him hugs. He learned that they had only arrived a half hour earlier.

When he had a plateful of roasted beef, fried potatoes, and beans, he sat down at the table. Monique indulged him and served his coffee and apple pie, patting him on the shoulder as she leaned over to place the mug and plate on the table.

"There are a lot of empty places at the table," Sam said. "I hope everyone is accounted for."

"They're not," Gage said. "We were just talking about our plans, and you need to be in on this. But first, you tell us what happened to Maddie and then the story about what you two have been up to."

"Maddie insisted I get back here to help, or I'd be with her. She's in a serious fix. Like a lot of folks, we got caught by surprise in the storm. Her feet got the worst of it. I think her right foot will come out of it, but the left, I don't know. I think she could lose at least part of it. I just hope Doc doesn't have to take the whole foot. And then you've got the possibility of infection and other complications." He swallowed hard. "And she could die."

The room went silent for a bit before Gage spoke. "Tell us the rest. Short version."

"The girl who went on the wagon with her is in worse shape. Little Alice Kleine. I don't see how they can save one leg, and both are at risk. Her sister died, and the schoolteacher, Mabel Norman, too."

Briefly, he told them of their experience.

Chloe said, "How sad. The Cedar Creek teacher died, too. The gals can tell you about that later. You're wanting to be with Maddie, ain't you?"

"Of course, but there is nothing I can do about her condition. That's up to Doc Svenson and fate. I'll do what's got to be done here, and then I'll be heading to town."

"Well," Gage said, "we've got plenty of work ahead of us the next few days. First comes the people. Alex and Jim made it back this morning, thanks mostly to Jim's skills, I'm thinking. The other new hands, Bing and Chub, haven't showed up and no sign of Smoky and Ricky Meeks. Alex and Jim said they heard gunfire from the west end of the K Bar K range, but with the wind, it was hard to judge the location. Jim found a cave to hole up in off one of the little canyons, and they claimed that while they could."

"Where are they now?"

"They went back out after they ate and supplied up. They're going to head in the direction of the gunfire and see what turns up. They're ready to stay out overnight if need be."

"Bruce made it in last night, and I'm thinking you and me and him ought to head out soon, if you're up to it, and look for Bing and Chub, maybe take a few extra mounts in case somebody ended up afoot. We'll check what cattle we can along the way, but we account for the people first. I'm thinking we'll spend the night at the line shack on Chloe's north border if we don't turn up Bing and Chub before nightfall."

He was not up to the venture. All he wanted to do was sleep. "I'm fine. I'll need a fresh mount. Bay's had some rough days."

Gage said, "Take your pick of critters in the stable."

"I'll see if Pirate has the gumption to join us. He's eating on the mud porch right now. I'm guessing he'll have a go. That hound has stood up to the storm better than any other living creature."

Chapter 56

THE RIDERS STILL had not turned up the missing cowhands as the sun began to drop below the western horizon, but Pirate spotted a white-stockinged, black gelding wandering by itself and led them to the horse. The gelding welcomed the company and trotted to them when the riders appeared.

"That's Bing's horse," Bruce Potter said. "Bing and that critter were like father and son. Ain't likely the horse would have wandered far from its owner."

Pirate had disappeared and was barking frantically from a wooded area along a spring-fed stream that split the flatter grasslands beyond them. Sam said, "I'm guessing he found Bing."

Five minutes later, they came upon a man sitting with his back against a tree, a few blankets wrapped around him, snow-covered hat pulled down above his eyes. First glance suggested he was napping. A closer look told the observers he was dead, his iced-over face giving him a ghostly look.

The men dismounted. Gage said, "He must have been lost and sought shelter in the trees. He took his bedroll from the horse but didn't tie the critter. Knew he wasn't going to make it and wanted to give his horse a chance. I was just getting to know Bing, but I liked him and bet on him to be a good hand, one who would have been with us for a spell."

After tying Bing's body over the back of one of the spare horses, they went to the line shack where they spent the night.

The next morning, while they drank their coffee and ate cinnamon biscuits Monique had sent along, Gage said, "Bruce, I would like you to head back to headquarters with one of the spare mounts and Bing's body. Take his tired horse, too. We'll keep the other extra mount in case it's needed and keep looking for Chub. We'll be back before dark regardless. I'm hoping Chub is there to greet us, and he could be. The two obviously got separated in the dang storm, and he could have ended up anyplace."

Bruce said, "Sun's coming up bright today. We should see some melt, but some of this is here till spring. I ain't never been in snow like this. And drifts some places twice as tall as a man. Some poor folks lost out there won't be found till spring, cattle and horses, too."

After Bruce departed, leading the body-laden horse and Bing's mount behind him, Sam said, "Gramps, we're not more than a two hours' ride from Bobcat Canyon. Maddie and I were heading there when the storm struck, so we never made it. I wonder if we might head up that way and see what's going on at the cabin, find out if the rustlers are still in business."

"I don't see why not. It's just as likely Chub wandered out that way anyhow if he kept moving."

The land was increasingly rough as they rode northwesterly, and the riders were forced to change course frequently because of drifted trails. Gage was encouraged, though, before they left Chloe's land to find small herds of cattle emerging from draws and canyons where they had found shelter. The haystacks scattered over the hills all were crowded serving nourishment to steers, heifers, and mature cows who could not find grazing beneath the snow. They came across dead cattle occasionally, most half covered with snow, and they would eventually find pockets with no survivors, but they had intentionally avoided destroying natural windbreaks over the years and were being rewarded for prudence now.

Before Gage and Sam entered Bobcat Canyon, they found a mostly windswept deer path to a spot overlooking the cabin. Gage pulled his spyglass from the saddlebags and scanned the area before handing it to Sam. "No smoke, two horses in the lean-to near the cabin. They're standing anyhow. Strange there is not a fire going."

"Yeah. I suppose they could have run out of wood, but it makes no sense they'd just be sitting there waiting for it to show up. I spotted cattle penned in what looks to be a dead-end branch of the canyon. If we can, I'd like to just open the gate. I'm betting most will wander home. We can come out later to round up strays, check brands and sort."

"Makes sense. I say we check the cabin. If there's nobody home, those horses need attention."

Less than a half hour later, they reined in within walking distance of the cabin and tied the mounts to cedars before advancing cautiously with rifles in hand toward the cabin. "No sounds from inside. Window's shattered, but I'm not inclined to stick my head in the darn thing and get it blown off," Sam said in a near whisper. "I'll knock on the door if you'll have your Winchester ready to fire."

"Just get out of the way if the door opens. Hard to believe somebody's in their sitting on their hands with a broken window letting the weather in."

Sam rapped on the door.

No response.

"Hello in there. We're just here to help folks that might need it." He looked at Gage and shrugged when there was no answer.

"See if you can push the door open but jump back."

Sam pressed down on the lever and pushed the door open. It only swung a few feet before it was blocked, but he saw a man's leg stretched out on the floor in front of him. "I'm going on in."

He put his shoulder to the door, shoving the body back that had been blocking it, and stepped inside. He stared at the man lying at his feet.

Gage stepped in behind him. "I've seen him before. That's Gar Ford, Wally Barnes's deputy."

"Former deputy. Maddie was sure he was in cahoots with the rustling outfit, maybe a leader. I haven't seen the man in the corner before, but I'm betting that's Roscoe Walton and that Colette's a widow now. I doubt if she'll be grieving much."

Sam had not noticed the corner corpse at first, the body sitting but slumped, eyes frozen open and head cocked to one side. One hand was clutched about a leather bag. Both bodies were glazed with ice and snow, and the fireplace was half full of the white stuff that had dusted most of the cabin's floor.

Gage said, "Let's see to the cattle in the canyon first and then swing by and see if we can load these carcasses. Our spare mount can haul Ford—he's a bigger man. Maybe our new additions can trade off, given they might be weakened some."

Sam said. "I'd leave them here to rot, but we need to get Walton identified. Chloe would know him if it's too much for Colette to handle. If they get to be too much, Ford gets dropped first. We can always try to beat the buzzards and coyotes to him later."

Chapter 57

SAM STAYED AT the headquarters house when they returned with the bodies. He and Gage went to the house after dumping the bodies in the barn. Bruce informed them that Chub had made it back, and that Ricky Meeks's mount returned alone. Chub and Bruce were there to help and put up all the horses while they had a late supper, before staggering off to bed.

This morning Chloe and Colette went to the barn with Sam to identify Roscoe Walton. Colette just stood beside the body staring at the man's face, her own emotionless. Finally, she just walked away silently. After breakfast, Sam intercepted her on the way to her bedroom. He handed her a leather bag and a belt with bulging pockets inside. "These are yours," he said, placing the items in her hands. "The bag was in your husband's hands, and

Ford wore the belt. My grandfather and I agreed they are yours, some of your inheritance refunded."

"I don't know what to say. This money was probably stolen."

"Could be, but it's impossible to say who from. We know that a lot more than this was stolen from you. I don't think it will get away so easily now."

"I can promise that. I don't deserve this, but thank you."

Midmorning, Sam, Bruce, and Chub were saddling up to search out distressed horses and cattle and to look for the other hands, when Jim Hunter and Alex rode in with Smoky. Another body slung across a horse's back followed. As Sam feared, it was Ricky Meeks on the trailing horse.

Bruce took the men inside for a late breakfast while Sam and Chub took care of the mounts. Sam examined Meeks's body and saw immediately the storm had not claimed him. At least three gunshot wounds had left splotches of blood on his chest, and he had taken slugs in his right shoulder and hip.

When he went into the house, Smoky was just getting started on the story. Sam saw that the old-timer's left hand and lower arm was wrapped with a blanket. Something was obviously wrong with the limb. Smoky had cleaned his plate and was downing coffee, Monique catering to him by adding a healthy dose of whiskey. His pale blue eyes almost matched the color of his nose and cheeks. He needed medical attention.

"Smoky, I'd like to look at your frostbite, see if you need some attention."

"Not till I say what needs to be said. I can do that much for poor old Ricky. He saved my worthless hide, and folks need to know. It should be me out there waiting to be planted under the ice and snow."

Gage said, "Fast then."

Smoky didn't know the meaning of fast, and he commenced speaking in his slow, growly voice. "We come on to some rustlers just as that dang snow hit. They was cutting out K Bar K cattle, maybe had a hundred head collected and ready to pull out. At least five rustlers, I'd guess. Anyhow, Ricky said we should hold up and think things out. I ain't good at waiting, and I dismounted, grabbed my Winchester and got off a few shots over their heads, thinking to spook them and the cattle."

Sam said, "Where was Ricky?"

"Behind me somewhere. Anyhow, I spooked the cattle and sent them running, but I scared the dang gelding, too, and he took off without me. I pissed the outlaws, and they turned on me. I started firing and knocked one out of the saddle but knowed the way they was coming, this was the end for me. Then Ricky steps in front of me, yanks my sidearm from its holster, pulls his own, gives me an elbow that puts me on my ass, and waits for the devils to get closer. He takes a slug before they get near enough for his liking, and then he lets loose. I never seen such shooting."

Gage said, "He never talked about his past, but he must have handled weapons in another life."

"Ain't no doubt. He took the whole bunch down. If they wasn't dead, the blizzard finished them up. I thought maybe Ricky wasn't hurt so bad, 'cause he turned around and took two steps toward me and fell over. He must have been firing them shooting irons after he was already dead. He was torn up by bullet holes, deader than dead. He saved my life, and I as good as kilt him with my foolishness. I got to live with that."

Sam said, "You told us your horse bolted and ran off. How did you get out of there?"

"Ricky again. His horse stood fast. That critter always was one of the best in the remuda. I climbed onto him, but I couldn't see a dang thing by now. I didn't know where to go, so I just give him his lead, figuring he might head for home. Well, guess it took him a spell, but he finally did—without me. I dropped off someplace and was hoping it would be over soon because my balls was froze solid by that time. Surprised they was there to come home with me. I don't remember nothing till Jim and Alex showed up."

Jim Hunter said, "He was burrowed in an old beaver den in what we call Dry Creek since Sand Creek changed course three or four years back. We found Ricky and the dead rustlers by the buzzards circling. After we got Ricky onto one of the extra horses, I tried to track Smoky. We picked up the trail twice from some scattered horse apples we uncovered, but the snow covered any real tracks. Of course, we couldn't tell where he and the horse parted ways."

Alex jumped in. "I'd pretty much given up, and night was closing in, but we decided to stay at that old one-room soddy somebody left behind years back and look for Smoky again today. Needed to get the one window covered and a fire going in the dark, but it was warming up pretty good. Well, I went outside to do my business before turning in, and danged if I didn't hear singing to the east along Dry Creek. Scared the blazes out of me. Ghost or something, I thought at first. I went in and got Jim. He said it was Smoky, and we took off alongside the creek bed. I'll be danged if we didn't find Smoky holed up in the beaver lodge."

Smoky said, "I don't recollect none of this. Maybe I passed through the Pearly Gates and decided to come back. Anyhow, the first thing I remember is waking up in the night between these two and a warm fire crackling nearby."

Sam said, "I want to see that arm you've got covered up, Smoky."

Smoky uncovered the arm, while everyone stared in stunned silence. The entire left hand was triple its normal size and the color of ashes from a dead fire and the forearm puffy and dark purple. Gangrene was setting in.

Sam looked at Gage. "Runners on one of the wagons?"

"Always have one ready when weather gets like this."

"Somebody's taking Smoky to Broken Bow to the doctor. We should double-team some mules."

"You're elected. I've got a hunch you might want to see another patient there. Boys, let's get that wagon out and mules hitched."

Smoky protested. "I'll be fine. I just need to rest up a few days."

"We'll be pulling out in a half hour," Sam said. "You need every man here right now. I can go it alone. The trail to town's been opened some by others. The worst of the drifts have likely been broken down by now."

Chapter 58

SAM WAS SURPRISED to find the street outside Doctor Svenson's big two-story house and clinic lined with buckboards, most bearing blanket-covered forms in the beds. Doc was outside, making his way from wagon to wagon as he examined patients. Young Lorelei Schoenbeck was at his side, taking notes with pencil and tablet in her hands as Doc gave instructions and gathered information from patients' family members. Two middle-aged men stood back with a stretcher at ready.

Sam reined the mule teams and wagon into line and waited. Some of the wagons pulled away after Doc's examination. In several cases, Doc would bark instructions to the stretcher bearers, and a patient would be removed from the wagon and borne into the clinic. It was late afternoon, and Sam worried about getting care for Smoky before dark. He looked back in the wagon where Pirate lay beside the old cowhand.

"Smoky, we're at Doc's. He'll be along shortly. How are you doing?"

"Ain't dead yet."

His voice was weaker, and Sam knew that time was critical. The man had yet to complain about pain, but Sam was not sure that was necessarily a good thing. The only thing he was certain of was that if Smoky survived, he would be returning to the ranch absent at least half of one arm.

Finally, Doc approached the wagon. "Sam, this is a surprise. What've you got for me now?"

"Smoky Fletcher. I would start with the left arm."

Doc stepped to the side of the wagon box. "That dog doesn't act like he's inclined to move."

"Pirate, here boy." Sam tapped on the back of the wagon seat, and the wolfdog leaped up beside him.

Doc leaned over the wagon and lifted the blanket to examine Smoky's arm. He dropped it. He turned and hollered at the stretcher bearers who were just returning from the house. "Stretcher." He turned to Lorelei. "This patient and Miss Sanford get billed to the K Bar K. Now, why don't you go in and get Maddie ready to move out. Sam here will be in for her directly."

"Maddie's fine then?"

"Will be. She'll be short two toes but will get used to it in time. She's one of the lucky ones. You are to take her to the Grand Central for a few days. I'm sending non-surgical and recovery patients there. They've set aside the main floor as a temporary hospital. You should know the place by now."

The stretcher bearers had Smoky on the stretcher now and were moving toward the house, where Svenson's wife would presumably take charge until the physician returned. "Smoky's in bad shape, isn't he, Doc?"

"I'll be taking the arm yet tonight. I just hope that's enough. In all the years since my Civil War service, I haven't taken as many limbs as I have the past few days. It's been as bad as the damn war, I tell you."

"The little girl that came in with Maddie—Alice Kleine. Will she make it?"

"Barring infection, she will recover. She will be missing a foot. I had to amputate to about six inches above the ankle on the one leg. Might have to take a toe on the other. She'll have to stay with us a spell yet. She won't like Maddie leaving one bit, but I've already got four patients in a two-patient room and others laid out on the hall floor waiting for a space. Now, I've got to move on. I'll be checking the hotel daily, and I'm guessing you will be nearby."

Chapter 59

MADDIE WAS SURPRISED when Lorelei told her that Sam and Pirate had come for her and that she was being moved to the hotel. She would be thrilled to see them both, yet she had reservations. Of course, she hated to leave Alice who was still struggling with recovery, morose and afraid at the loss of her foot and devastated by her sister's death. But she had promised the girl that they were forever friends and would see each other often. Maddie was determined to keep that promise. The girl was being heavily sedated now and was sleeping soundly. Her mother was to arrive this evening and would hopefully be at the bedside when Alice awakened or soon thereafter.

As to her own recovery, that would take time. Her right foot was nearly normal now, but the left, aside from her missing little toe and its companion, was still very numb.

Doc assured her that feeling would return over time, but she should be prepared to deal with the fact it would never be totally the same. He expected the missing toes to eventually go unnoticed, although she might sometimes feel their presence. Her shoes and boots might need cloth padding to support the foot, but she would learn to deal with that.

Lorelei came in with the crutches she would require for a week or two. They had practiced with them earlier, and she could support herself, but walking was another matter.

Lorelei said, "Doctor Svenson says you should not need these for more than a week, but you should obtain a cane for balance and support for as much as a week after that. He will visit you at the hotel to answer other questions you might have."

Dressed now in the laundered clothes she had been wearing the day of the storm, she sat on the edge of her bed, her right foot booted but the other dressed heavily with gauze and covered with a heavy wool stocking. Lorelei helped her pull herself up onto the crutches. When she stood unsteadily on her feet, she stared downward, plotting her first step.

Lorelei stepped away and Sam stepped into her place. She looked up and saw those gentle eyes and did not hesitate to fall into those arms when they wrapped around her nor did her lips resist when his sought hers. He smiled when one of her crutches clattered to the floor. "Lean on me while I pick it up."

Yes, she would lean on him. She would do so for the rest of their lives, and he would lean on her when he needed support. That is what a matched team did, was it not?

Epilogue

SAM AND MADDIE returned to the K Bar K within a week after her exit from Doctor Svenson's clinic. During the hotel stay, Sam and Pirate shared her room, and after two days Sam shared the bed with Pirate's consent after Maddie said to him, "Are you planning to marry me, or not?" He gave the correct answer and earned a place on the other side of Pirate, which ultimately sent him back to the floor.

Sam stayed at his cabin until they were married in a simple ceremony at the ranch on the first of March, and after the wedding, they shared her room at the headquarters. Calves were starting to be born, and there would not have been time for a wedding in the spring. Besides, Maddie was back on her gelding, Outlaw, and ready to work cattle by then.

Dalton Gage Kraft and Alice Chloe Kraft were born on Christmas Day 1888, shortly after the newlyweds moved into their new modest home a hundred yards from the headquarters house. Pirate had long since given up control of the bedroom, but he always enjoyed his own comfortable bed in the parlor and was allowed visitation privileges on occasion. The twins' birthdates gave Maddie ample time to be prepared for calving season.

Collette signed on as head teacher at Cedar Creek School for the 1888-89 school year and decided that teaching was her calling. She remained at Chloe's dugout with Inky and the barn cats. She used part of her "inheritance" to buy three brood mares and a bit more to build on an extension to the front of the dugout to provide a new kitchen and parlor space—with an oak floor. The remainder of her money was deposited in the bank, and she lived on her teaching salary although she found she could never be quite as frugal as her grandmother.

The young widow had many would-be suitors make appearances, but she was not looking for marriage for a long while, if ever. She first had to satisfy herself that she needed no man to provide for her. She found herself increasingly attracted, however, to one of the K Bar K hands who shared her love for horses and conveniently resided in the Circle D bunkhouse. Jim Hunter, a full-blooded

Sioux, was mutually attracted. For now, they settled for friendship. Even that thought would have sent Colette's mother rolling in her grave.

Gage and Chloe remained content sharing their lives at the K Bar K. Gage remained the official head of the ranch but intended to ease away from decision-making in the months ahead. They welcomed a one-armed Smoky back after his recovery. Thoughts of the deaths of the two other hands put him in a brief black mood on occasion, but Chloe would not put up with it for long and brought light back to his life quickly.

Combining the operations of the ranches worked out even better than expected with Sam proving to be a natural manager. Gage realized he should have given his grandson more responsibility sooner. He had deeded a quarter section to Sam and Maddie upon which the new house was constructed. Sam, of course, would someday inherit it all, but he was going to try and keep him waiting for a long time, not that it would matter to Sam, who was raised without any sense of entitlement.

One day in late spring, Chloe and Gage agreed to talk frankly about their financial positions and arrangements. He had never been very secretive about his finances and informed her he no longer owed the banks a nickel, but he still scratched for money to pay the hands and meet bills every month. A crisis could be averted occasionally by premature cattle sales, however. Part of the challenge was managing the business, and he lost no sleep over that anymore. Sam could figure it out.

He figured they suffered less than a ten percent cattle loss from the blizzard, far less than most ranchers and farmers. Gage felt that the consolidation of their operations would make for efficiencies that would keep the ranch afloat till better times. Optimism was a necessity for folks in the business.

Gage had no idea what Chloe would do with her property. Before their marriage, she had only said, "What's yours is yours. What's mine is mine."

He was not about to press her on her plans and knew it was none of his business. He had been surprised, though, when Chloe said, "I've got gold coins buried in three spots on my homeplace. I'll consider a loan if money gets short for the K Bar K. I would take your note and would only charge the going bank rate for interest."

Author's Note

THE BLIZZARD OF 1888 turned out to be an event that worked its way into Nebraska History textbooks required by that state's school curriculum rules. Statistics and data are imprecise and inconsistent, but it is estimated that well over one hundred Nebraska school children died in that unprecedented wintry explosion. Some estimates have been as high as two hundred.

Many accounts named the storm "The Children's Blizzard." Countless schoolteachers and older students performed heroic acts to save the lives of school children, and more than a few died. Numerous survivors suffered life-changing injuries carried as stark reminders of that January 12 to their graves. Parents died or were severely injured also when they ventured out to rescue their children, and stockmen succumbed trying to protect cattle, horses, and other livestock.

The blizzard struck many states throughout the Midwest, apparently hitting Nebraska and southern Dakota Territory, soon to be the state of South Dakota, the hardest per capita population. The storm extended south into Texas and east into Iowa and other border states along the north-south strip. Total fatalities are difficult to determine. Some reported accounts reached as high as a thousand, but others raised the figure to two thousand. Newspapers fought over the accuracy of their respective numbers.

Suffice it to say that that the human and livestock toll was tragic and unprecedented during a time of communication and transportation limitations. In Nebraska, many major train routes were blocked because of the ice and drifting.

The viciousness of the storm came from the lethal combination of wind, temperature, and snow. The wind ranged from 50 to 60 miles per hour in the area, and the temperature dropped rapidly from 35 degrees above zero to 35 to 40 degrees below in a matter of several hours. The shift of a warm, southerly breeze to a bitter-cold northwesterly wind occurred in a matter of minutes.

The amount of new snowfall, which was likely only three to six inches most places, was not the culprit so much as accumulated snow already on the ground. Earlier snows were scooped up by the powerful winds and added to the lethal, blinding mix. Some melting of the earlier snows formed an icy sheet of ice below the surface.

Such a blizzard today would be serious, of course, but new technology might provide more warning, and our motorized society and road systems would likely render it much less devastating in terms of human lives.

A valuable resource for this novel was a non-fiction book, "IN ALL ITS FURY, a History of the Blizzard of January 12, 1888," with stories and reminiscences of survivors, collected and compiled by W. H. O'Gara (1947). Articles in the archives of History Nebraska, formerly known as Nebraska State Historical Society, were also helpful in grasping the impact of the blizzard.

About the Author

Ron Schwab is the author of several popular Western series, including *The Blood Hounds, Lockwood, The Coyote Saga,* and *The Lockes*. His novels *Grit* and *Old Dogs* were both awarded the Western Fictioneers Peacemaker Award for Best Western Novel, and *Cut Nose* was a finalist for the Western Writers of America Best Western Historical Novel.

Ron and his wife, Bev, divide their time between their home in Fairbury, Nebraska and their cabin in the Kansas Flint Hills.

For more information about Ron Schwab and his books, you may visit the author's website at www.ronschwabbooks.com.

Made in United States
Troutdale, OR
06/19/2024

20694875R00289